MERCY RING  BOOK FOUR

RYKER

NYSSA KATHRYN

An NW Partners Book
Cover by Deranged Doctor Design
Developmentally and Copy Edited by Kelli Collins
Line Edited by Jessica Snyder
Proofread by Amanda Cuff and Jen Katemi

❀ Created with Vellum

Sometimes, the quest for vengeance can cost more than you're willing to pay.

Blakely Sullivan was a foreign aid worker in the Middle East when a deadly bombing took the lives of families she'd come to know and love, collateral damage in someone else's war. She's spent the last year coming to terms with the senseless loss, healing from the pain…and trying to ease the guilt of someone equally important—the special forces soldier she grew close to on her mission. Ryker blames himself for the deaths, and when he won't take her calls, she has no choice but to seek him out.

Ryker Harp's final mission as a Delta ended in devastation and loss. Not only did he and his teammates barely escape Beirut with their lives, but locals he'd befriended were targeted by the enemy. Since leaving the military, his life has taken more than one unexpected turn, but the guilt remains, and so does his ultimate goal: to annihilate the man who caused such death and destruction. He can't allow any distractions—least of all a beautiful aid worker he can't forget…and doesn't deserve.

When Blakely shows up in Lindeman, Ryker tries to keep his distance to ensure her safety. But it's too late. His enemy has found him. And history may repeat itself if Ryker can't protect everyone he loves most…starting with Blakely.

ACKNOWLEDGMENTS

Thank you, Kelli, for making sure every scene in this book was just right.

Thank you, Jessica, for your guidance, especially on the military elements.

Thank you, Amanda and Jen, for catching every little mistake and error. Your attention to detail is amazing.

To my ARC readers, you are wonderful, and your reviews always inspire me to write the next book.

Thank you to my husband and daughter, you two give me everything I need to be the writer I am.

And thank you to my readers, each and every book is for you.

PROLOGUE

One moment can change everything. Obliterate every carefully laid plan. Every hope for the future. Extinguish it all like a wildfire in a thunderstorm.

Maybe people weren't meant to make plans. Or maybe hearts weren't supposed to count on a tomorrow that was too carefully laid out.

Or maybe people *were* meant to make plans, then feel the devastating shatter of everything they thought they knew so that they were forced to grow. To thicken their skin.

Because everything *could* shatter. In fact, it often did. Break into so many pieces that some would never be found, let alone pieced back together.

She'd been a fool to make plans. To think that in a world of chaos and fluidity, she could actually create a blueprint for the future. That wasn't the reality of the world she lived in. It was a fairy tale. A story told to people, a *lie* to make everyone think they had some control over what happened in their tomorrow.

Sometimes, if she concentrated really hard, she could almost forget how devastatingly wrong her plans had gone. She could forget the searing white core of the flames. The tremble of the earth beneath her feet.

What she couldn't forget was the pain. The burn of the flames against skin. The heaviness on her belly.

But the physical pain was nothing compared to the senseless loss. The memories of the people who should be breathing today but weren't.

Because the loss *had* been senseless. And twisted. And ugly. Unfixable.

And wasn't that lesson number two? That she couldn't go back? She couldn't erase what had already happened and bring back the people who should still be alive.

Finally, she opened her eyes and looked at her reflection in the hotel mirror. Her gaze brushed over the simple black dress, barely seeing it. The chestnut hair that fell over her shoulders and the eyes that were too wide.

Then she focused on the bachelor auction pamphlet. She traced the intricate letters of his name with her eyes. A name that had refused to leave her head throughout the last year.

With a breath, she straightened and moved toward her hotel room door. A hotel she wasn't supposed to be at, in a town she shouldn't be in. But there wasn't anywhere else in the world she *should* be. Everywhere else just felt wrong.

She opened the door. Maybe she was a fool. Because even though she'd felt the collapse of her future, and with it, the cracking of her heart...here she was, making plans again. And hoping like hell these ones didn't end in another devastation.

CHAPTER 1

Ryker Harp stared at his reflection in the large rectangular mirror. Men surrounded him in the changing room, all getting ready for the same event. Sounds filtered down the hall of the event center. Voices. Music. The clinking of champagne glasses and the clicking of heels against marble floors.

The noises were almost quiet compared to the voice in his head. The damn voice that plagued him. *Had been* plaguing him for well over a year, since his last mission as a Delta operator.

His shirt was too fucking tight. He could barely breathe on a daily basis as it was, he didn't need his damn clothes choking him.

He silently cursed his sister, not only for forcing him to be here but forcing him to wear the damn shirt and slacks. A bachelor auction was the last place he wanted to fucking be. No one else could have talked him into it, and they certainly wouldn't have been able to get him on a stage to be sold off to the highest bidder.

He undid the top button of his shirt, trying to loosen the neck. "I know. They're uncomfortable as hell."

He turned to look at Erik. Over the last few months, the former Marine had become a friend to Ryker and the other guys on his team.

"How'd *you* get roped into this?" he asked, fingers twitching to tug at the shirt collar again. "Your sister isn't one of the organizers. You could have said no."

Erik stared into another mirror, an emotion Ryker couldn't place flickering across the guy's face. Sometimes Ryker thought he saw the shadows of demons there. The same shadows he had in his own past. But just like him, Erik was good at keeping his cards close to his chest.

"Trust me, I wanted to say no." Erik fiddled with the cuff of his sleeve. "But then your sister and her friends looked at me with those big eyes of theirs and told me what the money was going toward. I figured I could sacrifice my damn sanity for one date."

True enough. Tonight was about raising money for a good cause—women escaping domestic violence. And not only did the winner get a dance at the event, they also got a date during the upcoming week.

Erik nodded toward Ryker's chest. "You got a new tattoo."

Ryker glanced at the inked flames just visible in the V of his dress shirt. Beneath it, they burned across the left side of his chest. Some days, he swore he could feel their heat deep inside him. A reminder of the past.

"I got it last week," he said quietly. Even though he couldn't see the lines through his shirt, he knew every inch of its intricate detail.

He hadn't been there the day the bomb had taken so many innocent lives in Beirut. He was already back on US soil, after finishing that last shit storm of a mission. Yet he saw the flames when he closed his eyes like he *had* been there. When the world got quiet and his mind got loud, the flames were brighter. Angrier.

He swallowed the burn that came to his throat at the thought. When he looked back at Erik, he saw his friend watching him closely. He did that often. Sometimes Ryker wondered if he saw even more than his own former Delta teammates—Jackson, Declan, and Cole. Men he considered his brothers, who he now ran the Mercy Ring boxing gym with.

Ryker expected Erik to say something. Maybe ask a question he didn't want to answer. But he didn't. And before Ryker could say anything himself, the door flew open and River stepped in.

His gaze cut to his sister in the mirror. The corners of his lips twitched at the excitement in her expression and the huge-ass grin on her face.

"All right," she called, clapping her hands. "It's time, my sexy bachelors! You all know the drill, so let's get out there."

The men started moving, but instead of following them out, River crossed the room to stand behind Ryker. She clamped one hand on his shoulder and one on Erik's arm.

"Ready?"

No.

By Erik's silence and the look on his face, he felt the same.

River didn't seem bothered by their lack of response. Instead, she aimed her excitement at Erik. "I'm so happy you agreed to go first. They're going to go nuts for you."

Ryker lifted a brow, the corner of his mouth lifting. "You're first?"

Erik scrubbed a hand down his face, like the very idea of going out there pained him.

Join the damn club, buddy.

"Yeah. I'm first."

River gave a little squeal. "They're going to love you! Let's go."

Whether his sister didn't see the reluctance on Erik's face or was just choosing to ignore it, he wasn't sure. He was leaning toward the latter.

She yanked Erik's wrist and just about dragged the big guy

out of the room. Before stepping out, she looked over her shoulder at him. "Coming?"

"I'll be there in a minute."

He expected to receive an exasperated look. Maybe a humph or an eye roll. Instead, her expression softened and unspoken words passed between them. She knew this wasn't easy for him. Hell, she probably knew *nothing* was easy anymore.

When the door closed, it was just Ryker with his own company. He didn't mind being alone. In fact, he preferred it. He didn't have to hide what was inside him. Didn't have to force a smile to his lips or calm to his face.

His phone vibrated from the table in front of him. His heart thumped when he saw her name.

Blakely. Again. Because it wasn't enough that he already thought about her every damn day, she had to text and call as well.

He closed his eyes, begging the universe to give him a fucking break.

The woman had been an international aid worker in Beirut. They'd gotten close throughout his missions. They'd become friends, then that friendship had evolved into something more. Something deeper. And that night they'd shared together…

Fuck, he couldn't get it out of his goddamn head no matter how hard he tried. It was supposed to be the start of their forever. Only it wasn't. Because of *him.* Because he'd made the decision that Blakely was better off without…*whatever* the hell he'd become.

But ignoring her hadn't worked. Her calls and texts had only become more frequent, not less. And every time she made contact, it became harder not to answer. Every part of him wanted to pick up the phone. Connect. But he couldn't.

She'd been close with the locals in Beirut. And they'd died because of *him.*

His hands fisted as if he could somehow rein in the storm of emotions. Wrestle it into a box deep inside him. When he glanced at himself in the mirror again, his dark eyes stared back, looking tortured. Eyes so dark, if someone looked hard enough, they might think they could catch glimpses of his soul. But no one would ever know what lurked in its deepest crevices.

Sure, his sister and friends saw the anger...but they didn't know the depth of it. They didn't know his rage had become such a fundamental part of him that it was all he could see. All he felt. And they didn't know how tightly he held on to that anger. Pulling it close, terrified to let it drift or disintegrate. Because he needed it. To remind him of what he had to do.

That there was a man who existed in this world who Ryker needed to find. Kill. Destroy.

BLAKELY SULLIVAN STEPPED inside the Lindeman Event Center. The auction paddle felt heavy in her hand, and her heels pinched her toes. But she was here. And she was going to find and talk to Ryker.

She scanned the busy hall. The space was large, with a bar at the back and the stage at the front. People filled the room. Mostly women, each wearing a dress as beautiful as the next. They were smiling. Laughing. Some watching the stage with obvious excitement.

All Blakely felt was nervous. Her chest was too tight and there was the slightest tremble in her fingers. She hadn't seen Ryker in over a year. And God, that year felt like a lifetime.

She'd tried to make contact. Called and texted so many times she was surprised he hadn't blocked her number. She'd even called one last time just moments ago, before stepping inside the hall. Hoping to avoid any shock on his part by letting him know she was here. He hadn't answered. And even though she should be used to it by now, her heart still cracked a little more.

One time. He'd answered just *once* after learning about the explosion in Beirut.

To tell her they were done. That he was moving back to Washington and whatever they had in the Middle East was over.

Over. He'd said it like it was the easiest word in the world.

She swallowed, moving deeper into the crowd, slipping past the seemingly carefree guests.

Every word of that last call had sounded easy for him, in fact. Until his last two. *I'm sorry.* They'd almost been a whisper. But she'd heard them. She'd also heard the pain that laced his voice. It had slid through her and spidered in her belly.

He wasn't just saying sorry about them or the plans they'd made. His apology went so much deeper than that.

He believed it was his fault those families had died. As if *he'd* dropped the bomb.

He'd shared bits and pieces about that final mission. About his enemy finding him and his team. Trying to destroy them. And when the guy hadn't been able to kill Ryker? He'd killed the locals Ryker cared about. Locals Blakely cared about.

"Hi!"

She swung her gaze to the woman beside her, allowing the distraction to pull her out of her thoughts. A woman with aqua eyes and honey-blonde hair smiled at her.

She tried for a smile, hoping it didn't look as rusty and unpracticed as it felt. "Hi."

"I'm Aria," the woman continued, "one of the organizers of the event. I'm just introducing myself to some of the guests I don't recognize."

"Blakely."

"Great to meet you, Blakely. How'd you hear about our event?"

Pure dumb luck. "I'm visiting from out of town and staying at The Merchant Hotel. There were flyers on the desk."

She'd come to Lindeman with only Ryker's name and the

knowledge that he was here. And yesterday at check-in, there he was—his name on a flyer sitting right before her eyes. If that wasn't a huge, flashing sign from the universe that she was in the right place, she didn't know what was.

Aria beamed. "I told the girls those flyers were a good idea! In town for anything special?"

Special? She wasn't sure if special was the right word. Important? Scary? A huge risk for her already fragile heart that might not pay off? All those seemed to fit better.

"I'm just here to see an old friend."

It wasn't a complete lie. Ryker had once fit into that category. Until he'd become more.

"How lovely. Well, I hope you have a great time tonight." Before walking away, Aria leaned closer. "We've put the two bachelors we anticipate will be most popular first and last."

Ryker had to be one of those two. How could he not? He was six-four and all muscle. He was also this rugged type of beautiful, with a granite jaw and eyes so dark you could get lost in them and never find your way out.

She smiled at the woman. "Thanks for the heads-up."

"You're welcome."

Aria was moving away to greet another guest when a woman stepped onto the stage and spoke into the microphone. Blakely's heart sped up, the beats stumbling over one another.

She recognized the woman. Ryker's sister. Blakely hadn't met River Harp, but Ryker had shown her photos. They were very close, and only one year apart in age. Ryker had often spoken about missing her while he was away. He had this idyllic family, two parents who were still together and in love, and a sister he was best friends with. It was so different from her own divorced parents and a sister who barely had time for her.

"Good evening, everyone. I'm River Harp, one of the organizers. I'm thrilled so many people are here tonight!"

Blakely listened as River described the charity they were

raising money for. She spoke with confidence, her eyes lighting up with excitement. Eyes that were almost the exact shade of Ryker's, so dark they were nearly black. But also different. Where Ryker's gaze always had a cool calmness, this woman's looked more animated and open.

"Are we ready for our first bachelor?"

The crowd screamed around Blakely, some even throwing in a whistle.

River laughed. "Well, ladies, you can thank me later, because first off the ranks today is a man who's not only former military, he also did a stint in the professional boxing world. He's six feet, five inches of gorgeous bad boy. Everyone, help me in welcoming to the stage, Erik Hunter!"

Again, the crowd went crazy as a man stepped out from behind the curtain. He was tall and broad, his thick muscles pulling against his dress shirt. His hard jaw matched the hardness of the rest of him. A couple of visible tattoos and a brow piercing added to his vibe.

Yeah, the guy definitely fit his bio.

The shouts and screams lasted a little longer, the women standing a bit taller. The paddles in their hands rose to their chests, as if they were ready to go and scared others would beat them to the punch. And for good reason. Erik didn't do much in terms of flaunting what he had, but he didn't need to. Hell, he could just stand there scowling and the crowd would drool over him.

The bidding started high and moved fast. Paddle after paddle lifted into the air. River almost looked like she couldn't keep up. In the end, a middle-aged woman wearing expensive jewelry and thick makeup won. And she didn't hold back. After a loud squeal, she ran up the steps to the stage and wrapped Erik in a hug.

For the first time that night, Blakely laughed. It felt good. Also a bit unfamiliar. She hadn't done a lot of laughing in the last year.

Several more bachelors came and went. They were all cute, but not quite on Erik's level.

At the conclusion of each auction, Blakely held her breath, wondering if the next bachelor would be Ryker, even if she knew it wouldn't be. He was the last bachelor Aria had mentioned. She was certain of it.

Her foot started a quick, nervous tap against the marble floor as she waited.

Then, finally, it was time.

"All right, ladies, we're up to our last bachelor of the evening. At the conclusion of his auction, all bachelors will share a dance with their buyers so the couples can discuss specifics of their upcoming date amongst themselves."

Blakely's pulse didn't just speed up this time. It took off at a gallop. The air in her lungs felt so thick she couldn't take a proper breath.

Ryker was about to stand on the stage. She was about to lay eyes on him for the first time in so long. She'd only ever seen him in the Middle East. What did he look like as a civilian? The same? Different? More relaxed? Harder?

"This man is a former Green Beret," River continued. "He's also part owner of Mercy Ring, the new boxing gym in town. He's six foot four, ruggedly handsome and, for one date, he could be all yours."

He stepped onto the stage—and everything around Blakely slowed to a crawl.

Ryker. Memories bombarded her. Dinners together with locals. Shared walks. Shy touches.

She swallowed, trying and failing to calm her speeding heart. He looked so similar. Still big and tall, of course, like a warrior. But he also looked different. Harder. Like there was something deep and dangerous lurking in his eyes that hadn't been there before.

River was still talking, but the words were white noise. Ryker was all she saw, the thump of her heart all she heard.

She was still struggling to breathe, struggling to function, when suddenly, his gaze clashed with hers.

How had he found her in a roomful of people? His gaze made every strong part of her feel weak. Like her knees were ready to buckle under the weight of his stare.

His brows tugged together, and despite the distance, something passed between them. Some emotion she couldn't name.

A new breathlessness rocked her. She couldn't look away. His gaze held her prisoner.

It was only when paddles started to rise that she forced her attention back to River's words. The auction had started. Women were bidding.

Suddenly, her arm flew up. She needed to win this date. To spend even a minute of time with the man who'd once consumed her. The man with whom she'd planned to build a future.

CHAPTER 2

Ryker felt it the second he stepped onstage. The heat under his skin that spiraled like a blanket of fire. The burn from a gaze searing into him.

It wasn't the crowd he felt. It was someone specific.

He scanned the people in the busy room. Hundreds of women stood in front of him, but he kept shifting his gaze, kept searching.

His eyes stopped—and every muscle in his body went so hard he thought they'd snap.

Blakely. She was here. In this room.

Her lips separated, like she was surprised he'd found her. The woman could stand in a crowd of a thousand and he'd find her. Sense her. Feel her close by.

There was a time when he'd memorized every inch of her. Every millimeter, inside and out. She was a memory he couldn't erase no matter how hard he tried. Her long chestnut hair that flowed like a river down her back. Her olive-green eyes that darkened and lightened with her mood. Her soft curves and silky skin.

For a moment, the room faded. River's voice. The hum of

movement. Even the thoughts in his head…it all silenced. And he was taken back to a time when life made sense. When hell hadn't ravaged his very existence.

Then she blinked, and it seemed to pull her out of whatever trance she was in. She scanned the room, recognizing that paddles were rising into the air. Then she lifted hers.

She was bidding on him?

His legs twitched to move. Go to her. Demand she leave before he did something stupid. Like touch her. Kiss her. Fall into the depths of those gorgeous green eyes and let her take him away from the pain that drowned him daily.

There'd been a time when he thought he'd eventually see those eyes every damn day for the rest of his life. They'd made plans in Lebanon. Plans to give long-distance dating a go, once they both reached US soil.

What was that saying? Make plans and God laughs?

God hadn't just laughed at Ryker. He'd thrown wreckage on his damn doorstep.

Paddles continued to shoot into the air around the room, and they all seemed to be competing against Blakely. She didn't stop. Her arm kept moving, raising her bid, not seeming to care how high it got.

Even after the bidders thinned out, Blakely kept going until it was her and one other woman.

Janice. She'd had a drink with him at Lenny's Bar and Grill a few times. They'd even made out once. He'd never gone beyond that, though. He'd never gone beyond that with *any* woman since Blakely. He hadn't been able to.

Janice's eyes narrowed on Blakely until, finally, Janice stopped raising her paddle—and River declared Blakely the winner.

His lungs tightened to the point air flow seemed impossible. Because suddenly Blakely was walking toward him. Sliding through the crowd with the same lethal grace he remembered so well.

Damn, she was beautiful. She'd always been the most beautiful woman he'd ever seen, even in the casual pants and T-shirts she'd worn in Beirut. But tonight, she wore a tight black dress that hit mid-thigh. It hugged her curves and showed off too much damn skin.

His heart warred with his mind. A part of him wanted to turn. Run. Get the hell away from the dangerous woman. The other half wanted to meet her halfway. Touch her. Pull her into him and refamiliarize himself with every single part of Blakely.

He did neither. He stood so still that it almost felt like the rest of the world froze with him.

Too soon, she was in front of him, her sweet, intoxicating scent of lilacs mixed with strawberries infusing the air, toying with him.

River cleared her throat through the microphone. "Um, Ryker. Can you congratulate your winner?"

Suddenly, he remembered River's instructions. The auction winner was allowed a hug or a single kiss on the cheek.

The idea of touching his lips to this woman's skin almost brought him to his knees.

He ground his jaw, forcing his limbs to move as he took a small step toward her. He placed his right hand on her hip, feeling the race of electricity down his arm as surely as if he'd touched a live wire. Then he leaned in and pressed his lips to her cheek. Her skin was velvet against his.

It was more of a graze than a kiss. Still, her breath hitched, and he felt a tremble move through her body.

Before lifting his head, he lowered his mouth to her ear and whispered, "You shouldn't have come, princess."

～

A SHUDDER RACED down Blakely's spine at Ryker's words. At the way his breath whispered across her sensitive skin as he used the familiar endearment. He'd nicknamed her princess after their first meeting. She'd been standing in a field of dirt, and he claimed she looked like a monarch amongst the rubble.

When he straightened, she had to remind herself to breathe. To move her chest in and out and allow the air to flow.

"Okay, it's time for music! Bachelors, please take your winners to the dance floor." River's words barely penetrated Blakely's fog. It was only Ryker's arm, as it shifted to her back and nudged her forward, that propelled her to move.

She swallowed, careful to watch her feet as she walked down the three steps. Her legs felt like jelly and the rhythm of her heart wasn't even close to what it should be. Ryker's hand was on her, his hot body flush against her side. It was a body she remembered so well. What she *didn't* remember was the uncertainty in his eyes. He'd almost looked tortured as she walked toward the stage. Like he was on the verge of running. And even though she expected it after he'd ignored her for a year, it still hurt.

When they reached the dance floor, his arms skirted around her waist. He didn't pull her close enough that her body pressed to his, but she felt the heat radiating from his flesh. It surrounded her, pulling her into a cloak of Ryker.

"What are you doing here?"

A second shudder ran down her spine, this time at the rumble of his voice. The glint in his eyes. "You wouldn't take my calls or respond to my texts. I didn't have a choice."

His jaw visibly tightened before he glanced over her head like he was searching for something. What, exactly, she wasn't sure. But she was almost certain he didn't find it, because when he looked back at her, there was no resolution or calm.

"I didn't take your calls or respond to your texts because I'd said everything I needed to say in our last conversation."

His words were like physical blows, each more powerful than the last. But she didn't double over, and she certainly didn't let an inch of the pain show on her face. Instead, she told him what she needed him to hear. "You're important to me, and I needed to see that you're okay."

She didn't just care about him. Her feelings went so much deeper than that.

"I'm okay." His words came automatically and were so flat, there was no emotion behind them at all.

She could have laughed at his lie. Because it *was* a lie. One look at him had shown her he wasn't okay. There was a new darkness in him. One she desperately wanted to lighten.

She swallowed, trying to think of something to say that would bring out even a tiny glimpse of the Ryker she remembered.

As her gaze moved around the room, it caught on a small group of three men and three women—all staring at her and Ryker with interest. River was there. And the woman she'd met earlier, Aria. She didn't recognize the third woman, but she did recognize the three men. Jackson, Declan and Cole. Ryker's Delta teammates. She'd seen them in the Middle East but never really talked to any of them. Still, Ryker had spoken about them enough that she felt like she knew the men.

Not far from the group stood the woman who'd gone into a bidding war with Blakely over Ryker. Her eyes were narrowed. God, if looks could kill.

Did she know Ryker? Had they dated?

The thought made a sick feeling churn in her gut.

"I don't think that woman's happy I won the auction," Blakely said quietly.

"How long are you in town for?"

Her gaze shifted back to his. He wasn't looking at her. Because he couldn't? "I don't know. I bought a one-way flight."

By the flexing of the arms around her, he wasn't thrilled by that little fact.

"Is it really so awful that I'm here?" She tried not to let the hurt tinge her words.

God, there'd been a time when they'd seen each other every

chance they got. And when they weren't in the same country, they'd texted and called every night. *That* was the relationship they once had. *That* was the Ryker she remembered.

"Yes."

That single word cut like a knife across her skin, causing her to flinch. Her feet stopped and she started to step away, but Ryker's arms tightened, not letting her go. Instead, he pulled her against his chest.

His voice lowered, as if he was scared someone would hear. "It *is* bad that you're here. I'm not good for you."

If there was ever an incorrect statement, it was that one. Some days she'd almost convinced herself he was the *only* good. "What do you mean, you're not good for me?"

"You need to go home."

Home? Ha. Her apartment in Minnesota had long-since stopped feeling like home. And now she felt lost. Displaced.

They started moving again. Swaying to the music, his chest brushing against hers in soft, fleeting grazes.

"I'm not leaving." She curled her hand around his shoulder. Through his shirt, the thick cords of his muscles were tense. "Unlike you, I'm not running from this."

"I'm not running. I'm moving in the direction we've been forced to move."

"We haven't been forced anywhere, Ryker. *We* decide where we go and what we do."

She'd wanted to come sooner. But she'd been a mess after the explosion. She'd needed time. Space. To heal both emotionally and physically.

Ryker didn't know anything about the latter.

As if he'd heard her thoughts, his brows lowered. "Are *you* doing okay?"

Memories of that awful day attempted to swamp her. She'd been close to the explosions. Just a street away. Close enough to get there and see the flames. Feel them...

Her lungs tried to constrict again, but she forced her breathing to remain even…just. "I'm okay."

The lie fell as imperfectly from her as it had from him. But now was hardly the time to share that those flames haunted her even on her quietest days.

When he didn't respond, she looked up to see him watching her closely. Maybe trying to see the truth behind her words.

"Onstage, River said you run a boxing gym," she said quickly, not able to delve into her psyche here and now. "Mercy Ring. That sounds like an interesting business."

But it wasn't a surprise. He'd told her about the boxing gym he and Jackson had visited as kids. Plus, the man was former Special Forces. He was as lethal as they came and probably knew every type of hand-to-hand combat.

"It was Jackson's idea. The owner passed away, so we bought the building."

She had a feeling that was the short, condensed version of the story.

When his thumb shifted on her waist in a near-caress, her stomach did a little somersault. God, being near him again… His touch. His heat. The way he smelled of pine—earthy and all male.

"I missed you." The words slipped from her lips like a secret she wasn't supposed to share. And the muscles in his arms tensed against her.

"Blakely…"

She frowned. "Blakely?"

He *never* called her that. Or at least, hadn't for a long time.

She lowered her voice. "We had something." Hell, they *still* had something. Beneath the anger and hesitation, the connection still thrummed between them. The one that had always been there and neither of them had ever been able to deny.

"It was one night."

His words brought another knife to her flesh. Another flinch.

Was he hurting her on purpose? Trying to shock her into leaving? "Don't do that. Don't cheapen what we shared."

That night had been… Jesus, it had been everything. A culmination of the connection and affection they'd built over the year she'd spent in Beirut. He was trying to reduce their entire relationship to that one night of sex, but their connection wasn't just physical. It went so much deeper. An invisible link that drew them to each other, despite any distance.

Prior to that night, anytime they weren't together, their calls had lasted hours. Whether Ryker admitted it or not, they had something they couldn't just walk away from. At least, *she* couldn't.

"Ryker—"

He stopped, his hands dropping. The loss was like a bucket of ice water on her head.

He ran a hand over his face. "I have to go."

He took a step, but she grabbed his arm. "I know you're hurting. But I don't understand why that hurt needs to cause distance between us."

For a moment, he was perfectly still. Even his chest didn't rise. Then he turned toward her, lowered his head, and whispered into her ear. "Because my world has monsters lurking in the corners, Blakely…and I don't want you anywhere near them."

CHAPTER 3

"You gonna be silent all day or are you gonna tell me what's going on with you and Blakely?"

Ryker stilled at Jackson's words, the muscles in his forearms flexing as he tightened his hold on the focus mitts. He'd done a pretty damn good job of dodging his friend since they'd arrived at Mercy Ring this morning. It hadn't been hard. The place was busy. But now, it looked like he was out of time.

"Nothing."

Jackson wouldn't buy that for a second. Not only had the two of them served in the military together for sixteen years, they'd been best friends before that, growing up in this town together.

Jackson raised a brow. "The woman traveled here from Minnesota then paid a small fortune in the auction for you last night. *Something's* going on."

Ryker crossed the room and dumped the mitts in the box before turning. Jackson had his arms crossed and all his attention on Ryker.

He ran a hand through his hair as the sound of fists hitting bags and heavy breathing filtered through the room. "She said she came to check that I was okay."

"What did you tell her?"

More than he should have, even if he'd barely admitted anything. He didn't tell her about the anger that plagued him. The thirst for revenge he couldn't quench. Regardless, she'd looked at him with her intelligent green eyes and he *knew* she'd seen far more than he wanted.

He'd told her about monsters in the dark, hoping she'd stay away. He *should* have told her to go home and left it at that. Because the longer she was here, the more he'd reveal, and the more he'd be drawn back in to all that was Blakely.

"I told her I was okay."

"Are you?"

Gray, murky irritation swept through his limbs. He hadn't been okay for a long time. Jackson had seen some of that anger, but he didn't know the depths of it. And he didn't need to.

He definitely didn't need to know he'd received a call this morning from his informant, Cal, an old Army buddy who now worked in security and investigation. Ryker had hired him to find Sameed Saad, the man responsible for what happened in Beirut.

Saad was here, on US soil. That much Ryker already knew— and Cal would find him. He was the best at what he did, and Ryker trusted him completely.

Jackson didn't need to know any of that. It wasn't his war.

"Yes." One word. That was all he was getting.

He tried to walk past, but Jackson grabbed his arm and lowered his voice. "Don't lie to me. You put on a good face, but I see behind the mask. And I know you haven't let go of what happened in Beirut."

"Could *you?*" *Shut up, Ryker!* "If you'd sat at a family's table, let them feed you, welcome you into their lives. Then they died because of a war they had *nothing* to do with, killed by *your* enemy. Could you let that go?"

"First of all, he's *our* enemy, not yours. Second, I'm not telling you to let it go."

"Then what are you telling me?"

Jackson's chest rose and fell. "To be smart and let us in on whatever your plans are. River would never forgive me if I let you do something stupid. She already thought she lost you once." There was a heavy pause. "*Are* you gonna do something stupid and put your family through that pain again?"

He had no plans to die for real this time. He wanted to tear a man apart with his bare hands. But he needed to *get* his hands on the guy first. "Not right now."

Jackson's eyes narrowed.

Yeah, it was as good as he could give him, and certainly more honesty than he should have offered his friend.

Ryker pulled his arm from Jackson's hold and stepped away. Before he could go, Jackson's words rang out.

"*You* may not care about your life, but other people do."

Ryker paused, letting those words weave through his chest as they tried to puncture his carefully constructed wall. He wanted to tell his friend he shouldn't care so much. None of them should. It was caring about others that had gotten Ryker where he was.

Caring was dangerous.

But he didn't. Because he knew they'd be wasted words. Instead, he pushed them down and walked away, exhaling a long breath when Jackson didn't grab him again or follow.

He spent the next hour trying to forget what his friend had said. He went through the motions at work, circulating through the room, focusing on clients by correcting form and demonstrating hits. Even though he tried to block everything else out, memories skittered through his mind.

The entire team had been sent to Beirut to eliminate Saad's brother, a high-value target. It was a textbook operation, and they'd eliminated the target fairly easily. That should've been the end of it. And it would have been…if Saad hadn't learned their location and tried to eliminate *them* in retaliation.

That night had been the closest any of them had come to death. Declan had been shot. Cole had been shoved out of a second-floor window and broken his back. They almost hadn't made it back to their extraction point.

He'd never been so happy to hit US soil two days later. Unable to see Blakely beforehand, he'd shared what details he could with her during a call shortly before boarding the military aircraft, and she'd been worried. But his team's injuries weren't the worst fucking part.

The worst part was getting the call from Blakely just days later. Her voice still echoed in his head, broken and tormented. It was like she'd reached through the phone line and ripped his heart out when she told him about the people who'd died.

He'd never felt pain and outrage like that before. He'd demanded to be flown back so he could end Saad. But Captain Davis, his fucking commander, refused. Then he'd slapped a no-fly on his ass, so Ryker couldn't even return on his own.

In addition to the guilt and hurt and anger...there'd been deep hopelessness. It had all tangled inside him to obliterate everything he'd been before.

Slowly, that hopelessness, guilt, and rage had coalesced into a feeling of not being enough for Blakely. It was *his fault* she'd lost people she loved. *His fault* she'd sounded so broken on the phone. And that all amounted to one fucking thing—she deserved better.

At the very least, she deserved a man who didn't bring death and devastation to her damn doorstep.

A lot had happened over the last year, and the only reason he'd survived any of it was with the knowledge that, someday soon, the opportunity would arise for him to kill the man who desperately needed to die. And when that opportunity came, Ryker was gonna fucking take it.

He was still deep in his head when the door opened. He cursed and his pulse thudded in his neck when Blakely walked in.

BLAKELY TOOK a moment to study Mercy Ring. The place looked like an old warehouse, though the exterior paint seemed new. If it wasn't for the sign, she wouldn't know it was a boxing gym.

Nerves hummed under her skin. As soon as Ryker had stepped away from her last night, Aria had smoothly swept her away to sign some documents and pay for her win. It had cost a big chunk of her savings, but she'd gotten a few moments with Ryker, which was more than she'd been able to achieve in the last year. The win was also supposed to buy her a date, something he was clearly hoping she'd forgotten.

Well, sorry, buddy. I paid for a date, and I'm getting one.

Something had been different about Aria when she'd approached her the second time. More hesitancy in her conversation. Her gaze had lingered on Blakely, like she'd been trying to figure something out. The guys had obviously recognized her, and it seemed clear they'd told their women that Blakely had been in Beirut. Maybe even that she and Ryker had a history.

How much of that history, exactly, she wasn't sure. Because she had no idea what Ryker had told his team.

Before Blakely left the event, Aria had passed along her cell number, letting her know she was welcome to use it if she wanted someone to hang out with while in Lindeman. Not that Blakely knew how long she'd be here. The only thing she did know? She wasn't ready to give up. Not yet. She'd come here to see if Ryker was okay—and he wasn't.

Okay, maybe she'd come for another, equally important reason too. She'd missed him. And she cared about him. If she could, she wanted to help him. And maybe find out if he still cared at all about *her.*

Finally, she took a big, cleansing breath and pushed through the main door. The place was huge. One large open room, with a boxing ring that centered the space and heavy bags attached to the vaulted ceiling. There were several people in the gym, all wearing mitts and hitting bags like they were beating demons.

She felt the pull before she saw him. When she met his gaze, she glimpsed the same darkness she'd seen last night. Was that all Ryker was capable of feeling now?

Well, it wasn't going to deter her. In fact, it just cemented her need to be here.

With silent determination, she lifted her chin and crossed the room.

"What are you doing here?" he growled quietly.

She tilted her head. "Well, hello to you too, sunshine. Do you greet all your clients that way?"

His brows slashed together. "You're here to box?"

"Yes."

"No."

She almost laughed. Her lips definitely twitched. "No?"

"You don't know how to box."

"First, this is a boxing gym, so I would assume if I needed instruction, you or another staff member would be able to help me. Second—I've boxed."

A fitness class at her local gym in Minnesota counted as boxing experience, right? There'd been boxing gloves and mitts.

If looks could cut, Ryker's would be lasering straight through her right now.

"Blakely, it's good to see you again."

She turned at the gravelly voice coming from her left to find Jackson. She offered him a smile. "Hey, Jackson. It's good to see you too."

He crossed his arms over his wide chest. "Are you here to box?"

"I am."

"Great. I'll get you a form to sign, then I'll show you to a bag."

Actually, no, *now* Ryker's expression could cut. He looked like he wanted to kill his friend. Why, precisely, she didn't know. But his jaw was clenched so hard, she was scared it was going to break.

Jackson, on the other hand, had a smile that stretched wide across his face. He moved behind the desk and grabbed some forms and a pen. She signed the papers without reading them, then followed Jackson across the room. Ryker didn't move the entire time. He just stared, possibly hoping the I'm-so-angry-I-want-to-murder-someone look on his face would deter her.

Nope. Not even a little bit.

Jackson offered her a storage cube for her purse, then grabbed some mitts and took her to a free bag. "You can use this one."

"Thanks."

He stepped closer and strapped the gloves onto her hands. "You need any help?"

After she'd just told Mr. Grump she knew what she was doing? "I'll let you know."

A knowing smile teased his lips. "Keep your hands relaxed when you're not punching," he said quietly. "You can make a loose fist, but don't clench. When you punch, think of your fist like a brick. Your gloves start up by your face, then turn your fist horizontally for a straight punch."

She nodded, trying to remember all the information, even though at least a few words flew right over her head.

He leaned forward and lowered his voice another notch. "I'm glad you're here, Blakely."

She opened her mouth, not quite sure how to respond, but he was already turning and heading away.

She let his words roll over in her head as she turned toward the bag. Was he glad she was here because he knew what she suspected? That Ryker wasn't okay?

Well, of course. Ryker's friends knew him better than anyone. And Ryker had mentioned monsters last night. Monsters didn't lurk in the corners for people who were okay.

She did a few quick stretches before turning toward the bag, her heart aching for him. Then, with a long exhale, she lifted her fists.

"Hands like a brick and horizontal punches," she whispered, before stepping forward and hitting the bag.

Holy crackers, it was like hitting a brick wall. The thing didn't move an inch. Her gaze covertly swept to the man who was boxing beside her. He threw a fist into the bag, and it swung back about a foot like it weighed nothing.

Great. This was great. She couldn't even give the bag a nudge while the men in the room were practically shooting the bags to the roof.

She took a breath and threw another punch. Same thing.

She was just preparing for a third when large, warm hands touched her hips. Familiar hands.

It took everything she had not to melt against him.

"You need to turn your hips more side on," Ryker said in a deep rumble. He applied some pressure, and her heart stumbled. "Spread your legs wider." He slotted a foot between hers and tapped them apart.

Then he stepped closer, and she had to remind herself to breathe. To suck one breath in after another as his heat pressed into her back.

"Knees need to be slightly bent, and when you hit the bag, turn your hips toward your opponent, keeping your shoulders loose and exhaling on the hit."

More deep rumbles. She tried to take it all in, but she had to repeat his words in her head a few times to force them to make sense.

After a beat, she nodded. "Bent knees, turn hips, loose shoulders, and exhale."

When his hands fell away, she stilled, watching as his strong, thick fingers wrapped around her small wrists. The man dwarfed her. Made her feel tiny and fragile and just a bit...his.

The last word was a forbidden whisper in her head.

"Like this." He guided her fist toward the bag, his hips applying pressure to move hers as they went. And, Lord oh Lord, she wanted to drown in the feeling. "Good."

He stepped back. The heat disappeared. But she wouldn't forget it soon. She took a moment to calm her racing heart, then she punched the bag, incorporating everything he'd just shown her.

"That was good," he said quietly. "Again."

She struck out. It actually felt good. Frustration she hadn't realized she'd been holding onto poured out of her with each hit. Frustration at herself for taking so long to get here. At not knowing how to help Ryker, just knowing that being close felt right.

She punched again and again, expecting him to eventually move away.

Instead, he nodded. "Good, now try a cross punch with the other hand. This is often called a counterpunch."

He slipped his fingers around her wrist and guided the first hit. Then, again, he stepped back. Every time he stepped away, disappointment flooded her body. She pushed it away, replicating the hit on her own.

"You've got it."

They continued like that for a while. Him watching her; her doing as instructed. Every so often, stopping so he could show her a new hit or guide her actions with his touch.

Every time he nodded or voiced his approval, a small fleck of heat ignited in her chest. It was like a tiny flame that burned only for him, and every touch, every word, made it flare brighter.

It felt good. All of it. And there were short moments where she almost felt like she had the old Ryker back.

"You should stop now," he said when her breathing became labored. "Don't want to overdo it."

A part of her was disappointed, but the other part recognized her aching shoulders and heavy arms.

"I need you to go home, Blakely."

The flame dimmed. Or maybe it went out entirely, she wasn't sure. Whichever the case, the heat inside her definitely turned cold.

She looked at him, trying to decide on the right words and ignoring that he'd once again used her first name instead of her nickname.

"I can't," she finally said. "Not yet."

It was the truth. Not a single part of her felt capable of walking away from this man.

His jaw clicked. "Don't you have a job to return to?"

She'd *had* a job. Once she'd healed from her burns and felt up to the task, she'd taken a nursing position in a small hospital. She'd put in her resignation last week. Her head wasn't in it, and it wasn't fair to her patients.

She didn't want to tell him any of that, though. Not here. Not now, when he was trying to force her to leave.

"You owe me a date."

"No."

Instant. Unyielding.

She was getting pretty damn sick of this man saying no to her. "I won the auction. I paid the money. A date was part of the deal."

"I can't go on a date with you."

That frustration returned to her with a vengeance. "Can't? Or won't?"

"Both."

Then he turned and stepped away.

Really? He was just leaving *again*?

"I'm not leaving until I get that date, Ryker."

He paused—only for a second, and only long enough for the muscles in his back to ripple beneath his shirt. Then he continued, walking away from her without a backward glance.

CHAPTER 4

$\mathcal{W}$e're leaving in a few minutes. Are you sure you don't want us to pick you up?

Blakely smiled as she read the message. She was bored out of her brain and appreciated the invitation to a local bar with Aria and her friends.

Ryker was still ignoring her calls and texts, like he had been for the past year. Cornering him at Mercy Ring yesterday morning clearly hadn't changed anything. She might have no idea how to reach him emotionally, but leaving wasn't an option yet.

So yes, she wanted to go out. Aria hadn't said anything about Ryker being there, but a girl could hope.

She typed in a quick response.

I'm okay getting there. See you soon.

Her hotel was only a ten-minute walk. Everything seemed to be a ten-minute walk or less from here. Mercy Ring. The event center where the bachelor auction had been held. It was great since she didn't have a car. Must be a small-town thing.

Quickly, she swiped on some lipstick, then shoved her phone and room card into her pocket, automatically feeling for the key she always carried. Or at least, it looked like a key. It folded out into a knife. She kept it with her both for safety and for the connection she felt to Ryker when she had it.

He'd come to her room in Beirut and asked her to go for a walk. Along the way, he'd stopped and pulled out the device. Shown her the words he'd had inscribed on it.

Keep me close, princess.

And she did. Every day.

With a sigh, she checked the mirror one last time. Tight jeans and a pale green knit sweater over a white top, paired with some strappy heels—cute but comfortable enough to walk in.

She straightened her sweater as she left the hotel room. Ryker had once told her he loved her in green. That it made her olive eyes stand out.

But that wasn't the reason she'd thrown it in her luggage, and it certainly wasn't the reason she'd worn it tonight.

God, she wished she could reach him. Right now, it felt like there was a tall, thick wall blocking the old Ryker. Shielding him from the world.

She'd only been walking for a few minutes when a car engine sounded behind her. Blakely turned her head. A dark vehicle with tinted windows was behind her on the street. She frowned, an unease she couldn't explain closing over her.

Why were they driving so slowly? They were just about at a crawl.

Her heart gave a little thud as she faced forward and sped up her steps. One heartbeat. Two heartbeats. Three…

The car finally passed. But the feeling of unease didn't.

Who was that? And why had they inched along behind her for so long?

Walking back from the auction two nights ago, she'd felt like someone was watching her but wrote it off as being in a new, unfamiliar town. She probably shouldn't have been walking around by herself so late, but she'd had no idea if the small town had a taxi service, and her hotel had been so close.

She rounded a corner, seeing the sign for Lenny's Bar and Grill ahead. This time she sped up for a different reason.

She was just about to step inside when a car passed on the road behind her.

Dark. Tinted windows.

Frowning, she stared. Was it the same car? How common were black sedans around here?

She squinted to read the plate, but before she could get the entire thing, it disappeared.

She stood there for a few beats, waiting to see if it returned. When it didn't, she took a breath and stepped inside. Immediately, thoughts of the car went to the back of her mind as the smell of beer and the heat of bodies stole her attention.

The place was busy. Certainly busier than she'd expected for a Sunday evening. Another small-town thing?

She skirted around people, moving deeper into the thick crowd as she scanned faces. Aria was at a tall table with Erik, one of the bachelors from the auction, and Cole. Blakely had to school her features to hide her disappointment. No Ryker.

Well, at least she'd been saved from a lonely night in her hotel.

She was halfway across the room when a female voice from a table nearby called, "Well, look who it is."

She turned her head and only just bit back a groan. It was the woman from the bachelor auction. The one who'd bid against her. She stood at a table with two large guys, one with a sleeve of tattoos up his arm.

The woman cocked her head. "You don't have your prize with you tonight? He dump you already?"

She was trying to get a rise out of Blakely. She wouldn't get one. "I'm just here for a drink. You have a good evening."

Blakely moved away from the table. The woman said something else, but Blakely wasn't listening. Whatever it was, she was sure it wouldn't have been kind.

She smiled at Aria and the guys as she stopped beside them. "Hey."

"Blakely! I'm so glad you made it." Aria pulled her into a hug, surprising Blakely. When she pulled back, she nodded across the table. "This is Erik. And I believe you've met my partner, Cole."

Erik dipped his chin, while Cole grinned. "Nice to see you."

She smiled at the men. They both wore dark T-shirts that pulled tightly against their toned chests and arms.

"I'm gonna head to the bar to get our drinks," Erik said.

Cole pushed away from the table. "I'll help you."

Erik's gaze met hers. "What would you like?"

Aria bumped her shoulder. "I'm getting a Brown Derby. It's one of the only cocktails on offer here."

"That sounds great."

Erik nodded and moved away. Similar to the night of the auction, there was a hardness about him. A quiet intensity.

Blakely looked back to Aria. "It's busy."

"Yup. That's pretty much a constant here." Her gaze shifted to the bar. "The owner's a friend of mine. Kind of."

Blakely's lips quirked. Sounded like there was a story behind that. "Is he here?"

Her eyes turned sad. "No, he's recovering from a bullet wound."

"A bullet wound?"

Aria grimaced. "Yeah. It was kind of my fault. I was in a bad situation, and I ran in here to hide. The guy following me came in too. Lenny tried to help me and got shot."

Wow. Whatever she'd been expecting the woman to say, it wasn't any of that. Blakely didn't know how to respond. Sorry didn't feel like enough.

Aria shook her head. "God, I shouldn't talk about that tonight. Lenny's okay. Zac and I are safe. Cole and his team are safe."

She tilted her head. "Who's Zac?"

"He's my sixteen-year-old son."

"Sixteen?" This woman just kept hitting her with surprises.

"I know. I had him young, and now I have an almost-adult in the house. It's crazy."

Uh, yeah, it *was* crazy, because this woman did not look old enough to have a sixteen-year-old kid. Not even close.

Aria glanced over her shoulder before looking back at her. "So, tell me, have you had your date with Ryker?"

Ha. If only. She shook her head. "I went to Mercy Ring yesterday, and the man told me in no uncertain terms that he had no intention of going on a date with me."

Aria's lips parted. "But that was a condition of winning the auction."

"It was."

"An auction he signed on to do."

Blakely lifted a shoulder. "I plan to work on him, but it's looking pretty bleak." She'd never been a quitter, though, and she didn't plan to start now.

Aria scowled. "That's not cool, the backtracking butthole!"

Cole laughed as he set a glass in front of Aria. "Do I want to know who you're talking about?"

Erik set an amber-colored cocktail in front of her. She smiled at him. "Thank you."

Aria crossed her arms and all but growled to Cole. "Your friend, Ryker."

Cole and Erik seemed amused by that.

"What did he do?" Erik asked.

"He signed on to the bachelor auction, and now he refuses to fulfill the terms of his commitment." Aria swung an accusatory look Erik's way. "I hope you took *your* winner on a date."

He sipped his beer. "I did. Mrs. Albuquerque had a great night. I think I counted ten touches on my biceps and at least two ass grabs."

Blakely threw her head back and laughed at the image of this big, strong alpha going on a date with the older woman who'd won his auction.

Aria grinned. "She was *very* excited about her win. Possibly our most excited winner."

Blakely was just lifting her cocktail to her lips when a hard shove to her back caused her to fall forward, sending half the contents of her glass splashing onto her sweater.

"Hey!" Erik straightened beside her, fists clenched.

She turned to find one of the guys who'd been sitting with the woman from the auction. The one without tattoos.

The man raised his hands. "Whoops. Accident."

His tone told her it was *not* an accident. Blakely's gaze shot across the room to find the woman snickering at her own table. Definitely not.

Erik stepped forward. The air thickened and her belly tangled. She thought the guy would step away. Hell, any normal person would. Erik was big and muscular and had "threat" written all over him. Yet the man didn't even *look* away, let alone step back.

"Apologize," Erik growled.

When the guy remained silent, a nervous tickle spidered up Blakely's back. She touched Erik's arm, careful to keep her voice soft. "It's okay. I'll just go to the bathroom and clean up."

A heavy silence passed, where the men stared each other down. Blakely swallowed in an attempt to wet her dry throat.

Then, finally, the guy muttered the least sincere apology she'd ever heard before walking away.

The air whooshed from her chest. Erik remained where he was, keeping his stare on the other man.

Aria took her hand, finally pulling Blakely's attention. "Come on. I'll go with you to the bathroom."

Blakely allowed herself to be led to the back of the bar. It wasn't until they'd stepped inside the restroom that she let the shudder roll down her spine.

"Are you okay?" Aria asked quietly.

"Yeah, I was a bit scared the guys would break into a fight." Scared for the guy who'd bumped her, that was. He wouldn't have stood a chance against Erik.

She grabbed some paper towels and began to dab at her sweater.

Aria nodded. "Yeah, I felt Cole tense beside me like he was ready to attack the jerk too. The guys are all the same. They defend women and give men hell for being assholes."

"And the guy was definitely being an intentional asshole."

Aria snorted. "Oh yeah, he was a douchebag—and Janice clearly sent him over to mess with you."

"Do you know her?" The words slipped out before Blakely could stop them.

"I don't *know* her, really, but I've seen her and one of her friends crawling all over the guys in here before. I don't like either of them."

So it wasn't just her. Blakely grabbed the bottom of her sweater and tugged it over her head. It was too wet to continue wearing. She glanced at her shirt in the mirror. Argh, the liquid went through, and now part of her white top was wet and sticking to her. At least she'd worn a white bra.

"Oh no. I wish I had a spare shirt for you." Aria grabbed more paper towels for her.

"It's fine. It only got a little bit wet. It'll dry." She dabbed the material. It wasn't ideal, but it could be worse.

When she was done, she followed Aria out of the bathroom. Erik was just slipping his phone into his pocket when they reached the table. Over the next hour, they drank, talked, and the small group made Blakely laugh, which was rare these days. She realized quickly that Cole and Erik were quite similar. Both the dark, broody types, while Aria filled a lot of the silence.

Even though Cole didn't say much, he always seemed to be touching Aria with a hand on the back. On the hip. And when he looked at her, it was like she was the only woman who existed in the room.

It was sweet.

"You look deep in your own head."

She turned toward Erik. "Always." But the man didn't want to know what those thoughts were. She changed the subject before he could ask. "What do you do?"

It took him longer than it should have to answer. "I'm a government contractor."

She blinked. That didn't tell her much. She opened her mouth to ask him more, then snapped it shut. It was his business, and if he didn't want to share, that was okay.

"What about you?" he asked.

She sipped the last of her cocktail. After the spill, there hadn't been much left, so this was technically still her first. "I'm a nurse. I've worked in hospitals and did a stint as an international aid worker in Beirut. I'm taking some time off right now."

She'd loved her job as an aid worker, but she couldn't do it again after Beirut. And that fact hurt sometimes. More than she cared to admit.

"Hope you didn't venture to Syria. That would be dangerous."

She laughed. "You're a former Marine."

He nodded. "I was in special operations."

"See, *that's* dangerous. I just helped civilians."

"Didn't feel dangerous at the time. It felt important." An emotion she couldn't name flashed over his face. Had it *stopped* feeling important?

Again, she opened her mouth to ask, but he got in first, nodding toward her drink. "Want another?"

"Yes, but I'll get it. Want another beer?"

"Nah, I'm okay."

She turned toward Aria and Cole, who were looking at each other like they were about to run away and elope.

"Drinks?" Blakely asked.

They both shook their heads.

She moved toward the bar. She was halfway there when she was hit by that *being watched* feeling again, just like two nights ago. God, what *was* that?

She stopped and looked around the bar. When she saw nothing out of place, she shook her head and went to step forward—and walked right into a large body.

Oh, Jesus. It was the *other* man who'd been with the woman from the auction. Tattoos Guy.

"Hey, gorgeous."

She almost laughed. "What has she sent *you* over to do? I'm not holding a drink, so...trip me? Ask me to dance, then push me to the floor? Whatever it is, you'd be smarter not to."

She moved around him and kept walking, but she could feel him behind her. He was close. The second she reached the bar, he stopped beside her.

"Let me buy you a drink."

"No, thanks." That was a *hell* no, thanks.

He leaned his head closer. "Come on. One drink."

Argh. The guy's breath on her cheek was making her queasy. "I said no."

She shuffled away as the bartender stopped in front of her.

"What can I get you?"

"Just a soda, please." More alcohol suddenly seemed like a poor choice. Besides, she still had to walk home, and Janice didn't seem to be done messing with her. It was probably a good idea to keep her wits about her.

The second the drink was set on the bar, she lifted her card, but the guy beat her to it, swiping his own card on the handheld credit card machine.

He grinned at her, but the smile was calculating. "Now you have to dance with me."

"That's not how it works. I'm going back to my table."

She stepped away, but the guy snagged her arm and pulled her toward him, causing her drink to spill onto her hand.

"What's the matter?"

"The *matter* is that I'm not interested, and you're annoying me." She tried to tug her arm from his hold, but his fingers tightened. Instead of moving away, he invaded her personal space even more.

She scowled. "What are you—"

His head dropped and he mashed his wet lips against hers.

CHAPTER 5

*J*ab, *jab, cross punch.*

The bag flew violently at each hit from Ryker. But he didn't stop. He'd been in the workout room of his house, hitting the bag for a good hour. His body was tired, but not tired enough. He wanted exhaustion to weigh down his limbs. He wanted his arms to tremble and his mind to go numb.

Blakely's green eyes flashed in his mind. The disappointment. The hurt.

Jab, jab, hook.

Fuck, he needed to get her out of his head. Her eyes, her gentle voice, her skin that was so soft he worried he might scratch her with his calloused hands.

He growled and hit the bag harder.

She'd taken up residence inside him and he needed her gone. She was good and pure and perfect, and he wasn't any of those things. She was better off without him.

His fist connected with the bag again, every punch harder than the last. He hit it for so long and so violently that his arms finally started to ache and his breathing was heavy.

But she never left him. It was like she'd become a part of him. Like her very fucking being had entangled itself with his own.

The ding of his phone made him pause. It could be Cal with news of Saad's location. His heart hit his ribs in a hard jolt as he tugged the gloves from his hands and read the message.

Not Cal. Erik.

You should get down to Lenny's.

He clicked out of the message. Being around people was the last thing he felt like doing right now. He wasn't exactly in the mood for company. Hell, he rarely was these days.

He grabbed his water and chugged half the bottle before moving down the hall to the stairs. What the hell was he doing in this two-story, four-bedroom house now all by himself?

The place was too big for him. Originally, Dec and Cole had also lived here. And they'd let a homeless kid, Anthony, move in for a while. But one by one, his friends had found their women and moved out, and Anthony had gone to live with Cole.

He shot a glance at his phone before stepping into the shower. Still no message from Cal.

Dammit.

He'd always known it might take some time to find Saad, but knowing something and accepting it were two different things.

Ryker and Cal had been good friends for years. He trusted the man with his life, and more than that, he trusted Cal with his secrets. He didn't know how the guy found people, but he didn't question his skills. He had a lot of connections, and he was good at hacking into systems he wasn't supposed to hack. If anyone could find Saad, it was him.

As the heavy drops of water hit his back, Ryker closed his eyes and pressed his hands to the cool tile wall. He needed eyes on his enemy. He needed to know exactly where the asshole was so he could end him.

Would the voices in his head quiet once Saad was deep in the ground? Would the fucking torment tearing apart his insides ease? Probably not. No one could reverse time and bring back the dead. But maybe he'd be able to sleep again. Maybe he wouldn't feel like he was always on the edge of a damn cliff, seconds from tumbling off.

Ten minutes later, he stepped out of the shower. His phone dinged again.

Again, it was Erik.

Your woman's here, and Janice and some guys are watching her.

Ryker frowned. His woman as in Blakely? Had to be. Why was Janice watching her—and who the fuck were the guys?

He cursed under his breath. Dammit, why was she still in Lindeman? He needed her *gone*, and not just because being around him wasn't safe. Because he cared about her too damn much. He didn't know how to *not* care for her. But she needed to let him go and find someone safe. Someone undamaged.

Even if that thought felt like a dagger to his damn chest.

He grabbed jeans and a shirt, pulling them on before donning his shoes, grabbing his keys, and heading out. He should leave it. He should let Erik watch her. Erik was a good guy who wouldn't let harm come to a woman.

But when in the hell did Ryker ever do anything he was supposed to do?

He made it to Lenny's in half the time it should have taken. It would be packed inside judging by the number of cars in the lot and people milling around outside. But then, the bar was always busy, regardless of whether it was a weekend or weekday.

He stepped inside and spotted Erik, Cole, and Aria immediately. They stood at a bar table. Cole and Aria were talking to each other, smiling. Erik, on the other hand, was watching something across the room, an angry expression on his face, like he was about five seconds from hitting someone. Ryker followed his gaze.

A vein throbbed violently in his temple at the sight of some asshole standing so close to Blakely.

When she tried to step away, he wrapped a hand around her arm, stopping her abruptly enough to cause her drink to spill onto her hand.

What the fuck?

Ryker weaved through the tables, catching sight of Janice as he went. She hadn't seen him yet, too busy snickering while she watched the exchange. His muscles tightened. Was this her fucking doing?

He was halfway to the bar when Blakely attempted to tug her arm away. The guy didn't let go. Instead, his fingers visibly tightened.

Ryker moved faster, shoving a few guys out of his way, the anger in his chest weaving into an ugly, dangerous pattern.

Then the asshole dropped his head and pressed his lips to Blakely's.

Ryker saw red.

In three seconds, he had the dude's collar in one hand and was spinning him away from Blakely. Then he punched him square in the jaw.

The bastard fell to the floor, blood dripping from a cut on his face.

"You don't fucking *touch* her!"

The people in the bar grew quiet, even the volume of the music lowered.

The guy groaned as he rolled to his back. "I think you broke my jaw!"

Ryker reached down and yanked the guy up by his shirt. He lowered his head and his voice, so the words were just for him. "You touch her again, and I'll kill you with my bare hands. Got it?"

The man finally met his gaze, the pain starting to clear from his eyes. "Let me go."

Rage vibrated through Ryker, threatening to spill over a second time. He made sure the threat of danger was crystal clear when he said, "It's taking everything in me not to kill you right fucking now. So this is what's gonna happen. You're going to get your sorry ass up and leave, and you're never going to step foot in Lenny's again. You're also never going to touch or even *breathe* around her again. Do you understand me?"

The guy's eyes glittered. When he remained silent, Ryker's muscles flexed, and he was moments from throwing a second punch when soft fingers touched his arm.

"Ryker. I'm okay."

Her touch…her gentle voice…they went a little way toward calming the explosive fury inside him. But he didn't let up. He glared at the guy. "Tell me you fucking understand."

Fury. It burned bright in the asshole's eyes before he growled a response between gritted teeth. "I understand."

Ryker released him with a hard shove. "Get out."

The guy's nostrils flared, his fists clenching. Then, finally, he moved, standing and stomping across the room, brushing past Janice and the guy with her. Janice glared at Blakely, then she and the other man followed.

Ryker took a second to work through the storm of emotions swirling inside him—three long breaths—then he turned.

His gaze zoned in on Blakely's kiss-swollen lips. He growled, and his legs twitched to chase the fucker and beat his ass.

She stepped closer. "I'm really okay."

He lifted a hand and ran the pad of his thumb over the red marks on her arm. The fucker's fingerprints.

"I was actually a second away from nailing the jerk in the balls."

His eyes flashed back to hers, and the memory of a conversation flickered in his mind. They'd been in Beirut, and he'd told her if she ever felt unsafe, to go for the soft points and hit as hard as she could.

"I would have liked to see that." Finally, there was a semblance of normalcy in his voice. He wasn't completely calm. The image of that douchebag's lips on hers would be permanently etched into his head. But standing here, touching her, hearing her voice, got him close. "Erik would have stepped in if I didn't."

She smiled and glanced at his friends' table. "He's nice."

His gut twisted at her words, and an emotion that felt stupidly close to jealousy swirled inside him. Because he didn't like her thinking his friend was *nice*.

His attention dropped to her shirt. It was damp, and he could see the tops of her breasts through the thin, transparent white material. "Why's your top wet?"

Her eyes widened, her lips parting, then closing just as quickly.

It was when her gaze darted to the door and back that Ryker knew. The asshole was to blame.

Yep. He was going to kill him.

He stepped toward the door, but again, Blakely grabbed his arm.

"It was the other guy she was with. He knocked me in the back. Erik already did the tower-over-him-with-a-deadly-expression thing."

Good. Although if it were him, he would have done a hell of a lot more than tower.

She set her drink on the bar with a shake of her head. "You know what? I accepted Aria's invitation to come out on the off chance you'd be here, so we could talk, but after everything I've already been through tonight, I'm tired and my shirt is sticking to me so…I'm just going to walk back to the hotel."

"Walk?"

She nodded vaguely as she used a napkin to wipe her hand. "Yes. I don't have a car."

He blinked. "How did you get home from the bachelor auction?"

"I walked."

Goddammit. "Blakely, you left the center at eleven o'clock!"

She lifted a shoulder, as if walking around at night, in a town she wasn't familiar with, was nothing.

He growled and pressed a hand to her back. "I'm driving you."

"You don't—"

"I'm driving you, Blakely. You're not walking in the dark on your own." *Again.* The added word in his head was a jolt to his insides.

She sighed, obviously hearing the lack of leeway, then waved to Aria, Cole, and Erik. All three of them were watching, the guys on full alert. He had no doubt they would have stepped in if that altercation had gone any further.

Ryker nodded in their direction before escorting her out the door. He needed to thank Erik for both texting him and looking out for Blakely tonight. That could wait until tomorrow.

When they reached his car, he helped her slide in before moving around to the other side. "Where are you staying?"

"Just around the corner at The Merchant Hotel."

The hotel was close to both the bar and the event center. At least she hadn't walked far Friday night or this evening.

Still, his muscles bunched. Lindeman was a small town with a low crime rate, but River, Michele, and Aria had all found themselves in danger in recent months. Not to mention, he had a dangerous enemy and no idea on a location for the man. It wasn't safe for her to walk in the dark alone.

The ride to her hotel was quiet, and when he parked, she opened her mouth, presumably to say goodbye, but he was already out of the vehicle.

He walked to the passenger side and opened her door. She released another one of those soft, feminine sighs that slid right over his skin, making him want to groan.

He swallowed and closed the door behind her a bit too hard before leading her across the lot. He didn't miss the small shudder down her spine at his touch. And he didn't *stop* touching her as they entered the lobby, then an elevator.

When they reached her door, she swiped her card, but before she could enter, he stepped into the room.

"Ryker—"

Too late. He was already in, scanning every inch of the space. A large bed centered the wall on one side, while a mini fridge and bar sat on one side of the room, and a small wooden table, two old chairs, a dresser and TV sat against the opposite wall. Once he'd checked that the room was clear, he entered the bathroom. Empty.

When he turned back toward Blakely, she had a brow lifted and one side of her mouth kicked up. "You're still doing that?"

Always. "Better to be safe than sorry."

She closed the door behind her. "Want a nightcap before you go?" Before he could respond, she headed toward the minibar. "You like whiskey, right?"

"Blakely, you need to leave."

The muscles across her shoulders tensed. One breath of silence passed, then she turned slowly, her eyes hard and determined. "I told you, you owe me a date first."

His jaw ticked. She wasn't going to stop. He stepped toward her. Just one step. It was still too close. "If I go on a date with you, will you leave?"

Pain flashed over her face. It was so distinct, filling her olive-green eyes. It killed him. Made him want to take back the words. Tell the woman exactly what she meant to him. What she'd *always* meant.

Her features blanked and she straightened her spine. "Yes, then I'll leave." She blinked and turned toward the bar to open a tiny bottle of whiskey. "Although, it would be nice if my presence didn't cause you such revulsion."

"Revulsion?"

"Disgust. Annoyance. Frustration. Whatever it is, it all hurts the same way."

She poured two small glasses of whiskey, but before she could offer him one, he stepped behind her, grabbing her hips and letting the warmth of her back seep into his front.

"I'm not repulsed or disgusted by your presence."

Her breath stuttered and her voice lowered. "So, just annoyed and frustrated."

Yes. But those emotions were directed at *him*. At his reaction to her. At his *need* for her.

Slowly, she turned—and suddenly she was too close. Her sweet scent permeated the air, choking him. Her soft eyes looked so damn big, he felt chained to them, unable to look away.

"There was a time we'd count down the minutes and seconds until we could be together."

That felt like a lifetime ago. When a different Ryker existed in the world. A more whole Ryker. "A lot has happened since then."

"No. One thing happened since then. One thing that's changed us both. Changed the trajectories of our lives and forced us to relearn how to live. I wish you'd let us relearn together."

He wasn't trying to relearn how to live. He was trying to survive in a world so much bleaker than it had been prior to Beirut.

Her chest moved up and down, brushing his on each inhale. She placed her hand over his heart. "You're alive, Ryker. *Live*. Build memories." Her voice quieted. "Love."

The word had his vision tunneling. He stepped back. Her hand dropped and the light dimmed from her eyes.

He couldn't love. Love was dangerous. Love could be used against you.

"I have to go. Lock the door behind me."

He moved out of the hotel room, refusing to look back. Unwilling to see her pain again.

Outside, he crossed the lot quickly, damn near running from her now. He couldn't handle it when words like "love" left the woman's lips. Not when part of him wanted that love desperately, even while the rest of him chased demons.

He'd reached his vehicle when a glint of light from inside a dark car across the lot caught his attention. He could just make out a figure in the driver's seat. By the person's size, it had to be a guy.

Ryker took a few steps toward the vehicle, but the second he did, the engine switched on and the car left.

For a moment, Ryker remained exactly where he was, his gaze on where the vehicle had disappeared. Then he shot his attention back to Blakely's window on the third floor.

He didn't like her staying at the hotel alone. Hell, he didn't like *anything* about her being in town.

He cursed under his breath when he acknowledged what he had to do. Go on that damn date and be done with it. Be done with *her*.

A sour taste poisoned his mouth at the latter thought. Choked him. Destroyed him.

CHAPTER 6

I'm picking you up at six.

Blakely read the text for what had to be the tenth time that day. Ryker was picking her up. For a date. In fact, he was due to arrive in a few minutes.

Nerves skittered down her spine. They were familiar. They'd been buzzing through her system all day. She didn't know *why* she was so nervous. Ryker was the entire reason she was here, after all.

Maybe it was because this was so important. This was her last chance to get through to the man before she left. Because that's what she'd agreed to. One date and she'd leave.

Could she break through his wall tonight? It was so thick and formidable, possibly indestructible.

She gave herself a quick shake. No. It could break. And it would. She'd tear down the damn thing with her bare hands if she had to. Last night, she'd almost gotten through. She'd heard it in his voice. Felt it in his touch. Then she'd made a mistake. Said a word she shouldn't have said. And the wall had come back higher than before. Thicker.

Dumb. So dumb.

She adjusted her dark turquoise dress. It showed off her neckline with a deep V and hugged her waist before flowing to mid-thigh. It was pretty and had been a last-minute addition to her suitcase.

As she studied herself in the mirror, she tilted her head and let the previous night flow back into her mind. The thing was, she and Ryker had spoken about love before. Early in their acquaintance, he'd told her about wanting to find a love so pure and so real that it changed him. Made him better. Stronger.

Apparently, he wasn't willing to revisit that topic.

She blew out a breath and dropped her phone into her clutch.

A knock sounded at the door. Her breath caught, and her chest suddenly felt unbearably tight. He was early.

She crossed the room, each step feeling as big and important as the last. With trembling fingers, she tugged the door open—and her mouth went dry.

Ryker wore a white untucked dress shirt. Just like at the bachelor auction, the first couple buttons were undone, and there was a hint of a tattoo on his chest. A tattoo he hadn't had before. With intricate lines that she wanted to follow behind the material.

She forced her gaze to his as his earthy pine scent surrounded her, taking her back to a time when life with him was so much easier.

"Hey." The single word rasped out of her, shaky and low.

"Hey." His deep voice rumbled over her skin, causing the fine hairs to stand on end. "Ready to go?"

"Mm-hm." She moved out of the room, pulling the door closed behind her. Two steps down the hallway, his hand touched the small of her back. She swallowed in an attempt to wet her dry throat. He'd done that last night. And just like then, she loved how his hand took up almost her entire back. She loved the warmth and the sense of safety that surrounded her like a bubble.

Once in his car, as he pulled out of the lot, she stared at his strong fingers gripping the wheel with confidence.

She cleared her throat. "So, where are you taking me?"

"There's a little Italian restaurant called Farina's. They do good fettuccine Alfredo."

Her lips separated, a surprised puff of air sucking into her chest. Fettuccine Alfredo was her favorite dish. In Beirut, she'd dreamed about the stuff, telling Ryker that she planned to eat endless bowls of it every day for a week when she got back to the US.

"You remembered," she said quietly.

"I remember everything."

His words had her brows pulling together. Because he had a good memory, or because their conversations were worth remembering?

"I distinctly recall you saying you'd sell your left kidney for a bowl," he continued.

She threw her head back and laughed. Though she couldn't recall that particular comment, it sounded like something she'd say. "I really missed it. The extra parmesan too."

She expected another anecdote about something she'd said. Maybe she'd admitted to wanting to bathe in the stuff. When he was silent, she turned to look at him and frowned when she saw his knuckles had whitened on the wheel.

"I remember that laugh, too," he said, voice low.

She wasn't sure if he'd meant to say those words out loud, but the second they were in the air, they stole the smile from her lips. "And I remember yours."

It was a deep, throaty laugh. The first time she'd heard it, it made her belly do this funny little flip. She'd decided then that she'd do whatever it took to hear it as often as she could.

When they reached the restaurant, he pressed that same hand to her back as they headed into the dimly lit interior. The waiter led them to a corner table. Ryker took a seat so his back was to the wall, no doubt so he could see the entire restaurant. She was sure he'd asked for this specific table for that very reason. He'd once shared with her that he needed to see his surroundings. Be aware of who was near at all times.

She lifted her menu, searching for the Alfredo. Her mouth salivated just at the sight of the words. She *hadn't* eaten it every day for a week when she got home. In fact, she hadn't eaten much of it at all in the last year. Her appetite had been almost nonexistent for a long while.

She wet her lips, lowering the menu to the table. "So, you've come here before?"

Thoughts of the woman from the bachelor auction, Janice, suddenly took up unwelcome residence in her head.

He closed his menu and set it on the table. "Just takeout."

That little fact should not bring her as much joy as it did. Still, her traitorous mind wondered if he'd eaten that takeout alone or with company.

"What's Janice to you?"

Shit. She hadn't meant to ask that. Maybe she should just glue her lips shut for the night and be done with it.

"Nothing."

A one-word answer. Was that all he was going to give her? "A woman doesn't bid for a man like she did Friday night if he means nothing to her." And she certainly doesn't send her *friends* to harass and assault the competition.

"She's hit on me a few times at Lenny's Bar."

Hm. Sounded like there was more to it.

"What about you?" he asked. "Have you dated anyone?"

Yeah, right. Even if her heart wasn't hopelessly chained to this man, she had *not* been in a place to date. "No."

He lifted a brow like he was waiting for her to say more. He wouldn't be getting anything. Not tonight. The answer to why she hadn't dated teetered too close to why she hadn't been okay after the bombing.

Luckily, the waitress arrived at their table, saving her.

"Can I get you both some drinks?"

She smiled up at the woman. "Shiraz, please."

Ryker glanced at the server. "A beer would be great."

She waited for the waitress to leave before fiddling with a piece of material that had come loose on her dress. "So, how have the others been? Cole looks like he's recovered well from the broken back."

"Yeah, and he's more than made up for his downtime. He's active every day."

"And Declan?" She recalled Ryker telling her that he'd been shot.

"He's fine too. Everyone's okay."

Except you. The words stuck in her throat like glue. "Tell me about Mercy Ring."

That seemed like a safer topic.

They spent the next twenty minutes talking about everything and nothing. He told her about the relationships the guys had developed—in particular, the relationship Jackson had with his sister. He told her about a kid named Anthony, who Cole had adopted, and mentioned Aria's son, Zac.

When their meals were set in front of them, it was both too soon and not soon enough. She wanted to talk to this man, uninterrupted, without an expiration date. She wanted to learn everything there was to know, gather every minute lost and pull them all together.

But too soon, the smell of the Alfredo stole her attention. Holy heck, it smelled divine. Like a large bowl of heaven. Ryker had ordered seafood fettuccine, and it smelled amazing too.

She spun some pasta around her fork, and the second it hit her tongue, her eyes closed, and she groaned. A deep, satisfied moan of pleasure.

"Oh my God, Ryker, this is amazing." Maybe even worth the small fortune she'd spent on this date. She opened her eyes, smiling. "Tonight was definitely worth the fight."

Yet again, he wasn't smiling. Instead, his jaw was granite and his eyes steel.

For a moment, her world stopped, and the hushed voices of people around her faded. It was just her and Ryker, inevitably pulled together in ways neither of them fully understood.

When his gaze finally tore from hers and he took a mouthful of his pasta, she pulled her attention back to her own food. "So, how did the entire team come to live in Lindeman? From what you told me in the Middle East, this was your hometown, and Jackson's, but he never wanted to return."

"They came for my funeral."

The fork stopped halfway to her mouth, his words making the pasta in her belly churn. "What?"

The man was joking, right? Because only dead people had funerals, and Ryker certainly wasn't that.

He finished chewing before he answered. "It's a long story, but the short version is a few months after I got here, I found out about an underground cage fighting ring. I started fighting in it. Not long after that, a case agent from Homeland Security approached me. Said they were investigating some people in the club and asked me to help. I agreed, only it didn't go the way we were hoping. They discovered what I was doing and tried to kill me. To keep my family safe, I had to be dead for a while."

Her heart thumped with a new force. There was pain threaded through his voice. And guilt.

He cleared his throat. "I didn't like doing it. It hurt my parents and River and my team to think I was gone. But it kept them safe."

Breathing through the constriction in her chest was almost impossible. The world had thought Ryker Harp was dead. They'd attended his *funeral*. Cried for him. Celebrated his life.

And no one bothered to call her.

While she still saw this man as a big part of her life, to him, and to everyone he knew, clearly she was nothing.

The realization sliced into her skin like small shards of glass. Her throat suddenly felt thick, and tears she had no control over pressed at the corners of her eyes.

"Blakely—"

She stood, the pasta now the furthest thing from her mind. "I'm going to the bathroom."

She turned and walked away quickly, ignoring him when he called her name.

A funeral. Ryker had had a *funeral.* Did his friends not have her contact details? Or had they no idea what she'd meant to him once upon a time?

She pushed into the bathroom and gripped the vanity. What *was* she to him? Was she anything at all? He looked at her like he still cared. Hell, just now, he'd looked at her like she was the only woman in the damn room. But he was pushing her away. Hard. He hadn't been taking her calls. Hadn't responded to a single text. Did he *really* hope to never have any contact with her again?

The mirror showed her a face that was too pale and eyes that were too wide and wet.

For the first time since arriving in Lindeman, doubt started to kick at her ribs. Doubt about whether it had been the right decision to come here. About her determination to fight for Ryker, when he didn't even seem to be fighting for himself.

She traced the delicate lines beside her eyes. New lines of stress. Trauma. Lines that had only developed over the last year but had quickly become a part of her.

Was it all one-sided? He'd felt something for her in Beirut, she knew that, but he'd never said he loved her. And things were different now. He'd changed. They both had. What if they didn't fit together anymore? What if everything they once had was simply gone?

That certainly seemed to be what Ryker had been trying so hard to tell her.

Devastation pressed down on her, so heavy and unrelenting that her knees almost buckled.

He didn't care about her anymore. Sure, maybe he still found her attractive. But affection? You didn't push away the people you had strong feelings for.

The tears tried to escape, but she blinked them away. She couldn't force a man to love her any more than she could change the past.

Maybe it was time she left. The thought hurt, but she'd endured pain before. It had literally singed her skin, and she'd still gotten up to live another day. She would again.

With a nod, she scrubbed the tears from her eyes and left the bathroom. In the hall, a man passed her, moving quickly, his shoulder bumping into hers. Frowning, she stared as he headed toward a door at the end of the hall.

Raised voices came from the main dining room as she stepped inside.

She smelled the smoke before she saw the flames.

A chill swept over her skin, tunneling her vision and tightening her chest. Through the open kitchen door at the back of the restaurant, she saw flames dancing across a stove. For a moment, she didn't move. Didn't breathe. Instead, she let the brightness and sight of the fire thrust her back to a time she wished she could forget. A time when she'd watched flames dance across ravaged homes. When she ran toward them, despite knowing it was too late.

People surged around her in a panic, customers deserting their meals and leaving. Staff attempting to put out the fire as it spread up the wall behind the cooktop.

Blakely's feet were glued to the floor, her eyes locked on the flames as the air choked her.

Strong fingers wrapped around her forearm. Ryker's voice sounded, but his words were too far away for her to understand.

Then he stood in front of her, just inches away, blocking her view of the fire. She looked up and jolted free of the horrible memories.

Ryker's worried gaze turned dark. "We have to get out."

She opened her mouth, but there were no words. Instead, she nodded and let him pull her from the restaurant, away from the ghosts of the past.

Ryker glanced at her repeatedly. Her legs followed where he led, though she didn't really feel them.

She gave a final look over her shoulder, letting the flames take her back to that place one more time, before stepping outside into the cool night air.

CHAPTER 7

Ryker clenched and released the leather steering wheel, letting its cool surface calm some of the storm of emotions in his chest.

What the hell had happened back there? Every ounce of blood had left Blakely's face, and it was like she'd been in a damn trance, unable to look away from the blaze in the kitchen.

The fire department and police hadn't taken long to arrive. He'd stayed long enough to hear that a towel had been set on the stove. No one had noticed, and the small fire had quickly spread to grease in the nearby fryer.

Once he knew the cause, he wanted to get Blakely back to her hotel. She was too pale. Hell, she'd barely said two words to him outside the restaurant, despite his questioning her to figure out what was wrong.

He no longer pushed her to talk. He gave her time to process whatever was going on in her head. To gain some damn color back in her cheeks.

When they reached the hotel, Blakely was out of the car before he could get to her side. He cursed, hurrying after her.

She shook her head, not looking his way. "You don't have to escort me."

He sure as hell did, and he'd be finding out what the hell was going on. "I'm walking you to your door." His tone brooked no argument.

She sighed and continued toward the doors. He scanned the area as they moved, specifically checking the spot where that dark car had been the previous night. It wasn't there.

When they reached her room, he again stepped in first and checked the place. This time, she didn't react or comment. Instead, she closed the door and lowered to the bed, like her legs couldn't carry her any longer. When she started unstrapping her heels, his gaze caught on her toned calves. On thighs that were too creamy and tempting. He internally groaned.

"What happened back there?" he finally ground out, forcing himself to look away from the exposed skin.

Her fingers paused on the strap. Only for a second. Then she tugged off the heel and moved to the other. "Nothing. I just got caught up watching the fire."

Bullshit. It was a lie, and a weak one at that. She'd been looking at those flames like demons had been pouring out of them.

She pulled off the second shoe, but before she could stand, he lowered in front of her, hands going to her thighs.

"Blakely. Talk to me."

She shook her head, and when she spoke, her words were flat. "You don't have to do that."

"Do what?"

"Pretend to care."

"I'm not pretending."

She stood, and he was forced to rise with her, immediately reminded of their height difference.

She stared at him with eyes that looked so sad, he could

almost feel their hollowness. "You died, Ryker. Your loved ones mourned your loss and attended your funeral. And I had no idea."

His brow creased. "You were in Minnesota."

"And Declan was in Camden. Jackson was in Boston. Cole was in Chicago. People you loved were *told*, so they could attend. I wasn't."

Because he hadn't told anyone about her. Not really. His team had met her, of course. Knew he'd spent time with her in Beirut. They didn't know she'd burrowed her way so deeply into his life, imprinting herself on his very existence. They didn't know he lived for the moments he got to speak to her. Touch her.

He scrubbed a hand over his face. "They didn't know because I didn't share that part of my life with them. It didn't make you any less important. And I'm *glad* they didn't tell you. You really wanted to be told that I was dead? To go through that?"

"I wanted to be *important enough* to tell." She stepped back, blinking like she was holding off tears. "I wanted… God, I wanted so many things, but they all feel different now. It's like every time I breathe, I'm taking in some other woman's air. Living someone else's life."

"Blakely—"

"And *that*. That name. It's so unfamiliar from your lips. Like you're not even talking to me." Her throat bobbed, and she moved farther away from him. "I'm sorry."

"For what?"

"That I came. That I've been harassing you." Then she nodded, like in that split second, she made a decision. A decision he knew was going to torment him. "I'll stop. Stop calling. Texting. I'll go home."

His gut twisted into a knot that was so tight, it felt like it would never loosen. It was what he'd wanted. What he'd demanded she do since he'd first spoken to her at that auction. But now, hearing her say the words…hearing her refer to *any* place as "home" that wasn't with him…it hurt more than it should've.

She turned and got two steps toward the door before he snagged her arm. "Blakely, I…"

He what? What could he give her to make her feel better? To keep her safe from him and his world, but also make the knot inside him untangle? His mind scrambled for words he didn't have. Because there were no words in existence to make both his head and his heart happy.

"Tell me I'm wrong," she whispered, glancing over her shoulder, voice soft enough that he could barely discern what she said. "Tell me you want me here. Tell me you feel what I feel."

He didn't feel what she felt. He felt *more*. He was sure of it. He felt every fucking shred of her pull, like there was a physical rope between them, tugging him closer.

Words he knew would keep her here crawled up his throat, begging to break free. But then what? Let this woman stay and attempt to fix him? She deserved so much more than that. She deserved a man at peace. Someone whose calmness would spill over into her world.

His silence stretched, and the pain on her face, the hurt, it dragged his heart through the dirt.

"You should go." She pulled her arm from his hold and stepped again toward the door.

That loss of contact…it cost him so much more than it should.

She was almost to the door when he acted on instinct, snagging her wrist.

This time, swinging her into his arms and crashing his lips to hers.

For a moment, she was still, her tangible shock fusing with his desperation to hold onto her. Then her hands touched his chest, and her head tilted. It was everything. An instant ease to his torment. A puncture in the bubble that had become his prison.

A deep, primal growl ripped from his throat, and he lifted the woman into his arms. Her dress bunched at her thighs as he pressed her to the wall. When a throaty moan parted her lips, he thrust his tongue inside.

Blood roared between his ears, muting the world around him.

God, he remembered all of this. The taste of her. The feel of her skin beneath his fingers. The memory had gotten him through his worst days. It was the air in his lungs when he couldn't breathe, and the sun on his skin when there was only darkness and cold.

Her fingers moved up his chest and curled behind his neck, her touch soft and giving. He wanted more.

He curved his hand around her bare thigh before sliding up, pushing the soft material of her dress as he went, until it sat on her hip.

His tongue continued to fuse with hers, his heart thumping to a rhythm he hadn't felt for too damn long. The rhythm *she* created inside him.

"Ryker..."

Her throaty whisper as she said his name did things to him, dangerous things, that nothing and no one else ever could.

He trailed his lips down her cheek, her throat, every swipe of lips to skin like a new memory he'd plant inside his heart.

Why did this woman feel so right in his arms? Like everything she was, every tiny detail, was made just for him? Every inch of her a gift.

He skimmed his hand beneath the dress, up her waist—

What was that?

Smooth skin...yet somehow also rough. He ran his fingers slowly around her abdomen, feeling more of it. A new texture that hadn't been there before.

Like she suddenly knew he was touching something that didn't make sense, she stilled. Her limbs tensed, then she pushed at his chest, attempting to break free. "Put me down."

"What is this?" His tone was dark in a way it hadn't been before.

"It's nothing."

"Blakely—"

"Put. Me. Down."

"Not until you tell me what this is!"

Again, she pushed at his chest. Again, he didn't move a single muscle.

Her throat bobbed. "Fine. It's…it's a burn scar."

A new, dangerous pulse beat at his temple. "A burn from what?"

When she didn't answer, sick, ugly emotions began to churn inside him. Tear at him.

"A burn from *what*, Blakely?"

The quiet was so heavy, he almost choked on it. Then, finally, she looked up, meeting his eyes as she said words that would rock his world. "I was a block back when I heard the explosions. I ran down toward them. Saw the flames. I was trying to find survivors when a structure collapsed, and a beam fell on my stomach."

For a moment, he couldn't breathe. He let the weight of her words, the fucking utter shock of them, take root. Change him. Shatter him anew.

She'd been there. A street away. Seen the homes burning.

And she'd been *hurt*.

Guilt was like a snake, poisoning him. He slid her to her feet and stepped back. His gaze shot away because looking at her was painful. It was like an arrow to his chest, digging into every vital organ.

He'd just assumed she'd been at her local accommodation when the bombs hit. That she was safely elsewhere when the news had filtered back to her.

"Ryker—"

He stepped away. His fault. It was *his fucking fault*. How badly had she been injured? How long had it taken her to recover? He couldn't even ask—he was that damn angry at himself. He'd been angry for a long time, for well over a year…but this was different. And it confirmed everything he'd been thinking. That she deserved better. Needed better. She needed safe, something he would never be.

Suddenly, the urgency to find Saad burned hotter than ever. To personally wrap his hands around the man's throat and watch the life seep out of him.

Fuck!

"I need to go."

"Wait—"

He rushed out of her room, letting the door slam behind him.

This was why she had to stay away. He was the fucking kiss of death masquerading as a knight in shining armor.

A violent energy pushed him down the stairs, sparking painfully through his muscles as he stormed across the parking lot to his car. Inside, he slammed his head back on the seat so hard that every part of him vibrated.

He pulled his phone out and texted Cal.

Tell me you have him.

His friend responded immediately.

I've got a lead but not an exact location yet.

Ryker growled and threw the phone to the passenger seat. Then he leaned back against the headrest.

He didn't leave the lot for a long time, instead just watching her hotel.

A street away. Too close. She could have been in one of the houses. She wasn't, but she'd still gotten burned. Badly enough she was left with extensive scars. How long had they taken to heal? How badly had she suffered?

He had no idea…because he'd ignored almost all of her calls and texts for a goddamn year.

The anguish was so deep and vicious that he closed his eyes, not able to accept what he'd done by shutting her out. Or how Blakely could've died.

After several long minutes, he grabbed his phone from the other seat and sent a text to Erik. When his friend responded, he finally left the parking lot. But he didn't head home. Instead, he went to Mercy Ring.

The gym was dark and quiet when he arrived. Ryker went straight to the locker room and changed into shorts. He didn't bother with a shirt or shoes.

He'd just stepped into the ring and pulled on his boxing gloves when Erik entered. His friend didn't ask questions, just dropped his bag, pulled off his own shirt and shoes, and grabbed mitts.

Ryker waited until he climbed into the ring, then they danced around each other.

"You okay?" Erik asked, breaking the silence.

"No."

He jabbed. Erik reared his head back, narrowly avoiding the hit.

"Wanna talk about it?" he asked.

Did he?

Yes. He had to.

"Blakely was an aid worker in the Middle East. She and I grew close during my deployments."

Another jab from him. Another dodge from Erik.

"On our last mission, our target's brother attacked the team. When he didn't kill us, he attacked civilians I had grown close to by bombing family homes." He swallowed before saying the next part. "Tonight, I learned Blakely was close to the bomb site. She was hurt trying to save people."

He could still feel the rippled, disfigured skin beneath his fingers. He threw a hook, followed by an upper cut. The punch caught Erik, but he barely flinched, instead following it up with a hit of his own. It grazed Ryker's head.

"And you want to kill the fucker who hurt her." It wasn't a question.

Ryker threw three more punches before answering. "I want to burn him to the fucking ground."

Erik was good in the ring. He evaded most of the hits. Ryker got a few in, but he was almost certain it was because his friend let him.

When they finally stopped thirty minutes later, Ryker pulled off his gloves and ran his hands through his hair. "I hate this. I didn't used to feel like..."

Like what? Like he couldn't even express what the shit show of his emotions were?

"Like the darkness inside you is simultaneously your destruction, and your only reason for living."

Erik's words floored him. That was *exactly* what he felt.

And by the sounds of it, Erik was all too familiar.

CHAPTER 8

nxiety rippled through Blakely's body as she walked. Her bag of medical supplies sat heavy on her shoulder, ready for the wellness checks. It was a favorite part of her job, and usually she had a smile on her face, because families always welcomed her into their homes with open arms. But today, she couldn't muster a smile. Not since the call she'd received last night from Ryker.

He was back on US soil...but that almost hadn't been the case. His location had been compromised and the brother of the team's high-value target had attacked.

Cole had broken his back. Declan had been shot.

She had to drop her kit bag for a moment to catch her breath.

Ryker could've died.

It didn't seem real.

How could it? Just three nights ago, he'd walked her back to her room—and stayed. It was their first night together, but it wouldn't be their last. They'd made promises to each other. But now she had even more reason to want to see him when she was stateside again. She needed to know that he was okay, both mentally and physically.

A shudder raced down her spine.

The only downside was that she'd be leaving all the locals she'd fallen in love with. Her mind flickered to her favorite kids, Cyrus and Ara. She'd grown close to them during her time here. Today, she had a special treat for them—peanut butter cups. When she'd told them about the confection, their little faces lit up at the mention of chocolate and peanut butter mixed together.

She'd shared meals with a lot of families here in Beirut but had a soft spot for the Basers. At first, her significant time spent with that family had everything to do with Ryker, who'd also befriended them. But she'd quickly realized why he was so fond of them.

A child passed her on the street, and she forced a small smile to her lips.

The locals here were the most beautiful souls she'd ever met. They'd welcomed her into their lives, no questions asked. Shared the little they had.

Aid deployments were hard, but God, they were rewarding. She was a trained nurse, so her primary function was medical aid, but she also handed out care packages. Spent time with the locals. Integrated into the community.

Before coming here, she'd felt stuck. Stuck in a life that wasn't fulfilling. Plagued by the feeling that there was more out there for her but unsure where or how to find it.

She was just nearing a corner when a massive boom split the air, followed by two more. It was like fireworks times a hundred. The blast concussion buffeted her body as though she were inside her own heartbeat.

She stopped, her gaze whipping to the ground as it shook beneath her feet. There were other sounds now. Heavy sounds. Almost like bricks tumbling to the ground.

For a moment, her world slowed and she felt rooted in place. Then smoke filled the sky, shading the afternoon gray. And she saw something else. Fire. It burned just above the houses from a street away...

From right where the Baser family home was located.

Fingers tight around the strap of her bag, Blakely sprinted, feet slamming into the ground, air burning her lungs. A voice whispered in her head that she was too late, but she let her pounding heart drown it out.

She rounded another corner—and stopped.

The Baser house...it was gone. Rubble and flames. Crumbling walls and missing roof. And it wasn't just the Basers' home but also the structures around it, three on each side.

There was barely anything left. The Abadis...the Hadids.

The bag dropped from her trembling fingers. Her knees wavered and nausea crawled up her throat. Devastation gutted her. Cut a hole right in the center of her chest.

There was no movement coming from the destroyed homes. None.

Still, she ran forward, refusing to believe what her mind already knew was true. She shouted the familiar names. Begging for any signs of life.

Tears streamed down her face like a river, and she was vaguely aware of locals standing in the street. Crying. Screaming.

She moved from house to house, shouting until her voice grew hoarse. There were only flames. Angry, hot flames. Unforgiving fire. No calls for help. No one crying out in pain.

Until, from the corner of her eye, she caught a flicker of movement.

She ran, heading straight toward the flames, not caring about the heat or the instability of the remaining walls.

She was nearly to the Baser house when the roof and a wall collapsed in the neighboring home, a beam tumbling out of the building and falling on Blakely. It knocked her to the ground and landed on her midsection.

The plank wasn't on fire...but it was still so hot, it burned straight through her clothes into her skin. The pain was instant, and it was like nothing she'd ever felt.

It was the melting of flesh. She couldn't escape.

She opened her mouth to scream. At the pain. The heartache. The desolation. But she was almost certain the loud roar of the flames silenced her voice...

Blakely's eyes flew open, and she jackknifed into a sitting

position. Sweat beaded her forehead and her throat burned. Her gaze flew to her midsection.

Pink sleep shirt. No hot beams or fire or melting skin.

She closed her eyes, trying to find a scrap of peace. It was just a dream. But she knew the knowledge would take a while to compute.

She'd woken in a pool of her own sweat many times before, throat scratched dry from screaming through her nightmares. Too many nightmares.

The last few nights had been worse. Since she'd seen the fire in that restaurant, everything had come back to her.

With trembling fingers, she slipped her hands under her nightshirt and let her palm glide over her scars. She'd been lucky. Locals had tipped the plank off her body quickly and she'd received medical aid. Others weren't so fortunate.

She'd passed out from the pain and woken in the hospital, surrounded by her fellow aid workers. They'd confirmed the horrible truth. Lives had been lost. Mothers. Fathers. Children.

Safe in her hotel, she closed her eyes, a single tear rolling down her cheek. She'd cried so many tears, yet there were always more to shed.

Without thinking, she pulled out her phone, desperate to make contact with Ryker. It had become a habit. The need to text him after a nightmare. Call. Maybe it was because he was the only other person who'd known the Baser family like she did. The only person who could truly understand the pain of her loss.

She never followed through. Usually, her finger just hovered over the call button or, at best, typed a text she never sent. Oh, she'd called and texted plenty...but never after a nightmare. Never wanting him to witness this side of her.

Now, her shaking finger hovered over the key, like so many nights in the past. Then, feeling weak, she hit his number.

There was a single ring before she shook her head and

canceled the call. Then she lay back on the hotel bed and focused on evening out her breaths.

She hadn't heard from Ryker since their date three nights ago. For all she knew, the man thought she was back in Minnesota. She should be. But when she'd booked her ticket, she'd chosen one for the weekend, making excuses about the flight being cheaper or landing at the best time.

Lies. All of them. The truth was, Ryker owned a part of her, and leaving Lindeman meant leaving that part of her behind.

When her phone rang, her eyes sprang open. Ryker's name flashed on the screen.

He *never* called her.

She was so shocked, she just watched it ring, watched his name on the screen, until it stopped and his name disappeared.

She swallowed, unsure what to do. Then the text came through.

Answer the call or I'm coming over there.

Her eyes had barely brushed over the words when the phone started ringing again. She blew out a long breath and answered the call.

"Are you okay?" he asked before she could speak.

If the man had been asleep, his voice didn't show it.

She gazed at the clock on the bedside table, cringing when she saw it was four in the morning. Of *course* he was worried. She'd called him at an ungodly hour. "I'm fine. Sorry. My finger slipped."

She scrunched her eyes. As excuses went, it was a terrible one. It probably left more questions than answers, but she was too tired and upset by the nightmare to think of anything better.

"Your voice sounds hoarse and shaky. What's wrong?"

Sometimes she screamed herself raw during her nightmares. It was a little surprising she hadn't received a knock on the door or at least a call from reception.

She ran her finger over a crease in the quilt. "It's nothing. I just..." *Have demons that float around in my head and torment my dreams? Have memories I can't forget?*

"Tell me, princess," he said softly.

That endearment...it brought back just a flicker of warmth. A thread of calm. "I had a nightmare."

"About what?"

There was no point in lying. "Beirut. The sound of the bombs. The fire." *The heat of the beam on my stomach.*

The last sentence was a whisper inside her head. One she instinctively knew not to say out loud.

The beat of silence that passed was so heavy, she wanted to take the words back. Offer some lie that would roll off his shoulders like water.

His voice was gruff. "I'm sorry."

She shook her head, even though the man couldn't see her. "I don't want your apology. It's not your fault."

"What do you want from me then?"

The question caught her off guard. She'd been expecting some sort of proclamation of why it *was* his fault. She took a moment to turn the question over in her mind. What *did* she want?

She wet her lips, offering him more truths she probably shouldn't. "I want your smile. Not a fake smile or a forced one. A real one. I want to hear you laugh without hesitation or resistance. And I want you to touch me without a visible war raging in your eyes."

She'd seen it. The battle. Like part of him wanted to touch her, and the other part wanted to keep her far away from him.

"I don't know if I'm capable of any of that anymore."

Her eyes closed, pain slicing at her in brutal slashes. He was capable of so much more than he knew. "You are. You're capable of healing. Of having a life worth living. I just wish you could see it."

Silence followed. And the silence hurt more than any words or denials.

She swallowed. "I should go. I'm sorry I called you so late."

"When are you leaving?"

Those four words punched at her, heavy and painful. "My flight's Sunday afternoon."

Tell me to stay, she whispered to herself, wishing she had the courage to speak it. *Give us some time. Give yourself time to return to me.*

"I'm sorry I can't be what you want."

Her hope shattered into tiny fragments. Too many to put back together.

"And I'm sorry you got hurt in the bombing," he added, this time the familiar anger edging his voice.

Now *she* was angry. They'd had something. Something real and beautiful. And he was acting like it was gone forever when it didn't have to be. "Like I said, I don't want your apologies, Ryker. I want you to take what's yours."

She hung up before he could say anything else. Deny her words or give her another load of heavy silence.

She was his. She'd *been* his since the day they'd met, and they both knew it. Yet he was treating her like she'd meant nothing.

The weight of the blanket was suddenly suffocating, so she flung it away and stood to yank back the curtains. Maybe opening them would help her shake this off, give her some space. It was still dark, and she couldn't see much of the parking lot in front of her, but she wasn't looking for anything, really. The image in her head of Ryker was too vivid to see anything else.

She knew he was in pain. They both were. But why not heal together? Be what the other person needed and comfort each other?

She was just about to step away and head toward the shower when a flicker of light caught her attention. It came from inside a car across the lot. It was on the far side…and she could just make out a man in the driver's seat.

Frowning, she leaned closer to the glass. She watched for

another half second, then something thick and uncomfortable trickled through her belly. Quickly, she pulled the curtains closed and stepped away. She'd felt the sensation of being watched for days. And it was creeping her out.

Was the person in that car the one watching?

CHAPTER 9

River groaned. "Oh man, Ryker, you need to try these corn dogs. They're amazing! Mom, tell him they're amazing."

The corners of Ryker's lips quirked at his mother's grimace. While River seemed to be inhaling her corn dog, his parents didn't have the same enthusiasm. In fact, both of them had barely touched theirs.

"They're not terrible," Jody Harp said carefully. She glanced at her husband for help.

Grant Harp, a man who never told anything but the truth, shook his head. "They *are* terrible."

His father moved to a trash can and was about to drop it in when River yelped and rushed over, snatching it from his fingers. "Well, I like it. No need for a good corn dog to go to waste."

She popped the last bit of hers into her mouth before starting on their father's.

Ryker chuckled. Somehow, River had dragged him out to a family evening at the Friday twilight market. How she'd managed that, he had no fucking idea. He hated crowded events, and this definitely was that. Stalls lined a huge open area, making the space feel small, and he swore the entire town of Lindeman was here tonight being as loud as damn possible. Maybe all of Ellensburg too.

A rowdy group of shouting teenagers brushed past them, as if underscoring his thoughts.

It was probably the way River had looked at him with those puppy eyes. The ones that said refusing to come along would be the equivalent of stomping on her heart.

He'd been trying to spend more time with his family, anyway. After everything that had happened over the last year, they needed him. His alleged death and the ensuing funeral were more than any family should ever have to bear. It had taken a toll on them and his friends.

His mother shifted closer, her side almost touching his. "Darling, I'm so glad you came out tonight."

She was a shorter middle-aged woman who'd always been full of life, rarely seen without a smile on her face. Except for those first months after his "death" and resurrection. Another thing for which Ryker was to blame.

River smirked from the other side of their mom.

He sipped his coffee. "River wanted me to come, and what River wants, River gets."

"Damn straight," she said around a mouthful of food. She'd already finished half of her second corn dog.

His mother stared at him for a moment. "She mentioned you have a woman visiting."

He internally groaned but didn't miss the grin from his sister. Reaching behind his mother, he lightly shoved River's shoulder. "She's leaving soon."

He wanted Blakely gone. It was better that way. But whenever he thought about Sunday, about her getting on a plane and putting distance between them, his chest got unbearably tight.

"She's the aid worker from the Middle East?" his father asked.

Ryker eyed River again. She conveniently kept her head down and shoved more corn dog into her mouth.

"Yeah, that's how we met." And then, because he knew what the next question would be, he added, "She just came to Lindeman to check on me."

His mother's eyes glittered with interest as they rounded a corner of stalls. "We'd love to meet her before she leaves. Maybe she could come over for dinner?"

He swallowed at the image of Blakely in his family home, sitting at the table with his sister and parents. She'd fit. Too damn well. He could imagine the laughter. The smiles. The way she'd ease so perfectly into the fabric of his family.

His fingers tightened around the coffee cup. "That won't be possible, Mom."

He hated the way his mother deflated. How her lips changed from an upward curve to downward. All his mother had ever wanted was for her kids to be happy. And she knew—hell, everyone knew—he hadn't been happy for a long time.

He downed the rest of his coffee. "No proposal from Jackson yet, River?"

His question had the exact result he knew it would. His mother perked up and her attention switched from him to River. His sister's eyes narrowed on him as their mother started pumping her with questions.

His father moved to walk beside him. The man was tall, almost as tall as Ryker, and even though he was getting older, he was still fit.

"Your mother means well," he said quietly, the words just for his ears.

"I know." That was why he loved her so damn much. He knew how lucky he was to have the family he had, and he didn't take them for granted for a second.

"She just wants you to be happy." His father gripped his shoulder. "We both do."

Happy. An emotion he hadn't felt for a long damn time, and he didn't see it in his future anytime soon.

When his father remained silent, waiting for a response, Ryker cleared his throat. But instead of telling the man empty lies about emotions he didn't feel, he gave him the bald truth. "I *want* to be happy. And I want *you* to be happy too."

There was a tiny narrowing of Grant Harp's eyes. He'd clearly wanted reassurance that Ryker couldn't give him.

His father sighed. "You know us. Your mother and I have our schedule and haven't tired of it yet."

A smile stretched Ryker's lips. Small but genuine. His parents were nothing if not creatures of habit. Both retired, and both very fond of their afternoon coffee and cake. They had specific places around Lindeman and Ellensburg that they visited on certain days. They were comfortable and content. And he loved that.

He opened his mouth to respond but stopped at the ringing of the phone in his pocket. He pulled it out—and any lightness inside him turned heavy, his muscles going tight.

It was Cal.

"I need to take this, Dad."

He stepped away from his family and moved to a quiet area on the outskirts of the crowd. Only when he was sure there were no listening ears did he answer.

"Did you find him?"

"I'm close. I have a strong lead I need to confirm, but I should have a location for you by tomorrow night."

Ryker's fingers curled into a fist. "Can you give me an approximate area?"

He needed to know if he was going to have to be prepared to jump on a plane and travel across the country.

"That's why I called."

At Cal's heavy pause, Ryker's gut twisted. "Tell me."

"He's close to *you*. If my lead turns out to be correct…the location is about an hour from Lindeman."

Dread clawed at his insides. He searched the crowd for his family. His parents. His sister. It wasn't a fucking coincidence that the guy was so close. It couldn't be. And it had every part of him twitching with unease.

The asshole was hunting Ryker—just as he was hunting Saad.

Ideas started to scramble in his head. About getting his parents out of town. Making sure River was safe.

As he continued scanning for threats, his gaze caught on a familiar group of people across the market. Aria, Cole, the two teenage boys, Anthony and Zac…and Blakely.

"Tell me when you've confirmed his location."

He hung up, a new ache pounding at the back of his eyes. He turned—

And froze when he found Jackson standing behind him.

How long had his friend been standing there?

"Location for who?"

Ryker's jaw clicked. Jackson had to know so he could keep River safe. But the second he told him, the questions would come. And they were questions he didn't want to answer.

When Ryker was quiet a beat too long, Jackson stepped closer. "It's Saad, isn't it? And he's close?"

Another heartbeat. Then he answered. "Yes."

Dark emotions swirled in the other man's eyes. And something else. Fear. He looked for River, then back to Ryker. "You hired someone to keep tabs on him?"

"Cal." Jackson knew Cal. They'd all been stationed together a few times.

"Why didn't you tell us?"

"Because I didn't want to drag you into this."

Jackson's eyes steeled. "You and I both know he won't have come alone. He'll have a team. And more than that, he has connections. People stateside who'll do his dirty work. What was your plan? Go it alone and try to end him? You'll get yourself killed."

His plan was to do whatever it fucking took to wipe Saad off this Earth. "I'm not dragging you into this, Jackson."

His hands fisted at his sides. "I'm *already* in this. You think you're the only one who's angry? You think you're the only one who burns with the need to decimate that fucker? He killed dozens of innocent people because of *us*. Because *we* hunted and killed his brother—not just you."

"We're not in uniform any longer. We definitely don't have the authorization to kill him, and I'm not letting you go down for his death. There's too much risk involved, and my sister needs you."

What he was doing was dangerous, and not just because his own life was on the line.

He planned to kill someone. Yes, he'd killed before, but this time, the government wasn't on his side.

He tried to pass Jackson, but his friend grabbed his arm and tightened his fingers. "It's a morally gray area. And it's only dangerous if we get caught. You're not going alone."

Ryker took two deep breaths, glancing at his sister again. His parents. Even Blakely.

"I should have a location by tomorrow. Cal said it could be as close as an hour away." Another sharp ache in his chest at that information. "Blakely's leaving Sunday. I'm going to send my parents away." He'd organize some sort of protection detail, far from Lindeman. "But we need to protect everyone else."

Jackson's eyes narrowed as he probably had the same thought as Ryker—that the asshole was too close...and there were too many people in this town who were important to them.

~

"BLAKELY!"

Blakely stopped halfway to the bathroom at the sound of her name. She turned to see Aria heading toward her, Cole on one side of her, and two tall teenage boys on the other. It was almost comical how small Aria looked in between the three guys.

Blakely smiled at the group. "Hey."

"You made it!" Aria pulled her into a hug.

The other woman had been messaging Blakely all week, just checking in. She'd been the one to let Blakely know about this twilight market. She'd already walked around for half an hour, looking at the local goods and chatting with some of the stall owners. People were friendly here. She wasn't sure if it was a small-town thing or a Washington thing, but she liked it.

Aria turned toward the boy with dark eyes. "This is my son, Zac."

"Hey."

The kid smiled at her.

Cole nodded toward the other teenager. "And Anthony's mine."

Anthony dipped his head.

"Well, they're both ours," Aria added with a grin.

Cole slid an arm around her waist. "That's right."

Blakely's smile broadened. "Nice to meet you both."

"Have you grabbed a corn dog?" Aria asked. "That's where we're headed now."

"No, but I've been eyeing them." Not just the corn dogs. All the food stalls. It probably hadn't been the smartest idea to come to a market on an empty stomach, after skipping both lunch and dinner.

Or maybe it was, because now she could eat *all* the food.

"They're good," Zac said, staring longingly at the food area. "I usually eat a few."

She chuckled, following his gaze. But instead of finding the corn dog stall, her stare locked on Ryker. He stood beyond the stalls, away from others, phone to his ear and an expression on his face that was so hard and serious, he almost looked scary. The muscles in his forearms were thick and corded, and the hand not holding the phone was fisted.

She could just about make out his white knuckles from here.

She dragged her attention away. "I'm heading to the bathroom, then I'll come find you."

"Want us to grab you a corn dog?" Aria asked.

"No, it's okay. I can get it. But thank you."

Aria squeezed her arm then the group moved away. Before Blakely turned, she checked on Ryker again. He was finished on the phone and now talking to Jackson. She didn't have to be close to know the conversation was tense.

With a long sigh, she forced herself to continue toward the bathroom. Looking away was hard. Certainly harder than it should have been. Because every time she did, she wondered if it would be the last time she saw him. The last time she traced his handsome face. Saw the intensity of his steely brown eyes.

She stepped into the public bathroom and entered a cubicle. When she was finished, she was about to open the stall door but the conversation taking place between women who'd just entered the bathroom made her pause.

"It was a bidding war, Martha. You should have seen it! Both women were desperate to win Ryker Harp."

They were talking about her and Janice.

"Can you blame them?" a different voice asked. Presumably Martha. "He's the last of those Mercy Ring boys left. Of *course* women are falling all over themselves to get him."

"No, I don't blame them. But I've heard Janice has history with him. I don't know who the other woman is."

History? What kind of history?

"Jackie, we shouldn't listen to rumors."

"It's not a rumor if it's true. Janice has told everyone who'll listen that she's dated Ryker. I even heard they were kissing at the bar."

An ugly, sick feeling churned in Blakely's belly at the image of Janice and Ryker locked together in an embrace. At his hands on her body. His lips...

God, the woman was *awful*. Was that the kind of person he was into now? Was that why he was all but shoving her out of town?

She swallowed the bile in her throat and waited until the women stepped into stalls of their own before quickly stepping out, washing her hands, and exiting the bathroom. The earlier excitement for corn dogs and greasy market food was now gone. It was time to leave.

She was barely beyond the bathroom's threshold when she felt it. The weight of eyes on her.

Searching for the source, she caught the dark eyes of a man standing at least a dozen yards from the restrooms. After a very brief second, he turned and walked away.

Her feet were moving before she could stop them. There was something about his face that was oddly familiar. But not in a good way. In an all-the-hairs-on-your-arm-standing-on-end way.

She wove through the crowd, trying to keep the guy in her sights but losing him. He was too fast.

Almost jogging now, she shoved people out of the way, anxious to reach him, yet she had no idea why. Just this feeling inside her that she needed to follow. She needed to know who he was.

She cut through the masses, jolting shoulders and arms, before a tall body suddenly appeared in front of her, blocking her way. Unable to stop her forward momentum, her palms slammed into a wide chest, while fingers wrapped around her arms.

"Blakely? Are you okay?"

That deep, familiar voice. She looked up to confirm it was Ryker, opened and closed her mouth, then glanced around his shoulder.

Gone. The guy was gone.

But God, what the hell was she doing? Chasing a man she probably didn't even know? He'd been so far away, she'd barely seen him anyway. Just his dark features and some facial hair.

She swallowed, internally chastising herself for her impulsive behavior. "I don't know."

An honest answer, at least.

His eyes narrowed, and he looked at her as if he was waiting for more.

But before he could push for details, Aria was beside them, corn dog in hand. "I know you said not to, but I decided to get you one anyway."

Ryker's hands dropped and he stepped back. Because he didn't want others seeing him touch her?

The older woman's words in the bathroom came back to her, and she swallowed.

He's not yours, Blakely. You can't hate a man for not loving you.

Then why did the fusion of anger and pain and hurt threaten to drown her?

CHAPTER 10

*R*yker's fingers tightened around the bottle of soda as he watched Blakely throw her head back and laugh at something Erik said. It shouldn't bother him as much as it did. They were just talking. Yet he wanted to walk over there and tear his friend's head off.

The only reason he was still at this goddamn market was because she was here. She didn't have a car, and he needed to make sure she got back to her hotel safely, especially after witnessing her rushing through the crowd earlier. What the hell had that been about? Who had she been after…and why hadn't she wanted to tell him?

Aria, Cole, River, and Jackson stood with him, but he may as well have been alone. He only had eyes for Blakely.

She laughed again, this time grabbing Erik's arm as the man smiled down at her. The cords in Ryker's neck bunched. The image they presented was too fucking intimate. Michele and Declan sat with them, but that didn't matter. They may as well have been the only two people over there.

"Careful, big brother. You might crack the glass with that death grip of yours."

He tore his gaze from Blakely and Erik and glanced at his sister. She was looking way too smug.

"I was just talking to her," River said, her attention moving to Blakely. "She's nice."

Nice? She wasn't *nice*. She was gorgeous and loyal and honest and the very fucking definition of perfection.

"You know," River continued, clearly not requiring his participation in the conversation, "there's no harm in talking to her. She *did* come to see you."

He could have laughed. No harm? Every time he spoke to the woman, the longing nearly doubled him over with its sharpness. Because he wanted her so damn bad but couldn't allow himself to have her.

"We've said what we need to say. She's leaving soon."

At River's loud exhale, he reluctantly faced her.

She gave him a pointed look. "You need to stop punishing yourself."

Never. The word was a roar from somewhere deep and dark inside him.

River touched his arm, her expression as serious as he'd ever seen it. "Allow yourself some damn grace, Ryker."

If only it was that easy.

As Erik said something to Blakely, he touched her knee.

The last scrap of his calm dissolved, and he moved without thought or hesitation. River chuckled softly but he ignored it, dropping his soda bottle into the trash on the way. When he stood beside their table, all four of them looked up at him.

The smile on Blakely's lips dropped, while Declan's grew. "Hey, friend. Come. Sit with us. Blakely was just telling us about her flight over here."

His gaze swung to her. "Something happen?"

She wet her lips, causing his dick to twitch. "No. But I did have some interesting company. A drunk and a duck sat next to me. Not a real duck, but the drunk guy was talking to a stuffed animal like it was real. He even offered to let me pet him." Her smile returned and it was fucking radiant. "The duck's name was King Henry."

"And did you?"

Her brows rose. "Did I pet the stuffed animal? Of course. If a drunk guy offers to let you pet his royal duck, King Henry, you don't say no."

A smile tried to kick the corners of his lips up. That was the Blakely he remembered. Funny. Not afraid to be silly. "I'm heading out now. I'll give you a ride to your hotel."

He'd meant to ask, but it didn't really come out that way. Maybe because his fingers itched to grab her. Pull her away from Erik's side, where she was sitting too close for Ryker's comfort.

Her pink tongue poked out of her mouth a second time. Desire shot through him, his groin once again tightening at the sight of her wet lips…at their remembered softness.

"A ride would be great." Her voice was quiet at the even quieter table.

His tense muscles eased. And when she stood, he touched a hand to the small of her back. Her warmth seeped into his skin, snaking through his limbs, slowing his rushing blood.

Once they'd said a quick goodbye to everyone, he led her to his car, never lowering his hand. Mostly because he was weak, and he couldn't *not* touch her. His time with her was limited. Soon, he wouldn't be able to touch her ever again. Feel her calmness filtering into him. Hear her gentle voice.

His jaw clicked. He helped her into her seat, then he moved around the car and slid behind the wheel.

For the first few minutes, there was a comfortable silence between them. The kind that came from being with someone you knew well. Someone you were connected to.

Then she spoke, her familiar voice rolling over his skin. "Your friends are really nice."

"They're good people."

She nodded, fiddling with the phone in her lap. "How do you know Erik?"

His fingers tightened on the wheel at the mention of the man. At the image that flashed in his mind of Blakely touching Erik. "We fought in the same underground fighting ring. When I went missing, Jackson took my place in the ring, and Erik helped him train."

He could almost hear her rolling the words over in her head. "Sounds dangerous."

There was nothing left of that place now. Neither the ring, nor the nightclub that secretly housed it in the basement. "I needed dangerous. It helped me."

Helped calm the storm that was his emotions at the time. Getting into that ring and pummeling someone—and getting pummeled in return—gave him something to feel instead of something to think about. He'd come to Lindeman feeling caged by his anger, with nowhere to put it. First the underground ring, then his own boxing gym had saved him, but clearly not enough.

"Have you tried anything else?" she asked.

"Like therapy?" How many other people had asked him that question? His parents. His team. Hell, River still asked him all the time. "I don't want to talk to anyone."

He'd always been better with his body than his words. What would he even say to a therapist? Would he tell them he was responsible for the deaths of innocent people? About his plan for vengeance? About how he didn't *want* to feel better, because every dark emotion fed his need to find Saad? Hurt him? Kill him?

She was silent, and when he looked over at her, she was studying him, almost dissecting him. As if she not only saw his darkness but heard every black thought staining his soul.

"What?" he finally asked.

"I see it now," she said softly.

His gut churned. He shouldn't ask. He should keep his damn

mouth closed…but he wanted to know what was going through that beautiful head of hers. "See what?"

"You don't *want* to get better. You like the anger. You're holding onto it like a shield. Like if you lose it, you lose yourself or your will to do whatever you're planning to do."

Fire scorched his blood. How had she seen so much? How the hell had she dug inside his mind, placing enough broken pieces together to see the truth, when his own family and best friends hadn't?

"Unbelievable."

The word was a mumble under her breath, but he heard it loud and clear. "Got something else to add, Dr. Freud?"

She laughed, but the sound was twisted and wrong. There was no humor. "Everyone's worried about you. *Everyone*. And we're all racking our brains, trying to figure out how to help you. But you're not even trying to help *yourself.*"

"How?" he asked, suddenly matching her own frustrated tone. "How am I supposed to do that?"

"You *try*, Ryker. That's a start. You put in some damn effort."

"I've been too busy trying to survive, Blakely. Trying to figure out how to wake up every damn day, knowing my connection to people sent them to their fucking graves. Figuring out how to live with myself."

She shook her head, arms crossed over her chest in a defensive gesture. She didn't respond, but he could plainly see she didn't like his answer.

"Are you still leaving on Sunday?" he asked.

Acid flashed in her eyes as she pinned him with a stare so hot he was surprised he didn't melt in the driver's seat. "Stop the car."

"What?"

"Stop the damn car, Ryker! I'm walking."

"No." *Hell no.* It was dark, and it might only be a few more minutes back to her hotel by car, but there was no way he was leaving her on the side of a damn road.

Before he realized what she was doing, her seat belt was undone and she opened the door.

He cursed loudly, swinging the car to the side of the road and slamming his foot on the brake. Blakely was out and walking before the vehicle even rocked to a stop.

A growl rasped from his throat as he gave chase, catching up easily and grabbing her arm. "What the hell is wrong with you?"

"What's wrong with *me*? I'm worried about you! I've *been* worried. Desperately trying to make contact. *Connect* with you. For over a year. While you've been fighting in illegal rings and dating horrible women. Hell, you had a goddamn *funeral*, Ryker!"

"I've explained the funeral. And I never dated Janice."

"But you kissed her."

It wasn't a question, yet it had the muscles in his arms tightening. "Who told you that?"

She snapped her lips together in a firm line, yanking out of his grip and crossing her arms, gaze moving somewhere in the distance. "I've felt nothing but worry and sympathy for you since Beirut. But right now? Right now, I'm mad. So damn mad, I can't even look at you."

"Why? Because of Janice?"

Suddenly, like a balloon deflating, her shoulders sagged. She gave an almost resigned sigh. "Because people love you. And you're not even trying to come back to us." The anger was gone and only sadness remained in her tone.

"Blakely—"

"I'm angry because you made *me* love you, and then you cut me out of your life like I was *nothing*."

Any words he'd been about to say died on his lips, and a new emotion pulsed through his chest, threatening to cut into his heart. Fear mixed with dread mixed with something else. Something unfamiliar that he didn't want to name.

"Please don't say that," he almost whispered.

"What? That I love you? Sorry to disappoint, but I do. It's why

I'm here, Ryker. Why I've been refusing to give up on you for over a year, no matter how much you ignore me. No matter how much you try to convince me you're a lost cause. Because I love you, and I *need* you to be okay."

"You can't love me."

Tears welled in her eyes, but she blinked them away. "You can't tell me who to love. It's not your choice." She took a small step closer. "Why won't you let me?"

There were so many fucking reasons, but they all amounted to the same damn thing. "Because I don't deserve your love."

The last scrap of frustration leached from her eyes, replaced with a blend of empathy and sorrow. "You're not the villain you think you are, Ryker."

This time *he* wanted to laugh. At the damn absurdity of that statement. Because villain didn't even begin to describe him. "No, I'm worse. I'm the man dressed up as a hero who ends up wielding the knife. The kiss of death no one sees coming."

And there was not a single fucking thing he could do about it.

He turned, hoping she'd follow and get in the car.

Before he could get a step away, she grabbed his arm, and the second he turned back, she rose to her toes and kissed him.

He wanted to pull away. Every honorable part of him shouted at him to step back. Put distance between them. But the second her lips touched his, she softened his jagged edges.

Her kiss was vital. He needed her goodness and light to battle the fucking darkness that threatened to consume him every single day.

So instead of pushing her away, like his head demanded, he slipped a hand into her soft hair and another around her waist, and he kissed her back. Thrust his tongue into her mouth and tasted the sweetness that countered his sour.

The breathy moan that emerged from her throat drowned out the voices in his head. The loud, angry shouts that had become his companions over the last year.

Her delicate fingers brushed his cheek, igniting a fire in their wake.

Everything this woman was, he wanted. Had *always* wanted. Been hopelessly drawn to, unable to break the connection. But what, then?

Another moan sounded from her, and it finally penetrated his fog of desire.

She couldn't heal him.

He stepped back, dropping his hands. Her red lips were parted and her eyes hooded. It made him want to draw her back in. And he almost did…almost.

"We shouldn't have done that."

She blinked. "Ryker—"

"You're leaving on Sunday. And that's the way it needs to stay."

Devastation. It raced across her expression like wildfire.

He turned away, not able to look. Not wanting her desolation to seep inside him. He wasn't fucking strong enough to shoulder that on top of everything else.

He moved to the car and held her door open. He wasn't sure if she would get in. If she didn't, if she continued down the street, he had no idea what he'd do. Follow at a distance, maybe. He couldn't touch her again. He might lose himself a second time. But she wasn't walking in the dark by herself.

The soft thuds of her footsteps echoed through the quiet night, then she lowered into the passenger seat. He should feel relieved. She was letting him take her to the hotel, then she was leaving on Sunday. He was getting everything he'd asked for.

So why did his chest feel like it had been caught in a fucking bear trap that was squeezing the very life out of him?

CHAPTER 11

Ryker quietly slipped out of the car. The cool night air brushed against his skin. Even though he only wore a black T-shirt and dark pants, he didn't feel the cold. Not when his target was so close.

It was late. Or early, depending on how you looked at it. One a.m. Cal had sent him images of Saad in a warehouse less than ninety minutes from Lindeman. Ninety *fucking* minutes. Too damn close.

The man needed to be eliminated before he closed the remaining distance. Because he would sooner rather than later, if left alive.

The images had come to him only two hours ago, and he'd gathered his shit and left almost immediately. He couldn't risk losing him.

Ryker watched the wooded area in front of him as Jackson approached. He'd told his friend to stay the hell home. He hadn't listened, of course.

"Ready?" Ryker asked quietly and started forward. It would be a twenty-minute trek through forested land.

Jackson grabbed his arm. "I need to tell you something."

Unease spiraled in his gut. "What?"

"I called Davis."

His breath hissed from his teeth. Captain Davis had been their detachment commander. "Why?"

"We need someone on our side in case this goes bad."

A muscle ticked in his jaw. Davis had been the one who'd initiated Ryker's no-fly status. The reason his fucking well of hopelessness had become so deep, leaving him unable to cross the globe and kill Saad.

Jackson stepped closer. "Six months ago, he retired from the military and joined the FBI. He's backing us on this."

He'd known Davis had left the military, but not that he'd joined the FBI. But that didn't change anything. "He told me I wasn't allowed to kill Saad. And even if he didn't, we're not military anymore."

"They believe Saad's taken over his brother's organization and possibly planning terrorist acts on US soil. Saad's being careful, though. There's no concrete evidence that could lead to his arrest. Still, Davis will give us what support and intel he can."

He swallowed. "Calling him was a risk." Davis could have stopped them from going after Saad. Hell, he could have put eyes on Ryker's entire team.

"A risk I thought worth taking."

Ryker took a deep breath. "Anything else you need to tell me?"

Lights flashed from the road behind them. They'd chosen an isolated area of the countryside. There should be no one else here.

"Yeah," Jackson said. "I also told the guys."

The car stopped behind Jackson's, and Declan and Cole climbed out of the front.

Then the back door opened and Erik exited.

"I told you," Jackson said quietly. "We're in this. We want this asshole as much as you. And we've got your back."

The three guys joined them, Declan pushing a gun into a

holster. "Haven't had a good rumble in a while. This should be fun."

Trust Dec to try and bring humor into this.

Ryker's gaze cut to Erik. "You don't need to be here."

"You think I'm letting you old, washed-up Delta boys go out there and get yourselves killed?"

Cole scowled. "Hey, we got out *after* you."

"Yeah, but you're all a bit out of practice. I'm not." Declan shoved him, and Erik laughed before turning his gaze to Ryker. "So, what's the plan?"

"I got confirmation via photo evidence that Saad and about five members of his team are two miles west of here in an abandoned warehouse. The building is owned by a Lebanese family with ties to his organization."

He pulled out his phone and sent them the location. They studied the route, each man committing it to memory.

Jackson went back to his car and returned with earpieces and bulletproof vests. He handed them out to the others.

Ryker may not have wanted to pull anyone else into this mess, but he couldn't deny it felt good having his team here. Men he trusted to watch his back and protect him.

Once they had agreed on a course of action, Ryker tipped his chin toward the woods. "Let's go."

They didn't communicate as they moved. They naturally spread out, each jogging toward the location on their own path.

His feet pounded the ground, leaves and branches whipping against his body. The closer he grew to the target, the harder his heart thrashed against his ribs. He'd always been good at keeping his emotions in check during missions. All of them were trained to switch off and maintain pinpoint focus. But right now, switching off wasn't easy. This wasn't some unknown target. This was a man he was intimately familiar with. A man who'd brought him the closest to death he'd ever been, then killed people he cared about.

This was personal.

When he saw the building ahead, he forced his feet to move faster. It wasn't until he reached the line of trees forming a perimeter around the building that he stopped.

Jackson had stayed closest to him and was about ten meters to his right. Though no one said it out loud, Ryker knew that Jackson would never be far away to ensure he didn't do anything stupid. He didn't care. Tonight, Saad was his only concern.

"I have an armed guard with a pistol by the east wall," he said quietly into the earpiece.

"I have another on the north wall," Cole added.

The other men confirmed there were no visible guards where they were stationed. So only two guards on the exterior. Saad didn't think anyone had his location, so he wasn't playing it safe.

Worked for Ryker.

He gauged the distance between himself and the guard. Watched his movement. The guy paced the side of the building, never looking at the trees. He was watching the dirt in front of him as he kicked it. When he reversed his direction, Ryker moved quickly and silently, approaching from behind.

He wrapped an arm around the man's throat and squeezed. The guy didn't have time to shout before his air cut off. He struggled for several heartbeats, then went limp.

Ryker lowered the body to the ground before pulling the Glock from his holster.

"Target on our side's out," Jackson said quietly, as he moved into the clearing, pulling his own weapon.

"Let's move," Declan said.

Ryker's adrenaline spiked as he crept silently to one side of the warehouse door. Jackson stopped on the other side.

"In position," Erik said.

"Go on three," Ryker whispered.

He quietly counted to three in his earpiece, each number

bringing a harder thrash of his heart and a louder roar of blood between his ears. Then he kicked the door open.

Half a dozen men immediately scattered inside, all of them shouting and reaching for weapons when they spotted Ryker's team.

Ryker aimed and fired, killing the first man he saw. He got off another shot but missed his target as the guy lunged for the floor.

Then came the return fire.

Ryker dove behind a wide stack of crates as bullets hit their surface. To his right, Jackson took cover as well.

He waited two beats, then eased his head out slightly, getting one man in the leg, then the gut, before sliding behind the crates again.

Where the fuck was Saad?

Another two breaths, then he rose and fired. The guy he aimed for dove but the bullet hit him in the side. Erik, Cole and Declan were each shooting from their positions, trying to take out three men who were returning fire—but Ryker still didn't see the asshole he'd come here to kill.

The thought had barely entered his mind when a large rolling door opened across the warehouse. A second later, a smaller door flew open, revealing an office of some kind near the bay door, and two men ran out—covering a shorter man like human shields.

Everything in Ryker slowed to a crawl, and the rest of the room darkened as his vision tunneled.

The shorter man was Saad.

Ryker ducked behind the crates as a bullet flew toward him. His body was at war with his heart. Every inch of him wanted to get moving. Hunt. Kill. Every second he waited was a second too long. But he needed to be smart. Getting himself shot wouldn't help.

He waited for a short break in the gunfire. For Jackson to rise and cover him. When the moment came, Ryker sprinted out the door they'd breached.

The men were in the distance, heading into the trees. The gap between them was wide.

Fuck.

He holstered his Glock and ran faster, arms swinging, propelling him forward. He was gaining on them, but it wasn't enough.

Someone fired from behind him—he fucking prayed it was one of his own guys—and the guard on the left stumbled but kept moving.

Ryker sped up again. When the guard turned and aimed, Ryker threw himself behind a tree. By the time he was running again, any made-up ground had disappeared. Frustration and fury filled him, propelling him forward, faster than he'd ever run. He jumped over the stump of one tree and rounded another.

The roar of a car engine pierced the night, and a second later, he saw lights. The car was ahead in the distance, on a narrow access road.

No! If the asshole got in that vehicle, Ryker would lose him. He'd have to tear the fucking world apart to find him a second time.

He raised his Glock and fired, but he was too far away and there were too many goddamn trees between them.

He watched as Saad and his men slipped inside the vehicle. The door had just closed when Ryker finally got a clear shot. He fired, but the bullet didn't shatter the glass. Bulletproof.

He fired again just as someone gunned the engine and the car sped off.

Still, Ryker didn't stop running. It was like he was physically incapable of doing so. He pushed his body to limits it had never reached. When his feet hit asphalt, he stopped to aim at the tires, but they were too far away. A second later, the sedan disappeared around a curve.

The silence that followed splintered every part of him that had been even remotely whole. His fury had claws, and those claws dug deep at his insides, threatening to tear him in two.

When the raw disbelief had passed and he could finally move again, he spun, reared his fist back, and smashed it into the body of a tree—hard. Pain radiated up his arm. It wasn't enough. His body burned and bled, and he couldn't do a fucking thing about it.

The asshole was still alive. Still breathing. And yet again, out of Ryker's reach.

CHAPTER 12

Blakely traced the outline of the waterfall with her eyes. It was just a photo on her phone, but the blue specks of water were as clear now as the day she'd seen them in person, and the green plants bursting around the falls just as lush.

Beautiful. Lebanon was so damn beautiful, and she missed it. She didn't just miss the country though. She missed the person she was when she was there, before the bombing, when the anxiety and sadness hadn't been pulling her down.

She flicked to the next photo. It was of her and Carrie, a fellow aid worker. They'd become quick friends. They still texted sometimes. But rarely. When Blakely had stopped being okay, their relationship became strained. It was her fault for not answering her friend's calls. Not putting more effort into keeping in touch.

She flicked again, this time finding a group photo. She studied each face. The faces of the other aid workers who'd been in Beirut with her and tried to ensure she was okay after the blast.

It was late. She should be sleeping, but every time she closed her eyes, she saw flames. Bright, angry flames that infiltrated her dreams and rocked her sanity.

She'd been having more nightmares than usual lately, not just because of the fire in the restaurant earlier in the week, but because she was here, with Ryker, and it was bringing it all back.

Tears pressed to the corners of her eyes when she reached a photo of her, Cyrus, and Ara. God, she'd loved those kids. They'd been so full of life. Like little rays of sunlight.

She swallowed the lump in her throat and blinked until the wetness in her eyes dried. She'd already cried so many tears over losing them. She'd asked her therapist when the hole in her chest would heal. When she'd be able to remember them without her heart cracking and her throat closing. She'd expected a *soon.* Maybe a *give yourself time.* The answer she'd received had been harder to accept.

You'll never be whole again. You'll rebuild yourself around the loss, but you'll have a few cracks. And then you'll be a new Blakely. Different.

She'd wanted to scream at the woman that she didn't *want* to be different. She liked the old Blakely. The one who could smile with ease and look at the simplest fire without losing her breath. The Blakely who hadn't been exposed to war and death and devastation. She wanted the life before the loss.

She swiped to the next image. Her breath caught. This photo was almost identical to the last, but there was one very large difference. It included Ryker. He'd snuck up behind them, popping into the photo just as she'd snapped. And his smile... God, it was so big and real and uninhibited. Devastatingly beautiful.

This time, she didn't just trace the photo with her eyes, she reached out a hand and ran her fingertip over his face. If only she could reach into the photo and pull him back to her. Hold the man who'd openly cared for her and beg him not to leave again.

Another impossibility. What was that saying? You never know the value of a moment until it becomes a memory? But she *had* known the value of that moment. She just hadn't known how fleeting it would be.

Her heart clenched at the thought of tomorrow. Actually, it was past midnight, so today. Of stepping into that plane. Leaving Lindeman. Leaving Ryker. She might never see him again. And that hurt so much that new cracks formed in her heart.

She'd told the man she loved him. And his response? That she *couldn't* love him. He wouldn't allow it. It hurt as much now as it had then.

It wasn't like she'd expected a declaration of love in return, but she'd hoped for...something. Some emotion other than that dark anger.

She swallowed and was about to move to the next image when a text appeared. Her heart catapulted into her throat.

It was Ryker.

Open the door.

For a moment, she remained perfectly still, convinced she was seeing a message that wasn't there. A message she'd created in her mind from her deep desperation to have the man close.

An entire thirty seconds passed, then another message popped up.

Blakely...I need you to open the door.

It was real. He was here.

Almost on autopilot, she dropped the phone onto the bedside table and stood. She didn't think about the fact that all she wore were panties and an oversized shirt. She didn't care that her hair was a tumbled mess over her shoulders and her eyes red-rimmed.

When she reached the door, she didn't even look through the peephole, just pulled it open.

And there he was. Ryker. Standing in front of her, his hair windswept. Black T-shirt tight around his thick chest. When she looked down at his hand, she gasped. Dried blood was smeared across his knuckles.

"Ryker...are you okay?"

When he didn't respond, her eyes flew back to his—and she almost stepped back. There was something drastically different about him tonight. An intensity in his gaze. A dangerous edge that felt so sharp it could slice her in two.

"Ryker—"

The whisper had barely left her mouth when he stepped forward, wrapped a possessive hand behind her neck, and kissed her.

She gasped again, and his tongue swept into her mouth, tangling with hers. The kiss was firm and warm and completely devoid of hesitation. It made her forget to breathe. It made her freeze and burn all in the same fraction of a second.

Her stillness lasted for a beat longer, then she leaned into him, meeting him swipe for swipe. Stroke for stroke. Tasting him.

He groaned and pulled her body against his. The door thudded closed, then he spun them and pressed her against the wall.

"I shouldn't be here," he growled between kisses. "Tell me to leave."

His hand smoothed up her thigh, her hip, pushing her top up and settling on her waist before inching around her front. His fingers almost spanned her entire stomach. Her scarred, disfigured stomach. He caressed that skin like the scars were a precious part of her. Like he wanted to feel every inch of her suffering. Memorize it.

His fingers tightened, his tongue sweeping over hers, and when he spoke again, his voice was guttural. "Blakely. *Tell me to leave.*"

She slid her hands up his chest, where the strong beat of his heart thudded beneath her palm. "No."

This time, his growl was primal, almost animalistic. He whipped her shirt over her head, and she gasped as cool air whispered across her bare breasts. But they were only free for a second, because then Ryker was cupping them, his head dropping, lips wrapping around one hard nipple while he thumbed the other.

She threaded her fingers through his hair, throwing her head back. The cry that wrenched from her lips was one of need, but also agony. Agony because she needed him closer. To feel his lips on her forever. She remembered them so well. They may have only had one night of bliss, but that long night had carved itself into her memory.

His tongue swiped over her hard peak, his thumb circling and teasing her other nipple. She was on fire. The good kind. The only kind of fire that brought her peace. The heat so raw and intense, she wasn't sure she could catch a single breath.

He switched his mouth to her other tight bud, and she moaned, tugging at the soft locks of his hair.

Suddenly, the wall disappeared from her back and air slid across her skin. Her hands went to work, tugging at the base of his shirt, pulling it over his head. Then she felt him. His warmth. His strength. The smooth planes of his chest.

He lay her on the bed but didn't part from her as he shifted over her body. His weight was like a blanket of safety. Salvation.

He kissed her again, this time softer as his hand moved down her side before slipping inside her panties. Her blood sped up, rushing hard and fast. He swiped her clit, rocketing pleasure through her, and she cried out his name.

"You're so fucking beautiful." His voice was deep and raspy, begging her to crumble. To fall apart for him. *With* him.

He caressed her again, and she clutched his shoulder, digging her nails into his flesh. "Ryker, I need…" She couldn't finish because she didn't know *what* she needed, beyond just him. It had always been him.

"Yeah, princess. I've got you."

Princess…the nickname that was his alone. Because *she* was his.

His mouth moved across her cheek, down her neck, below

her ear. His finger never stopped moving against her bundle of nerves. Touching. Torturing.

When a finger slid down to her entrance, desire flared in her lower abdomen. Then he pushed inside. Her back arched, and it brought more of her flesh against his, causing her to groan with a new desire. Every time he gave her more, she wanted more.

He dragged his finger in long, rhythmic thrusts, while his thumb worked her clit and his mouth teased her neck. He was everywhere. Caging her. Marking her.

"Ryker, please!" she cried, reaching down to grasp him through his pants.

His muscles tensed and expanded. She could feel all of him through the material. He was hard, and he was large. She stroked and massaged, and his heated breath hissed across her skin.

He leaned to the side, causing her hand to drop, and quickly removed his boots, pants, and briefs. He started to wrestle his wallet out of his pants, but she grabbed his arm.

"I'm on the pill." And she wanted to feel him. His thick length against her walls with no barriers.

He cupped her cheek, the hard calluses brushing her skin as he shifted back between her thighs. God, he was big.

"Last chance, princess. Tell me to leave. Tell me to walk out that goddamn door so you can find a man who doesn't teeter so dangerously close to the dark."

She returned her palm to his heart, feeling their beats sync. "Pull me into the darkness with you."

His eyes blackened, and his lips crushed hers. Then he slid inside her, filling her so completely that she finally understood why she'd felt empty for so long.

∼

Blood roared between Ryker's ears, and it roared for *her*. For the woman whose softness made him feel a little less jagged. Whose sweet heart made his feel less broken.

Her body closed around him, tight and wet and warm. He pulled out of her almost completely before driving back in.

It was fucking heaven. A heaven he hadn't known for too long. There was still the ugly voice inside him that howled that he shouldn't be here. That coming to her was a mistake and would end in her ruin. But he shut it out because he was a selfish bastard. Because he needed her.

He cupped her breast, playing with her hard peak with the rough pad of his thumb as he continued to move. Her mouth tore from his and she threw her head back. The cries that escaped her lips destroyed him. Silenced the world around him. The silence was peace. It was harmony. It was a flood of salvation in his soul.

At the sight of her delicate neck stretched before him, he lowered his head and latched on, sucking the creamy flesh.

She met him thrust for thrust, lifting her hips, welcoming him deeper inside her.

Fuck, she felt like home. And she brought just a flicker of the old Ryker back. The Ryker he barely remembered. The Ryker who had long since disappeared.

Her back arched, and he slipped an arm around her small waist, pulling her body closer.

"Yes!"

Her soft, raspy voice was something he fucking dreamed about. Dreams he'd classified as forbidden. She'd become a fruit he wasn't allowed to touch or taste. But tonight, he was allowing himself all of her and he was ignoring tomorrow.

Her fingers dug into his shoulders and her eyes scrunched, like she teetered dangerously close to the edge of pleasure and pain. He felt it too. The pleasure of having her, the pain of knowing this moment couldn't last forever.

He swiped his tongue back up her neck and grabbed her

hands, interlacing their fingers. His lips paused on a spot behind her ear. This time she whimpered, a tender, vulnerable sound that he wanted to capture. Replay a hundred times in his head.

He increased the pace of his thrusts. His. This woman was his fucking everything.

"*Mine*," he growled, unable to keep the vow to himself.

"*Yours*," she breathed.

His heart clenched so hard, he could almost feel her fingers around it, digging in.

He trailed a hand down her body and his thumb rolled over her clit. Suddenly, her back arched and her walls clenched around him. Her scream slashed through the otherwise quiet night.

The vision of his woman losing herself to pleasure, combined with the feel of her muscles pulsing around him, stole his last shred of control. He managed two more deep thrusts before his entire fucking world exploded. A primal growl that sounded unfamiliar to his ears erupted from his throat as waves of ecstasy crashed through his body.

He continued thrusting until he had nothing left. Until he was a shadow of the man he'd been when he walked in here.

Finally, he stopped and touched his forehead to hers, letting the stillness of the moment seep inside him and still his racing heart.

Again, she touched her hand to his chest, right over his heart. "Are you okay?"

Okay? Not even close. But then, he didn't know *what* he was. So he lied. He gave her a simple yes in an attempt to not break the moment apart with an annihilating truth. Then he dropped down beside her.

Her gaze was heavy as she watched him, but she didn't attempt to move or touch him again. That was his own fault for pushing her away. But he needed her closer, so he wrapped an arm around her waist and tugged her to him. Immediately, she nestled into his side.

And there it was. The peace he'd been searching for when he'd come here in the middle of the night, furious and frustrated and desperate. The glue that pieced him back together.

He shouldn't have come, he knew that. But the second Saad had disappeared, the second the sedan was out of his reach, the hopelessness had dropped him into a hole so deep, he couldn't find his way out.

He'd come here in search of salvation. Needing to touch her more than he needed to save her.

Yeah…he really was a selfish bastard.

Pain. Fear. Torment. It thickened the air and took Ryker from deep sleep to wide awake, his eyes flashing open to see the hotel room cloaked in darkness.

He pushed up, his muscles rippling as he expected to find an enemy. The room was empty. He turned his head to see Blakely, eyes closed, face pinched in agony. Her chest moved up and down so quickly it was like she was running a marathon in her sleep. And those sounds. Intense, sorrowful whimpers pulled from somewhere deep inside her.

Her head thrashed to the side. That's what had woken him. She was having a nightmare.

He touched her shoulder. "Blakely."

Her eyes didn't open. Her panting intensified.

He lowered his head, cupping her cheek and touching his temple to hers. "Princess. You're safe."

"They're gone!"

The tremble in her voice crumbled his insides. Squeezing. Crushing. She was talking about Beirut. About the people they'd lost. He knew that with everything he was.

He moved his lips to her ear, grazing her flesh ever so softly as he repeated, "You're safe."

Finally, the thrashing slowed. Her erratic breaths eased, and for a moment, she was just still.

"Ryker."

He closed his eyes, letting the sound of his name on her lips soothe the savage inside him. "Yeah, princess. I'm here."

A small, familiar hand touched the back of his head. He didn't move, and neither did she. They just remained as they were, tangled but separate. Caught between a nightmare and reality, allowing the two to fuse together.

He wanted nothing more than to wrap her up and protect her from the world. But then who would protect her from *him*? It was a battle he continued to fight the longer she was here. A battle he'd lost last night. Or maybe he'd won. He wasn't sure anymore.

When they finally separated, he found her gaze, and similar to when she'd lain in his arms before they slept, he felt it. Peace.

How did she do that? With one look, make him feel almost human?

"Are you okay?"

She swallowed, her green gaze shifting between his eyes. "I'm okay."

He wanted to ask her about the nightmares. To know if they stole her sleep often. But he didn't want to force her back into that darkness. Not now that she was calm.

Instead, he trailed the pad of his thumb down her cheek. "Good."

He turned his head to find the bedside clock. Six a.m. He wouldn't be getting more sleep. "I might have a quick shower."

She yawned, exhaustion weighing on her features.

His heart softened. "You go back to sleep."

Then he did something stupid. He leaned down and kissed

her. Slid his mouth over hers, letting the warmth of her lips anchor him to this moment.

Rising from the bed was harder than it should have been, and the only way he made it to the bathroom was by not looking back. The second the cold water of the shower hit his shoulders, he dropped his chin to his chest. Hopefully the cold would shock his body out of whatever trance it was in. He needed to gain some damn perspective.

The cracked skin on his knuckles stung as the water hit it. But it was nothing compared to what was going on inside him.

Saad had been there. Right. Fucking. There. And he'd slipped away.

His insides coiled at the unfairness of it all. A few things had to go into place today—as soon as possible. Get his parents out of town. Make sure River was protected.

And Blakely…

He closed his eyes, letting hopelessness wash over him. He'd run to her last night, needing her to take it all away. The anger. The pain. The fucking desolation. And she had. God, she'd taken it away so easily. The second he'd touched her. Hell, the second he'd lain eyes on her, his lungs had released and he could breathe again. He'd switched from surviving to living.

He scrubbed a hand over his face and stepped out of the shower. Quickly, he dried off before returning to the room. Blakely's eyes were closed, and her chest rose and fell with even, deep breaths. She was asleep again. He'd suspected she would be. By the time they'd fallen asleep earlier, it had been damn late.

For a moment, he just stood there and watched her, transfixed. She was like nothing and no one he'd ever met. And it was both a blessing and a curse.

With a sharp inhale, he pulled on the same clothes he'd worn last night. She was leaving today. When, exactly, he wasn't sure. And he had no fucking idea what to do about it. His head was a mess.

A part of him wanted to ask her to stay. Hold onto her with both hands and never let go. But nothing had changed. Saad was still alive. His emotions were still a dark, tangled mess. And she was still the picture of perfection and deserved the damn world.

A few rounds in the ring would help him focus. But even that probably wouldn't entirely clear his head.

He was walking to the door, about to leave, when something on the small table caught his attention. A piece of paper with a few scribbled notes.

He moved closer, eyes narrowing on a time and date. Then the writing below. It was messy, like she'd written it in a rush. Like she'd needed to get it down before it slipped from her mind.

Landed in California. Hired car to drive north?

Family and friends in San Francisco and Seattle.

Access to cash and weapons.

A heated exhale blasted from his chest and his vision dulled. He fought to maintain the calm he'd felt before his shower, but it was rapidly fading.

He couldn't believe what he was seeing.

Blakely was tracking Saad.

THE SOUND of movement pierced Blakely's sleep. She inhaled, breathing in a deep, earthy scent. Ryker's scent.

A smile played on her lips at the memory of last night. Of what they'd shared. Slowly, her eyes opened, first taking in the ceiling of the hotel room, then searching for him.

Ryker stood across the room, back toward her. He was wearing his clothes. Black shirt. Dark pants. The tight fit of both made her insides flutter.

She pushed up to her elbows, gaze lowering to whatever he was looking at.

The flutters became a nervous squeeze.

Shit! She'd forgotten about that.

She swallowed. "I didn't mean for you to see that."

Ryker turned, his intelligent eyes as fierce as she'd known they would be.

She sat up slowly, pulling the sheet over her bare chest.

"Tell me this isn't what I think it is, Blakely."

They were back to Blakely. Trying to lie to him would be futile. He knew what it was. "I spoke to a lot of the surviving families before I left Beirut. Went to a few funerals." She shifted her gaze from the note, back to him. "It wasn't hard to learn who was responsible and why he did what he did."

Ryker's jaw clenched, danger practically rolling off him. "And now you're *tracking* him?"

"Not tracking, per se. I asked some of the locals to keep tabs on him and let me know if he left the country. Once he did, one of them gave me a contact for someone in the States who knew of him and where he might be heading."

He cursed, the fury behind it filling the room. "If the news got back to him that you're asking for fucking reports on his activity—"

"The locals are as angry about what he did as I am. They wouldn't tell him."

He stepped forward, suddenly looking every bit the dangerous former Delta operator that he was. "You can't be sure of that. Is that why you're here?"

"Partly. You wouldn't answer my calls or texts, so I was always planning on coming. But when I found out he was on the West Coast...I *had* to make sure you were okay." *Physically and emotionally.* "And make sure you didn't do anything reckless."

It was as if every part of her needed to confirm he was safe. That Saad and Ryker hadn't destroyed each other. If she had eyes on the terrorist, she knew Ryker did as well. And she also knew Ryker well enough to know he wouldn't let this drop. The second it became possible, he'd enact his revenge.

Suddenly, it hit her—the late-night visit. The blood on his knuckles. The rage and desperation on his face.

"That's where you were last night," she whispered, her words a statement, not a question. "You went to kill him, but…you lost him?"

The puzzle pieces fit together. Why had he come to her afterward, though? Because she eased his torment as much as he eased hers?

Ryker stepped forward, his eyes black. "Stay out of this, Blakely."

"If you're in this, *I'm* in this."

He flinched like she'd struck him. "*No.* You're going home. Today. And you're staying far away from that bastard."

Every word felt like a carefully placed blow, each heavier than the last. He'd told her to leave so many times, she should be used to it. Expect it, even. But after last night? It hurt worse than ever before.

It wasn't just the danger that she'd be leaving. It was *him* and *them*—and he knew it. And then what? She just had to twiddle her thumbs at home and wonder if Saad would kill Ryker or Ryker kill Saad?

She swallowed in an attempt to dislodge the emotion that clogged her throat. "You're really telling me to leave after last night?"

For a moment, she thought she saw a flicker of emotion in his eyes. Then he blinked. "You're not safe here."

"Then why do I feel safest when I'm with you?"

Ryker moved toward the door. Blakely flew out of bed, grabbed her discarded T-shirt from the floor, and pulled it over her head. She made it to the door just as Ryker pulled it open and barreled in front of him, slamming the door closed with her back. "Why did you come here last night?"

"What?"

"You were angry and desperate. I could feel it in you. You could have gone anywhere, yet you came here. Why?"

His hands fisted. "You need to get out of my way, Blakely."

"Answer my question first."

She saw it in his eyes—the snap of his final shred of restraint. Then his voice raised, his words anguished. "Because *you're* here, and I'm fucking chained to you, Blakely! I needed to feel okay, and that's what you do for me!"

Five seconds of truth so raw and powerful, her knees threatened to cave.

"And has it ever occurred to you," she said quietly, "that maybe I need *you* to help *me* feel okay? That maybe you're my safety as much as I'm yours?"

She hadn't been okay for so long, but last night, with him, those cracks that had formed in Beirut had started to fill.

"Every single morning, I wake up and I see my scarred, mutilated skin." She reached for his hand, slid it beneath the material of her shirt, and pressed it to her burned stomach. "The scars are a daily reminder of what happened. I hate them. I hate the memories. The nightmares. And more than all of that, I hate that when this happened, I didn't just lose those who died—I also lost *you*."

And not just the man himself. The future they'd been planning when they returned to the US. It had all just disappeared, and she'd been powerless to stop it.

His throat bobbed, and she was almost certain she could feel the slightest tremble in his fingers.

"Don't push me away," she whispered. "I need to be here to know that you're safe from Saad. And we want and need each other, you know that as well as I do."

She slid her hand up his chest, around his neck. Then she pulled his head down, hovering her lips over his.

"You're trying to save me from something I don't want or need saving from. *You*."

Slowly, she lifted her head until their mouths touched. It was barely a graze. A fleeting stroke of lips. When he didn't pull away, she did it again, this time getting a small nibble from him. On the third swipe, his arm slipped around her waist, pulling her against him.

Then he kissed her with the same passion he'd shown her last night.

She leaned into him, letting the connection sweep her away from this room. To somewhere else. Somewhere just for them.

This kiss wasn't wild or desperate, despite the intensity. It was cherishing. And it melted her. It turned her into liquid heat that she prayed never solidified.

Too soon, he tugged his head back. She opened her eyes to see Ryker's still closed, and an expression on his face that made him look lost.

Choose me, Ryker. Choose us. She whispered the plea inside her head. It was loud and it was desperate.

His eyes opened, but he didn't look at her. Instead, he looked past her, to the wooden door, as if the plain surface would give him answers.

She knew the exact moment he made his decision. That guarded expression returned, and he stepped back. "I need to go."

Her heart dropped.

Silently, she stood to the side. Watched him open the door and leave. Walk away from her, and with him, every inch of her that still belonged to him.

Ryker's feet pounded the pavement. He pumped his arms, forcing his body to continue, hoping to outrun everything that chased him. The thoughts. The emotions. The fucking torment.

Every word Blakely had spoken to him was true. So damn true, he'd all but run from her as well.

Don't push me away.

He clenched his fists harder, the feel of her scars against his palm still alive on his skin.

You're trying to save me from something I don't want or need saving from. You.

He ran faster, not caring about the tightening of his lungs or the ache in his muscles. He welcomed the pain. The damn exhaustion. He hoped his mind would get there too.

He still believed with everything he was that she could do better. That with another man, she could find love and peace. Someone who'd fall to his knees in front of her without a suitcase of baggage trailing behind. But despite believing that, the idea of her actually being with this other perfect man ruined him.

He turned the corner, and up ahead, running toward him, was

Cole. It wasn't a surprise. His friend only lived a short distance away, and he was a regular runner. He usually went much earlier though.

When he got closer, Cole stopped and turned, matching his strides to Ryker's. "Hey."

"Bit late for your run, isn't it?"

Cole nodded. "Yeah, woke late after last night."

Most people would have just skipped the run altogether. But he knew Cole better than that. The man had broken his back in that hellish last mission. Being unable to run, barely able to move at all for so many months, had affected him deeply. Made him appreciate his fitness and mobility that much more.

They ran in silence for a few minutes, but the second he felt Cole's gaze on him, he knew what was coming.

"Are you doing okay after last night?"

No. He was far from okay.

They'd called Davis the second Saad had slipped away, and he'd taken care of the aftermath at the warehouse. Ryker hadn't stuck around for long. He'd needed to get the hell out of there. Find something to bring him even a shred of calm. He hadn't realized he was driving toward Blakely until he'd parked in the lot. Everything between Saad disappearing and showing up at the hotel was a hazy blur.

"No," he finally answered, letting the ripples of frustration coat the single word.

"I feel it too, my friend. It's heavy. But we'll get him."

Ryker was silent. He'd heard that before. Hell, he'd been telling himself the same thing since the bombing. But *when*? He needed a date. Time. A fucking road map.

"Where'd you disappear to, after?"

Ryker considered lying, but there was no point, and his friends knew him too well anyway. "Blakely."

Cole was good at keeping his emotions in check, and right

now was no different. There was no change to his features. "Everything okay there?"

Another resounding no. "My head keeps telling me going to her last night was a mistake. That if I cared about her as much as I think, I'd stay far away."

Fuck, his insides rebelled against that statement. Against the word *mistake* in reference to Blakely. Against the idea of staying away.

"And the rest of you?"

"The rest of me feels bound to her. Tethered with a chain so strong, it's fucking unbreakable."

"So, give yourself permission to have her."

Permission to have her… Cole made it sound like it was actually a choice. But choices weren't that simple. He didn't *choose* the dangerous emotions inside him. He didn't *choose* to have an enemy he couldn't kill.

"She's been tracking Saad," he said instead.

His friend's brows slashed together. "What?"

"She knew when he touched down in the States. Knew he had family connections in San Francisco and Seattle. It's part of the reason she's here. Because she's worried he's coming after me."

"Shit."

His thought exactly. "It's another reason she has to go. It's safer for her to not be here."

"By that reasoning, it's safer to send River away, and everyone else you care about."

"River has Jackson. And I've already booked flights to Cradle Mountain for Mom and Dad and made a call to Blue Halo Security. They're going to protect them."

His team had a connection to the Blue Halo boys. Jackson, Declan, and Cole had helped them out when one of their women had been taken in a hostage situation. Idaho wasn't too far away, but Ryker trusted those men to keep his parents safe.

"And Blakely could have *you.*"

Ryker nearly choked. He didn't trust himself to keep *anyone* safe, let alone someone as important as Blakely.

When he remained quiet a beat too long, Cole grabbed his arm and eased him into a walk. "You need to stop."

"Stop what?"

"Punishing yourself." Cole stopped them altogether and stepped closer. "You were doing your damn *job*, Ryker. It is not your fault the target's brother killed people to hurt you."

"I could have kept my distance from the locals. I *should have* kept my distance." It was a regret that had scarred his soul. Scars that would remain for as long as he breathed.

"And he would have killed someone else close to you, if not them. Or someone close to me, or Jackson, or Declan. As devastating as it is to accept, those people in Beirut were chosen because they were easy targets for Saad." Cole's voice lowered. "You can't save everyone, and you can't control the actions of a killer."

Ryker clutched at his hair in frustration, trying to gain some goddamn clarity. There was none. "I need him to die, Cole! Until he does, I can't forgive myself, or forget what he's done."

"He will. But it won't bring anyone back."

The words cut new wounds into his flesh.

Cole's jaw tensed. "You have to separate the events. Separate Blakely from those deaths. What happened in Beirut doesn't define you, and it doesn't define your relationship with her." He shook his head, seemingly frustrated. "From what I can see, you're both exactly what the other person needs. And you both deserve to be happy."

Happiness was an emotion that felt so far out of the realm of possibility, he didn't even dare reach for it. He opened his mouth, not sure if he was about to agree with his friend or push the narrative he'd been living by for over a year. Before he could do either, his phone rang from the strap on his arm.

He pulled it out. Every other thought in his head disappeared at the sight of Cal's name flashing on the screen. He'd sent his friend a text, summarizing the mess of last night. That was just before his run.

"Cal?"

"I put a tracker on his vehicle when I took the surveillance pictures at the warehouse," he said, in lieu of a greeting. "Assumed it was his because it was the fanciest one." He snorted over the line. "When I saw your text, I took a look at the program. Vehicle's sitting on a rural property half an hour north of Ellensburg. We did a check on the ownership of the property, and the man's a longtime friend of Saad's family."

Ryker's heart throbbed in his chest. "Send me the location."

The second he hung up, the address came through.

He looked at Cole. "We got another hit."

Another *chance*. They couldn't waste this one.

BLAKELY STOPPED in front of a shop. The sign read *Meals Made Easy*. She wanted to see Aria and the other women before leaving town, and this was where she said they'd be.

Through the glass, she could see Michele standing at a counter in a kitchen, and River and Aria sitting at a table. Blakely pushed at the door. When it didn't open, she looked through the glass again to find Michele looking back. Her face transformed into a smile and she reached for something below the counter. A second later, the door clicked, and Blakely stepped inside.

"Hey!" Aria stood and hugged her. The embrace was warm and almost familiar, which was crazy. She'd known the woman such a short amount of time. She'd miss Ryker when she left, but she'd also miss this woman.

Blakely smiled and exchanged hellos with River and Michele before sitting at the table.

"Tell me you're not really leaving today," Aria said.

Blakely had told them about her plans Friday night at the market. Everything in her had been hoping that between then and now, things would change. That Ryker would ask her to stay.

She lifted a shoulder. "I am. I'm here to say goodbye."

The women looked as disappointed as she felt. It was River who finally spoke. "Argh! My brother is making a huge mistake. He cares about you. I know he does. I can see it."

She could see it too. And every time he touched her, the emotion seeped through his skin into hers. But she could only put herself out there and ask a man to love her so many times. "I told him how I felt. And last night…" She stopped, not sure how to articulate everything that had happened. "Last night, he came to me, and we shared something incredible. But this morning, he told me to leave again."

The final nail in the coffin.

Michele's lips angled down. "I'm so sorry."

Aria reached across the table and squeezed her hand. "Maybe he just needs more time. It took Cole a while to get to a place where he was open to a committed relationship."

"Jackson too," River said softly. "Those men pretend to be fearless, but really, love scares the shit out of them."

Oh, Blakely could see his fear. She just couldn't shift it. It was too heavy and too firmly in place. "Well, he has my number if he suddenly has a change of heart."

"You can't just stay in town for a bit longer?" Aria asked.

"He's been pretty insistent he wants me gone, and honestly, I don't know if my heart can take any more rejection."

In fact, she knew it couldn't. That he could kiss and touch her as if she was the center of his world, then just walk away without a backward glance…

No. She couldn't do it again.

She spent the next half hour talking to the women. They were incredibly kind, trying to take her mind off everything she was leaving here in Lindeman, and then it was time to go.

After giving each woman a hug, she stepped out of the shop and started down the street. Her hotel was only a five-minute walk, she'd already packed her things, and her digital ticket was on her phone, so all she had to do was ask her hotel to call a car to take her to the airport and leave.

Her heart gave a little squeeze, but she ignored it and forced the pain down, focusing on putting one foot in front of the other. If there was anything she'd learned in the last year, it was that she was stronger than she thought. She'd withstood pain that should have knocked her to the ground with every step she took, and on the occasions when she *did* fall, she was capable of standing again.

Maybe after some time, losing him wouldn't hurt so much.

What she absolutely did *not* want to do was return to Minnesota, sit at home, and pine for him. She wasn't close to her family, so they weren't a reason to stay in her hometown. The idea of moving to a new city had been playing in her head for months. Getting a fresh start felt smart.

Ha. Like that would help. Ryker was basically tattooed on her heart.

With a long exhale, she walked faster and turned the corner toward her hotel.

A cloud of dust flew into her face.

She scrunched her eyes, coughing and spluttering as the stuff entered her nose and mouth, choking her. She blinked rapidly, barely able to make out a man in front of her, shoving something into his pocket that looked like...a straw?

The man mumbled something that sounded like an apology, then he kept moving.

What the hell?

She frowned as she turned her head and watched the back of him as he rounded the corner. His accent reminded her of the locals she'd known in Beirut. Was he Lebanese?

Whatever she'd breathed in burned and she coughed more as

she continued down the street. She brushed a hand over her face, frowning at the white powder on her fingertips. What was that?

Her steps slowed as the path suddenly blurred in front of her.

When a wave of dizziness hit, she stumbled.

Footsteps sounded behind her. She turned to see the same man walking back toward her. He wasn't looking at her, but she suddenly knew he was coming for her. Knew he'd blown that powder in her face on purpose.

The need to get away from him had her heart racing. She moved faster, but her feet were clumsy, her vision clouded.

Too soon, a thick arm slipped around her waist, and a car seemingly came out of nowhere, stopping beside them. She opened her mouth to say no, to cry for help, but no sound came out. She tried to push away from the man, but her arms were uncooperative.

When two teenage boys rounded the corner at the other end of the street, a flicker of hope leapt into her chest. Even with her vision blurring, she recognized Zac and Anthony, Cole and Aria's kids.

She opened her mouth to scream, to call to them, but again words wouldn't leave her. She felt like a zombie, unable to speak. Unable to fight.

The guy had just opened the door when one of the teenagers met her gaze. She mouthed *help*, tried to communicate to them with her expression that she was in danger. Too soon, she was shuffled into the back of the sedan.

CHAPTER 15

Ryker's team situated themselves around the large property, staying out of sight. His gun was a familiar weight in his hand, and he had two more strapped to his waist and ankle.

The property was well hidden within the woods, just as the warehouse had been. The guy clearly had connections to people who knew how to remain hidden.

Erik hadn't been able to make it today, so it was the four of them. Worked for Ryker. Years of training and working together as a Special Forces team meant that they knew each other inside out. And, more than that, he trusted these men to have his back like he had theirs.

There'd been no movement outside the large house, but a car sat in the drive.

Cole's voice sounded through the earpiece. "Clear on the east side."

"Clear on the south," Declan said.

"Clear on the west," Jackson added.

Ryker's blood flowed a bit faster in anticipation of what was to come. "Let's go."

He moved out from behind the trees, pistol drawn and aimed forward. The house was two-story, so he kept his gaze between the floors. At the front door, he tried the knob. Locked.

One hard kick breached the door. Wood splintered as glass shattered from both sides of the house. Something crashed in the back. Declan.

Ryker stepped inside, keeping his gun up while scanning the space. He stood in a long hallway with a formal dining room to the left and a living room to the right.

Jackson dropped in through the window on one side of the house while Cole climbed in another. They remained still for two heartbeats. The silence was loud, and it prickled Ryker's skin.

"Clear," Jackson said first.

Cole shifted toward the kitchen, weapon still raised. "Clear."

Declan stepped out of a room at the end of the hall, immediately shaking his head. "Clear."

Shit.

Cole and Jackson moved slowly around the lower floor while Declan hit the stairs. Ryker followed him up.

His muscles were so tight, they were on the verge of snapping, and his gut churned in sickly spirals.

Something wasn't right. The house didn't look like it had been taken over by a terrorist organization—or a family, for that matter. Everything was clean and tidy. There was zero clutter, no photos on the walls. The place almost looked like a show home.

But Cal wouldn't lie. The man was a friend, and he was damn good at his job.

On the second floor, there was another long hall with doors on either side. One by one, he and Dec entered each room, checking every inch of the space. Beneath beds, inside closets.

Empty. Every damn one. And that eerie silence still clogged the air around him, nearly overwhelming him with dread.

He reached the last room in the house, the master bedroom. He knew what he'd find before he opened the door. Still, he stepped inside. A large king bed on one wall, a small bathroom attached. He moved toward it, every step as quiet as the last, then checked the space the same as he'd done to every other room.

Saad wasn't here. No one was. And not just that. There was no evidence of terrorists ever *being* here.

Fuck. What the hell was going on?

Declan stepped into the room, gun lowering to his side. "They're not here," he said, confirming Ryker's thoughts.

They jogged downstairs and found Cole and Jackson looking just as frustrated.

Something wasn't right about this. About any of it.

They moved outside, each of them eyeing the car parked in the drive. As his team moved toward it cautiously, Ryker whipped out his cell and called Cal.

The second he hit call, an explosion detonated.

The blast threw him against the house. Pain ricocheted up his side and down his leg, but he ignored it, cursing under his breath as he pushed to his feet. He searched for the gun that had been in his hand and lifted it quickly, almost expecting Saad's team to fly out of the woods.

There was only more silence.

He shot a look around at his team. There were smears of blood and ripped clothing, but everyone was alive, standing with weapons drawn, and their wounds looked superficial.

"The call to Cal's phone triggered the explosion," Ryker growled as he scanned the wooded area.

Had Cal been in the damn car? His fingers tightened on his pistol.

"Let's search the area," Declan said, his voice low, holding the threat of danger. "There's something here. Some clue he wants us to find. There has to be."

Ryker nodded, his limbs shaking with a fury he couldn't tame. The four of them spread out, each searching a quadrant of the woods around the house. How had the fucker gotten Cal's phone? And why blow up the car?

As a message? To say he knew he had eyes on him?

Three minutes had passed when Cole's voice sounded in the earpiece, calling the others to his location.

Ryker found Cole, saw what his friend had, and his skin iced. That sick feeling in his gut churned with renewed intensity, his breath freezing in his lungs.

Cal's body sat on the ground, tied to a tree. His face was covered in bruises and a bullet hole pierced his forehead.

Every part of Ryker rebelled. A war raged inside him, urging him to find Saad. But not just to kill him. To dig his hand into the asshole's chest and rip his cold heart from his body.

Jackson knelt and gingerly pulled at a note that had been nailed to Cal's chest.

The fucking animals.

Jackson's eyes narrowed. "It's in Arabic."

He pulled his phone from his pocket and typed in the words. The veins on his neck tightened, his knuckles whitening as he squeezed the device. When he looked up at Ryker, there was the expected anger, but there was also something else. Something he'd rarely seen on his childhood friend's face before.

Fear.

Ryker grabbed the phone and read the translation.

My road to revenge is long, and not even close to over. I have her. And you can only pray that she survives my hell.

The narrowing of Ryker's throat suffocated him. Choked the fucking life from him.

He was just pulling his phone out, debating who to call first—his parents? River?—when Cole said, "Aria's calling me," and answered the silenced cell.

There was a beat of quiet, then he met Ryker's eyes.

The dread in his gut spidered through his body like a poison, turning his blood to acid.

"Blakely's been taken."

BLAKELY TWITCHED HER LITTLE FINGER. It was the first movement she was capable of in…she had no idea how long. Time had stopped existing, along with her last memory of being pushed inside this car. Since then, everything was a blur. The trees that passed the window. The vibrations of the car beneath her. The conversation of the men around her. The voices—deep and unfamiliar—sounded like they came to her through a tunnel.

She almost felt like she was sitting in a dark hole, and she had no way of crawling out and pulling free. It seemed like hours had ticked by before she was finally able to twitch her pinkie. The movement was so small and slight, it was almost nothing.

She kept going. Kept trying to move and make sense of what she saw outside the window, and bit by bit, the blending colors started to form shapes. The green turned into grass and the brown into tree trunks, racing by the window.

She was coming back to her body—which meant soon she'd be able to fight. Because no way in hell would she let these men do God knew what to her while she did nothing to stop it.

The words spoken around her began to filter in. Not words she understood, but familiar words all the same.

The fog tried to return, dimming the voices.

Come on, Blakely, concentrate.

She scowled as she worked hard to differentiate the voices. Three. Three voices. All male.

Images flashed in her mind. Familiar images of the past. Kids playing by the water in Beirut. Smiling parents. Everyone chatting…

Arabic. They were speaking Arabic.

She tested her neck, trying to shift her head away from the window, catch a glimpse of her captors. God, her head was heavy…but she did it. At first they were blurs, like the shapes outside.

She blinked. Once. Twice. Slow, heavy blinks, in an attempt to turn the fuzzy lines into men. She could just make out the shoulders of the man behind the wheel. On another blink, she focused on the man in the passenger seat, then the man beside her in the back. He sat by the other window, so big he took up most of the middle seat.

They were talking faster now, almost shouting. She caught one of the words. A word she knew. *Poles.*

It was Arabic for police.

Were the police here? Oh God, please say yes!

Before she could give it more thought, her body was shoved to the floor of the car and darkness cloaked her. It took a moment to figure out the darkness was a sheet or blanket over her body.

Sirens sliced the air. Loud, piercing wails that hammered at her aching skull. There were other sounds too. The roar of the engine. The squeal of tires.

They were being chased by police.

More yelling in Arabic. She could feel the tension humming and churning through the small space.

The car made a hard turn and her body flew to the left, slamming into her captor's legs. She flexed her fingers, blowing out a silent breath of relief when they worked. Next, she tried fisting her hand. Again, she managed. It was a loose fist, but she'd take it.

Good. This was good.

She moved a hand to her pocket, her fingers brushing something small and hard. She paused, her fuzzy mind scrambling to work out what it was.

Realization slammed into her.

It was the outline of a key. The key Ryker had given her that was actually a switchblade knife.

Her heart hammered. She had a weapon.

She blocked out the voices. The tension and fear and uncertainty. Then, with fingers that barely felt like her own, she inched them toward the opening of her pocket. As quickly as she could manage, she dug inside and slipped her fingers around the small weapon.

The car turned again, and she was thrown to the opposite side. Her face collided with something hard. The door? She bit back a groan of pain as she pulled the key from her pocket and clenched it in her fist.

Piercing shouts, at least five decibels louder than anything previously, came from the men. The car swerved again—but this time it crashed into something, bringing them to an abrupt stop.

Her head slammed into something she couldn't see. The pain was instant and jarring. She couldn't hold in her moan, but the sound was washed out by the loud cries around her anyway. The pain almost pulled her back into the fog, but before it could, the covering was gone and she was yanked from the car.

She would've dropped to the ground, her knees like jelly, but a man clutched her neck, holding her firmly against his body. She blinked, just making out the police surrounding them.

The man was using her as a shield.

She spared a fleeting glance at the police cars. There were three of them, surrounding the vehicle she'd just been pulled from, which now had a huge dent in the side.

They stood on a suburban street surrounded by houses.

The police shouted at the men to drop their weapons. Her heart stopped, her eyes scrunching shut as gunshots rang out.

Oh God! She was in the middle of a shootout being used as a human shield!

She opened her eyes to see a police officer drop to the ground, blood blooming on his chest. Her lungs seized.

The guy holding her inched backward. It took her a moment to realize the officers weren't shooting back because she was covering the man.

The key dug into her palm.

Screw that. This asshole needed to die.

She clicked the little tab, flicking the knife out.

Then, without hesitation, she flung her fist up and back.

The weapon met resistance as it dug into her captor. Where exactly, she wasn't sure, but she knew she'd hit his face.

He shouted, dropping her to the ground. She rolled away, then turned to find him, make sure he wasn't coming after her again. His eye bled where the little knife had stabbed in.

A bullet hit him in the shoulder, then another in the gut.

Her breaths stalled in her chest at the sight of so much blood. At the death at her feet.

The other two men were still shooting haphazardly as they ran toward a small path between two properties. One of them had blood pouring from the back of his shoulder, but he didn't pause.

The second they disappeared into the alley, there was a stampede of feet. Police officers, on the chase.

Everything around her started to blur again, the trees and people losing their shapes. When an officer dropped beside her, she could barely make out his features.

"Hey. Are you okay?"

She opened her mouth to say yes, to breathe, but everything swamped her at once—adrenaline, that powder, the pain in her head, relief.

She was with the police. She trusted these people to get her to safety.

The second that trust settled into her chest, she let the darkness take her.

CHAPTER 16

The vehicle jumped forward as Ryker pressed his foot harder to the gas. The last few hours had been a nightmare he couldn't wake up from. The one saving grace was that Zac and Anthony had seen Blakely get shoved into that car and had remembered the plates. The second Aria told Cole, he'd called Davis, who'd gotten in contact with local law enforcement agencies in the towns surrounding Lindeman. In turn, they'd spread a BOLO far and wide, including into Oregon and Idaho.

The APB on the car saved her. By the grace of whichever God was watching over Blakely, an officer had pulled up behind the car without even knowing about the APB, and when her captors sped up, the officer had given chase while calling in reinforcements.

She was safe in Providence Hood River Memorial Hospital after the assholes had driven her south, into Oregon. Safe but injured, with a gash on her head. She'd also passed out at the scene.

His fingers tightened on the wheel, knuckles white. The drive was almost three hours. He'd make it in two.

He needed to know *everything*. How she'd gotten the gash on her head. How the assholes had gotten her in the car. The boys said she didn't fight her attacker. The only way they'd known something wasn't right was the fear in her eyes and the fact she'd silently mouthed the word *help*. Did they have a gun on her?

The sign for Hood River appeared. The exit was a mile ahead.

"Turn right from the off-ramp," Cole said quietly.

Declan trailed behind, while Jackson had stayed in Lindeman to watch over River. They'd also called Erik and asked if he could stay with Aria, Michele, and the boys. They didn't seem to be in danger, but fuck, the team wasn't taking any chances.

My road to revenge is long, and not even close to over. I have her. And you can only pray that she survives my hell.

Those words were burned into his memory, turning every part of him to stone. The fear he'd felt upon reading them, the utter desolation, had been like nothing else. And what the hell did Saad mean when he said his road to revenge was long? What was the asshole planning?

More questions that needed answers. And until he had those answers, no one was safe.

He turned right at the end of the ramp.

"Dec and I will take the ends of the corridor when we arrive," Cole said.

Cole hadn't said much during the drive, and Ryker had said almost nothing. Words were beyond him until he could touch Blakely. Take her in his arms and check that she was okay.

They were all bruised and bloody from the explosion. Ryker's shirt was torn and Cole had a gash on his cheek. Neither of them cared about any of that.

A couple of turns later and the hospital came into view. The second he parked, he was out of the car and running.

~

BLAKELY SCRUNCHED HER BROWS TOGETHER. She'd woken ten minutes ago with a headache so severe, it felt like tiny hammers were pounding inside her head.

She was in a hospital bed, and small flickers of memory had begun returning. Of police. A car chase. Guns. But it was all hazy, indistinct, and it almost felt like memories that weren't her own. Like her life was a movie for a brief time, one she'd only seen snippets of.

Police officers stood just outside her door, eyes alert as they scanned the hall. It made both safety and fear roll through her chest like a waterfall.

For what had to be the hundredth time, she scanned the room for her phone. It wasn't there. Neither were her clothes.

She was just struggling into a sitting position when a nurse entered the room. A gentle smile curved her lips when she saw Blakely's eyes were open. "You're awake."

She swallowed, her throat so dry it felt like sandpaper. "I am."

The woman inclined the top half of the bed and helped her sit up. Then she wrapped a cuff around Blakely's arm just above the elbow. "I'm just going to check your blood pressure."

She pumped the bulb as Blakely searched for words. A hundred questions took up space in her head, but before she could ask a single one, the nurse nodded and unwrapped the cuff. "Perfect. Now, I've been told a loved one has been notified you're here and is on their way to pick you up."

A loved one? Her parents were back in Minnesota, and she barely spoke to them. Unless they meant—

The nurse lowered her head, interrupting her thoughts. "And when you're feeling up to it, the police would like to talk to you."

She swallowed nervously. "I barely remember anything. I feel like I have a black hole in my memory."

Sympathy softened the woman's eyes. "Considering the drugs that were in your system, I'm not surprised. The doctor will be in soon to talk to you."

Drugs? A memory came to the forefront. The powder the man had blown into her face as she'd rounded the corner while walking back to her hotel.

She was just opening her mouth to ask what it was when raised voices sounded from the hall.

"Get the hell out of my way. *Now!*"

Ryker...

She straightened. "I know him. I think that's my...the loved one you were referring to." She stumbled over her words.

The nurse nodded and slipped out of the room. There were quiet words spoken in the hall that Blakely couldn't make out. A few seconds later, Ryker stood in the threshold. Her breath caught at the sight of him. At the dirt on his jeans, the tear in his shirt. And there was a cut on his arm that looked hours old, covered in dried blood.

"What happened to you?" she gasped.

He crossed the room, looking fierce and unstoppable, like he dared someone to get in his way. Perched on the edge of the bed, he reached for her hand, his touch warm but hesitant, like he was scared he'd hurt her.

"Are you okay?"

She opened her mouth to speak, but she wasn't sure what to say. The black holes in her memory felt scary. Her head hurt. And the police at the door made her feel more nervous than anything else, as if whatever had happened to her wasn't over.

But now with Ryker here?

"Yes, I'm okay." She leaned forward and rested her head against his chest. His arms immediately went around her, pulling her close, not a wisp of space between them. It was safety. It was peace. It was everything she'd been missing.

They stayed like that for long, calming minutes, Blakely cocooned in his warmth, and Ryker holding her like he was scared she'd slip away if he loosened his grip.

It was only a tap on the door and footsteps into the room that had her pulling away. Ryker kept his arm around her as a middle-aged woman in a white coat approached.

"Hello, Miss Sullivan. I'm Dr. Palmer."

Blakely tried for a smile but was sure it came out all kinds of wrong. "Hi."

"I'm Ryker," he said. He didn't sound like himself. His voice was gruff, and she heard…fear?

"It's nice to meet you both." The doctor directed her gaze at Blakely. "How are you feeling?"

"Confused." Actually, she felt many things, but that emotion was at the forefront. Although, she was pretty sure that wasn't what the doctor was asking. She wet her lips. "Physically, my head hurts, but I hate that I can barely remember anything."

Her snippets of memory didn't give her the road map of events that she desperately needed.

"That's to be expected. We found Scopolamine in your blood. Some people refer to it as Devil's Breath. It's an alkaloid that has therapeutic effects, but it can disorientate the user. Affect language, perception, behavior. And memory."

Blakely swallowed while Ryker's arm tightened around her.

"We only detected a small trace of it in your blood," the doctor continued. "Which is a big reason people use it. It doesn't stick around in the body for long. After several hours, it's basically untraceable. The substance itself is colorless and has no smell or taste."

"I rounded a corner on a street, and this guy blew a powder into my face from a straw."

Ryker's entire body hardened.

The doctor nodded. "A fairly common method of getting it into victims. Thankfully, we didn't find many injuries, just the blow to the head, which caused a mild concussion. That was likely from the car crash."

The doctor spoke to them for a couple more minutes about care after the concussion, letting her know she'd need someone with her overnight so they could wake her every couple of hours. Then she discussed Blakely's discharge.

Her mind raced the entire time. Trying to come to terms with the reality of the situation when it didn't feel close to being real. She'd been drugged. Kidnapped. She remembered seeing the police once she was out of the car but didn't remember how she'd escaped.

The second the doctor left the room, Ryker turned back to her.

"Will you tell me what you know?" she asked quietly, suddenly needing to know everything she couldn't recall. All the minutes and memories that felt stolen. Ryker wouldn't have all of them, but he might have some.

His jaw clenched. He didn't want to tell her. She could see it in his dark eyes. "I asked a guy I knew in the military, who'd gotten into private security, to locate Saad. He did, and we found him last night, but he got away."

She frowned. She'd assumed that's what had happened last night.

"Cal found him again this morning. Again, the guys and I went to the location. He wasn't there. Cal was, though…" At his pause, Blakely's chest grew heavy, like her heart knew what was coming. "He was dead, with a note on his chest."

Nausea coiled her belly. "I'm sorry." She shoved down the uncomfortable scenarios in her head and asked the question she didn't really want the answer to but knew was important. "What did the note say?"

Ryker's gaze went to the gash on her head and his eyes narrowed. "He said he had you."

When he paused, she knew there was more that he didn't want to say.

"Then we got a call from Aria. Zac and Anthony told her they saw you get into a car and mouth *help*. They couldn't get to you in time, but they memorized the plates. We managed to get an APB on the car. I got a call two hours ago that you'd been found."

"The men hit a police car, I think. I remember a dent."

Then what? God, she *hated* that her brain didn't work.

Ryker's hand shifted to her thigh, and he slipped his thumb beneath the material of her hospital gown to swipe the rough pad against her skin. "I was told Saad's men hit a police car when one pulled out in front of them. They got out of the car and fired on the cops. One of the men was holding your body in front of his."

She touched her neck, remembering…something. The feel of a hand or arm around her? Holding her in place? "How did I get out of his hold? Did the police shoot the guy?"

For the first time, there was a spark of something other than rage on his face. One side of his mouth lifted, and he almost looked…proud.

"You stabbed him in the eye with the switchblade I gave you."

She looked at her hands. An image floated up in her mind—they'd been crimson with blood. Then she'd dropped. Shifting her legs, she could almost feel the softness of the grass against them. She'd been in someone's yard, on their lawn.

"I remember. Only snippets…but I remember."

His fingers clutched her thigh tighter, holding on, his thumb continuing its gentle caress. She watched that thumb intently. The way it slid over her skin. Brought heat and comfort.

"I'm glad you're okay."

Her gaze shot back up. The intensity in his expression made her pulse speed up.

"I'm so fucking sorry." Pain leached into his words. "It's my fault you were targeted. I should have known you would be. I should have protected you instead of pushing you away—"

"No." A single whispered word, cutting him off. She cupped his cheek. "It's not your fault. None of what he's done has *ever* been your fault."

He stared at her, so many emotions playing over his face. Then he lowered his head, touching his temple to hers.

"He will pay." The words were a quiet vow. And they sent wild shudders racing down her spine. "And until he does, I'll protect you. I swear."

CHAPTER 17

Ryker glanced at Blakely in the passenger seat. Strands of hair had fallen onto her cheek and the day's last remaining rays of sunlight shone on her through the window. She'd fallen asleep about an hour ago, and he'd barely been able to keep his eyes on the road.

He wanted to watch her. The rise and fall of her chest. The flickers of emotion on her face as she slept. To remind himself that she was here. Alive. That she wasn't at the mercy of his enemy, holed up God knew where and out of his reach. He needed that assurance. It was as vital as oxygen.

But even though he had her back, the war wasn't over. In fact, it had barely begun. The asshole was still gunning for Ryker as much as Ryker was gunning for him. Only Saad had an advantage. He knew Ryker's kryptonite. His family. His loved ones. *Her*.

He swallowed hard as he took a right. They were almost at his house. Thank God. After such an emotionally charged day, the drive was too long. Declan was stopping by her hotel to grab her stuff, and he'd also stay the night at Ryker's place, just as backup, while Michele stayed with Aria and Cole.

He'd already made contact with Blake from Blue Halo Security, in Cradle Mountain. The man confirmed Ryker's parents had arrived and were safe.

He turned onto his street, only starting to feel the ease of relief in his chest when he saw his house. He wanted to get her inside, protected by his high-tech security system, and never let her out again.

He'd already spoken to Davis, who was talking to his team about the next steps. One thing he already knew—Ryker wouldn't be allowed to hunt down Saad again. Certainly not on his own.

It bothered him a little less now. Which was a shock, considering Saad had been his main focus for so long. But he could no longer deny his priority had shifted to something far more important—Blakely. And anytime he wasn't with her personally, he was going to make damn sure someone he trusted was.

When he pulled into his drive, he pressed the button for his garage door and drove in. Darkness surrounded them as the door closed. He climbed out of the car, but instead of grabbing Blakely, he tugged out his Glock and moved into the house. First, he checked the lower floor. The living and dining rooms. The kitchen. His bedroom. Silence and stillness.

Quietly, he moved up the stairs, never lowering the weapon. Again, he checked every corner of every room. Only when he was sure he was alone in the house did he return to the garage. When he opened the passenger door, it was to see Blakely still asleep. Her breathing was rhythmic, those same strands of hair caught on her cheek.

Gently, he brushed the hair behind her ear, grazing her skin. There was a small flutter of her eyelids, but other than that, nothing.

He unbuckled her and gently lifted her against him. There was a small moan from her lips, then she burrowed closer. It made every protective, territorial part of him stir to life. Every crevice of his being shouted that this woman was *his*. Even though just this morning he'd been pushing her away, now he felt absolute torment at the idea of her being out of his reach. Because he'd pushed her away thinking she'd be safer without him. Now he knew she wasn't.

She still deserved more, but his need to keep her safe and alive outweighed the need to send her away.

When he reached his bedroom, he lowered her to the mattress. Carefully, he removed her shoes and pants. He'd just pulled the sheet over her when his gaze caught on the cut on her forehead.

A deep, gravelly growl ripped from his chest. It was a minor graze, but it was also a reminder that today could have been worse. So much fucking worse. An image slashed through his mind of the car exploding and sending his team flying. Of Cal's body in the woods.

What had Saad been planning on doing with Blakely? The man who'd used her as a shield from the bullets had been alive on the way to the hospital but died an hour later, both from the bullet wounds and the stab to his eye. His identity had been confirmed as Charbel El-Din. A member of a prominent Lebanese family that had a lot of money and even more connections. The FBI was looking into his family members and their properties to see if they could use that information to locate Saad.

A vein throbbed in Ryker's temple. He straightened, but before he could leave, small fingers wrapped around his wrist.

Blakely's eyes were half open. "Don't leave me," she whispered.

Something loud and primal roared in his chest. He lowered to the edge of the bed and cupped her cheek. "I'm just going to wait for Dec, then I'll be back." He swiped a thumb over her soft skin but couldn't look away from her head wound. "Do you need more pain medication?"

She shook her head, her gaze sweeping between his eyes. "Are you okay?"

She'd asked him that a couple of times today, and every time he'd cleverly avoided answering, knowing she wouldn't like his answer. But right now, he felt too damn weak to hold back.

"No."

Her green eyes turned sad. "I'm sorry."

"I'm so fucking proud of you, though, Blakely."

Her brows flickered. "Proud of me?"

"You fought through the drugs. You stabbed that asshole in the eye. You got away. You're alive because of your strength." If she hadn't, that bastard might have gotten away with her, and Ryker would be a shadow of the man he was at the moment. In saving herself, she'd saved him, too. "Thank you."

She turned her head so her mouth was pressed to the palm of his hand, then she kissed his skin. He felt that kiss everywhere, right into the deepest, darkest corners of his heart. "I'd do anything to return to you."

A sharp exhale escaped his throat.

Gently, he pulled her up, tugging her into his arms, and he just held her. He didn't deserve this woman. He'd spent so much energy trying to save her from everything his life entailed. But he was all out of fight.

He wasn't ready to release her, but then, he knew that moment would never come. So he kissed the top of her head and forced his hold to loosen. "Declan will be here in a couple of minutes. I'll just check on him, make sure we're all locked up, then I'll be back."

"Okay."

The second her head was back on the pillow, her eyes closed. Damn, she was exhausted.

He rose and moved out of the room. He'd just reached the living room when the text came. Declan was out front. He let his friend in before closing and locking the door and switching on the alarm, then he took Blakely's bag.

"Thanks for grabbing her stuff."

"You got it." Declan headed to the kitchen and grabbed two bottles of water, tossing one to Ryker. "She holding up okay?"

"She says she is, but I think she's in shock. I know it bothers her that she can't remember all the details."

"Yeah, that would bother me too. She's strong, though. Christ, to stab her attacker like she did…" Declan shook his head. "That took some strength."

He wasn't wrong, and Ryker would be forever grateful for that. He downed half the bottle of water. "Michele get to Aria and Cole's okay?"

"Yep. And Jackson's with River."

Good. "I'm going to bed early. Your old room's still set up."

"Thanks. I'll stay up for a while. Watch the streets."

Ryker grasped his friend's shoulder. "Thank you, brother."

Declan dipped his chin.

Ryker returned to the bedroom, glancing at Blakely before moving into the connected bathroom and taking a quick shower with water hotter than he could actually stand. He *wanted* his skin to burn. To take his mind off the shit show that had been today.

Clean and dry, he slid between the sheets. He didn't hesitate in tugging Blakely's still form into his body, finally letting himself have some peace as he held her.

CHAPTER 18

$\mathcal{A}$ ray of light hit Blakely's eyelids. She groaned and rolled onto her belly to escape the zing of pain. Man, her head ached. And she was tired. Her sleep had been riddled with nightmares, but for once, the nightmares hadn't been about the explosions in Beirut. Little bits of the car ride had started to come back to her. Her fear. The stench of tobacco, charcoal, and leather. And the voices. Deep voices speaking words she didn't understand.

Ryker had been there throughout. Waking her every couple of hours, per the doctor's instructions. Holding her. Whispering gentle words of comfort into her ear. Giving her that feeling of safety she'd needed to drift back to sleep.

Slowly, she rolled to her back once more and her eyes fluttered open. A white pendant light hung from the ceiling. She turned her head, scanning the room to find a wooden chest of drawers, two bedside tables, and a wooden bed frame. Beneath her were dark, rumpled sheets...but there was no Ryker.

Her gaze shifted to the connecting bathroom. The door was open and the light off. He wasn't here. Was he in the kitchen or living room?

Carefully, she climbed out of bed. Her muscles were sore, and there were small flashes of pain in her skull. Her gaze caught on the glass of water on the bedside table, accompanied by two small pills.

She lifted them, swallowing the pills and letting the water soothe her dry throat.

Then she eyed the shower, almost groaning at how good it looked. She desperately wanted to get clean. Hell, she wanted to stand under the stream of water for hours and let it wash away the entire day before.

She still wore the T-shirt the guys had grabbed from a shop near the hospital. Her previous shirt had been covered in blood. Not *her* blood.

Her stomach pitched at the thought. She'd stabbed a man in the eye. A man who'd later died. The very thought felt surreal in her head. She looked down at her fingers, questioning their capability of doing something so brutal. But the alternative would have been worse. Being taken. Allowing God knows what to happen to her.

She blew out a ragged breath, then noticed a bag by the door. *Her* bag, from the hotel.

Thank God. Clean clothes and a shower.

The second she stood under the spray, she closed her eyes and tipped her head up, letting the heat warm her chilled skin.

What would have happened if Zac and Anthony hadn't spotted her when they had? If an APB hadn't been put out on the car and the police hadn't found them?

She didn't know. And that almost felt *worse* than knowing. Because the realm of evil was wide and it was deep, and there were too many scenarios to contemplate.

She reached for the bodywash and used it to scrub her skin until her flesh was red and sensitive. It didn't scrub away thoughts of the men touching her. Kidnapping her. But nothing would.

When she stepped out of the shower, she dried quickly before throwing on some jeans and an oversized sweatshirt. Comfort was definitely needed today. She pulled her wet hair into a ponytail to keep it off her face before applying a thin layer of moisturizer.

The bruise on her forehead was far worse than the cut. It was purple and blue and angry-looking.

Unable to stop herself, she touched it, prodding the small laceration at the center and immediately wincing in pain. The headache had lessened since taking the pills, but it was still there, and she had a feeling it wouldn't be leaving her for a while.

Straightening her spine, she left the room, expecting to find Ryker in the living area. Instead, she stopped at the sight of Declan standing by a window, cell to his ear as he spoke.

When he saw her, he said a quick goodbye to whoever was on the other end of the line and hung up. "Hey. You sleep okay?"

She took slow steps into the room. "Not really." She glanced around. "Is Ryker here?"

She was pretty sure she knew the answer, but maybe…

"He went to Mercy Ring this morning."

Her heart did a little dip. She'd been hoping to wake up to him. Or at least have him in the house. But it was probably better this way. Just because the man had picked her up, injured and scared from the hospital, didn't mean they'd fall back into a relationship.

Hell, he'd told her to leave—again—as recently as yesterday morning. Maybe now he felt responsible for her safety because her enemy was his enemy, but she wouldn't make the mistake of assuming his sense of responsibility would translate into anything deeper.

The smart part of her brain knew she needed to protect her heart.

She'd been quiet a beat too long.

Declan tilted his head. "I may not be Wonder Boy Ryker, but when I heard the shower running, I did something that'll make you glad it's *me* here, and not him." He nodded toward the kitchen, and she followed when he headed that way. "I made you pesto eggs."

The pan of green scrambled eggs made her chuckle. "Pesto eggs?"

"Michele taught me. Now, I'm not saying they'll be as good as hers, the woman's a damn goddess in the kitchen, but they beat cereal, right?"

"Definitely right." Her gaze shifted to the other pan. "You made bacon too?"

"Hell yeah, I did. What's eggs without bacon? And of course, we have the drink of the gods...coffee." He grinned at her. "How am I doing? Better than Ryker yet?"

Her lips curved. His intent was clear—he was trying to distract her. Maybe even cheer her up a little and give her something to smile about.

And she appreciated it. She touched his arm. "Thank you."

His smile softened. "Of course. Now let's eat before I dwindle away to nothing. It's been a good hour since my first breakfast, and I'm starving."

She laughed again before grabbing a plate and loading it up with eggs, bacon, and toast, then sat at the small kitchen table. When she looked across and saw Declan's plate, she almost gaped. The man had heaped his plate like he was preparing to serve a small army.

Throughout the meal, Declan made her laugh and smile, doubling his efforts anytime her grin faltered. He recounted various old military stories, usually involving Ryker doing something he shouldn't that ended with him in some hilariously bad situation.

Declan was exactly what she needed this morning.

She'd only cleared half her plate when he got up to get seconds. He'd said this was his *second* breakfast? Where did the man put it?

When they were done and the dishes were in the washer, he drove her over to Mercy Ring. The nerves hit as they grew close.

"Is Ryker in the office or the ring?" she finally asked, nibbling her bottom lip.

The question had been on her mind all morning, but she was fairly certain she knew the answer. He wouldn't leave her so soon after the incident for work. He'd only leave if he needed to be physically active. Exorcise emotions he had no other way of expelling.

That's what boxing was to him. It was the sanctuary he turned to when he needed an outlet.

Declan pulled into the gym's parking lot, then finally turned to answer her question. "We closed Mercy Ring to the public today. Ryker's boxing."

She gave a slow nod. "I figured as much."

Which Ryker would she get today? The man she'd seen last night, who didn't dare allow an inch of space between them? Or the man who was emotionally distant because of some deep-rooted need to protect her from himself?

When they stepped into the building, she immediately spotted Ryker and Erik in the ring, both bare chested, wearing only shorts and boxing gloves, and both looking like they'd been at it for hours. Sweat dripped from their flesh while their chests heaved. And the looks on their faces...

Fierce. Dangerous. Deadly.

Erik swung and Ryker dodged before throwing a punch of his own, aiming for Erik's gut. The hit landed, but if Erik felt any pain, he didn't show it. Just danced around Ryker again.

Blakely didn't realize she'd gone still near the door until Declan touched the small of her back, encouraging her forward into the room with gentle pressure. Her gaze never left the big men in the ring. Every blow came with a force that would knock an average man to the ground. And each time a fist swung, she held her breath, scared at the possibility of it landing and causing some serious damage.

~

RYKER KNEW the moment Blakely was close. The door opened, then he felt her presence as a thickening in the air and a tightening in his chest.

But he didn't look at her. He didn't dare take his eyes off his opponent. Erik had been in the ring with him for a while. It wasn't enough. He was trying to chase away the demons that had returned with a vengeance upon waking this morning. It wasn't going to happen, but that didn't mean he should stop trying.

Ryker lunged forward, throwing punches with force and momentum. Erik dodged. His friend returned a volley of his own with the same precision and training. Every hit that landed, Ryker absorbed. He let the pain and ache fuel him. Push him to swing harder. Force him to be more strategic.

The pain was nothing compared to the emotional and mental load of yesterday. It was a drop in the ocean.

The two of them went at it for another ten minutes. It was only when Erik got him in the cheek and his head flew back that he stopped. But not because of the pain. Because of the loud gasp from Blakely.

Erik lowered his fists. "You okay?"

"I'm fine. Let's call it though."

He'd texted Erik early this morning and the guy had come, just as Ryker had known he would. Erik was always up for a round, always seeming to have similar emotions to expel.

Ryker pulled the gloves from his hands before climbing out of the ring. He expected Blakely to approach. Instead, she turned and asked Declan something before crossing to the kitchen at the back of the gym.

"Thanks for the session," Erik said, throwing his gloves into a box. "Let me know if you guys need any help with anything."

"Will do. Thanks, Erik."

He lifted his bag and left, nodding at Declan on the way.

Declan, in turn, gave Ryker a nod. "I'm gonna head out and see Chele now. You need me, just call."

"I appreciate you staying the night."

"Anytime, brother."

Declan was almost at the door when Blakely came out of the kitchen, tea towel and ice pack in hand. Declan pushed the door open, shouted goodbye to Blakely, and was gone.

She paused and frowned, seeming surprised that Declan was leaving, before heading toward Ryker. Without speaking, she grabbed his arm and tugged him toward a seat. When he sat, she wrapped the ice pack in the towel and pressed it to his cheek.

"Are you okay?" she finally asked, not meeting his eyes.

"I'm fine." He studied her. "Sorry I left you this morning. I needed to get in the ring."

There was a small marring of her brows. "So you *aren't* okay."

It wasn't a question, and she wasn't talking about his cheek, or any other hits he'd sustained in the ring. "No, I'm not. But I'm used to not being okay. How are *you* feeling today?"

Her brows pinched further. She didn't like his answer, but he didn't have any honest ones she'd like better. "Considering what happened, I guess I'm okay."

Fuck, that killed him. She deserved better than okay. She deserved the fucking world. "I'm so—"

She touched a finger to his lips. "Don't say it. You've apologized more than enough for things that aren't your fault."

He gently took hold of her wrist, pressing a soft kiss to her finger.

An emotion he couldn't place swept over her face. She tried to step back, but he grabbed her thigh and pulled her closer. "What's going through your head right now?"

She swallowed. "I'm worried about you. I've been worried about you for a long time. Watching you in that ring…it reminds me that you're fierce, but also that you're breakable. And now there are dangerous people after me. Dangerous people who I know you'd shield me from by letting them destroy *you* instead."

Damn straight he would. Every single time.

This time, he tugged her onto his lap so her legs straddled his hips. She still held the ice pack to his face, and still, she wouldn't look him in the eye, instead fixing her gaze on his injured cheek like it was a puzzle she needed to solve.

He touched her chin, holding it until she met his gaze.

"Hey. I may be breakable, but I promise you, I will *not* break. I'll protect you, and myself…and us."

Confusion darkened her eyes. "Us?"

"Yeah, princess. Us. I've been pushing you away since you got here. And I'm so damn sorry for that. I'm sorry I ignored your calls and texts for over a year. I'm sorry you had to feel the pain of losing people you loved, and I wasn't there."

It fucking tore at him. Every part of him had felt like she was better off without him, but he hadn't known the depths of her love for him. He should have. He should've tried to be more for her.

"I still think you deserve better," he said quietly. "You deserve a man without baggage, not the truckload that I have to offer. But almost losing you yesterday…it changed things."

She shook her head. "I don't want you to make that decision while you're recovering from almost losing me. I want you to want me when you don't *have* to have me close. When you can leave my side and not be scared someone will take me. I want you to want me as much as I want you, for no other reason than you love me."

"I—"

Again, she touched her fingers to his lips. "I don't know if you're about to say it right now or not, but if you are…please don't. If the day does come when you love me, I want you to tell me when there's no Saad. No danger. Nothing but you and me to consider."

Though delivered gently, the words landed like a jab. *He'd* created this hesitation in her, and he deserved every bit of the distance she was attempting to create now. It was up to him to work to get her back.

He cupped her cheek. "Okay. We'll do it your way. But when this is over—because it *will* be over—I'll tell you everything I feel. And you'll know I mean the words forever."

Then, because he wasn't sure if she'd accept his touch on her lips, he kissed her cheek. A light kiss. A cherish. A promise.

CHAPTER 19

*B*lakely stirred the curry bubbling on the stove. River stood beside her, stirring her own pot and chattering about her morning with Jackson, while Michele moved around the shop's kitchen. Declan sat in the front customer area of Meals Made Easy, working on his laptop. He'd remained fairly quiet, bar the occasional chuckle or comedic comment.

She glanced out the door. Ryker would be here to pick her up soon—and yeah, she was nervous. A few days had passed since her kidnapping, and the man had been nothing short of amazing. Attentive. Kind. And he'd respected her boundaries. Oh, there'd been small touches. Grazes of his thumb on her cheek. A hand on her back. His arms reaching for her in the dead of night when she woke, since they were still sharing a bed. But that was as far as it went.

She wanted to give him all of herself, but her heart was still reluctant to believe she could ever be a permanent fixture in his life. She just wished this damn danger would end so she could know for certain, either way.

"River, you're doing more eating than cooking," Michele groaned.

She looked beside her to see River's head over the pot, spoon to her lips. Blakely chuckled. While Michele had given her the task of stirring the curry, River was responsible for a marinara sauce that smelled divine. They'd be lucky if there was any left for the customers.

"I can't help it," River groaned. "You know how much I love this sauce."

Michele and River had both gotten her number from Aria and encouraged her to come to the shop whenever she wanted. Just like Blakely, River was on strict orders to remain with one of the guys at all times. So while Jackson worked this morning, River was at the shop. When he picked her up, he'd go to a photography job with her.

Blakely enjoyed spending time with the women. They were friendly, fun to be around, and they took her mind off, well... everything. The danger. The relationship stuff.

Michele swapped River's spoon for a clean one. "I'll give you some to take home, but right now, no more."

River huffed. "That'll require restraint, something I'm scarily low on."

"It *is* good, Chele," Blakely pointed out, feeling compelled to defend River. "Everything here is. Your cooking's amazing."

Michele's annoyed frown softened. "Thank you. And I'm sorry. With everything going on and no one being safe, I'm just a bit..."

"Stressed," River finished for her, tugging her friend closer to her side. "We know. We're all feeling it. Luckily, we have each other."

"Feel free to take my mind off it. Is Jackson still perfect?"

"Hey!" Declan's voice boomed through the room. "Did you just refer to a man other than me as perfect?"

Blakely grinned at Declan's deep frown and fake pout.

"Perfect for River," Michele clarified as she moved over to

him, massaged his shoulders, and pressed a kiss to the top of his head. "You know you're the only perfect man for me."

"Damn straight," he said as he tugged her to his lap.

River sighed. "Yep. My perfect man is still perfect. The other night, he could tell I was a bit down, so he sat through the entire length of *Pretty Woman* while we drank pink champagne and ate chocolate-covered strawberries."

"Oh gosh, I love that movie." Blakely sighed. Julia Roberts in anything was amazing, but her and Richard Gere? Perfection.

River nudged her shoulder. "Make Ryker watch it with you and then report back to me. Knowing my brother sat through the entire thing will bring me so much joy."

She laughed. "Right now, I think he'd sit through that, *Legally Blonde* and *A Walk to Remember*, all in one sitting."

He'd done a complete flip from the man she'd been greeted with when she'd stepped into this town. And that was precisely what scared her. If he could flip one way so quickly, what would stop him from flipping back?

River's eyes softened. "What happened to you scared him."

"I know. And he's been great since, but…I can't trust that the way he's behaving toward me now is long-term."

"Because he pushed you away for so long?" Michele asked.

"Yeah. I care about him so much." God, she *loved* him. And she'd told him so. "I put my feelings out there, basically begged him to return them, and he *still* pushed me away. Hell, before I got here, he ignored me for over a year. And it wasn't just because Saad's out there. It was because he's dead set on heaping too much guilt and responsibility onto his shoulders. That kind of self-condemnation doesn't just disappear because of a little scare. He has to forgive himself before we can ever hope to take things further. And then I want him to choose me when my life isn't at risk."

Was she asking too much? It sounded like a lot to her own ears, but she couldn't help what she was feeling.

"That's completely understandable," River said. "But I should warn you, when my brother decides he wants something, he doesn't stop. And I can see it in his eyes—he wants you."

God, she hoped that was the case. That he saw them creating a life together. Loving each other without hesitation or effort.

Michele moved to a cupboard and grabbed some plastic containers. "How are you doing after your kidnapping?" she asked gently.

Her belly soured at the reminder. "Not great. I'm always looking over my shoulder. Constantly reminding myself that any stranger coming toward me from the opposite direction isn't likely to drug me and snatch me off the street."

A sickening shudder rocked her spine just thinking about the fear that had been plaguing her.

"You're well protected," Declan said quietly from where he sat.

She turned her head, offering him a smile. While he could be the jokester of the group, he had eyes of steel and could switch over to deadly soldier in the space of a heartbeat.

"Thank you." She turned her attention back to River. "How are *you* doing with everything? I'm sure you're worried about yourself and your parents."

"My parents are in the best place possible right now. As for me, no walking anywhere alone. I always have a tall, sexy former Delta soldier in tow. It's not all bad." Some of the humor fizzled from her eyes. "But yeah, it's still a bit scary."

Of course it was. Everyone felt the fear. The heaviness that uncertainty created.

Before she could respond, the buzzer on the shop door rang, and she looked up to see Ryker and Jackson. Little flickers of awareness tickled her belly. Man, he was beautiful. The rugged, wide-shouldered, sexy kind of beautiful.

Michele hit the button to unlock the door. Immediately, Ryker pinned Blakely with his gaze, and those tingles in her belly turned into pops of fire.

River and Jackson met each other halfway across the room. She wrapped her arms around his neck while he held her hips. Blakely glanced away as they kissed. And even though she wasn't looking at Ryker, she could feel him moving toward her. Closing the distance. Every step made her heart hammer harder.

When he reached her, he touched her hip, leaned in, and kissed her cheek. A light kiss. Almost a whisper on her skin. Then he spoke quietly into her ear. "I missed you."

She swallowed, a big, Lord-give-her-a-voice kind of swallow. She wanted to say she missed him too, but the words didn't come. She looked at him as he raised his head, and his attention almost felt more intimate than any kiss could ever be.

"Are you doing okay?"

Better now. His presence alone brought so much comfort and warmth and safety. "Yes."

He grazed the back of her hand with the rough pad of his thumb. "Ready to go?"

In this moment, she'd walk anywhere this man led her. To the damn moon if he had a path. She nodded and pulled her bottom lip between her teeth.

His gaze shot down and blackened.

Oh, Jesus. She was screwed.

Finally, he took hold of her hand.

Blakely cleared her throat and turned to Michele. She was watching them with a knowing smile.

"Would you like me to stay and help a bit longer?" she offered.

"No, no. I'm almost done. You two go."

Declan stood and moved over to Michele. "I can help. Some people refer to me as a god. Good at all things without any effort."

Michele rolled her eyes, but that same smile played on her lips. "No one calls you that but you."

"Oh, you've called me that in—"

She covered his mouth before giving Blakely another smile. "Thank you for your help today."

She laughed for what had to be the tenth time that afternoon. Man, she loved these people. "Anytime."

Ryker didn't release her hand after they exited the store. If anything, once they were on the sidewalk, his fingers tightened, and he inched closer. So close, his earthy pine scent was all she could smell. His warmth all she could feel.

She swallowed. "Did you speak to your old commander? The guy who's in the FBI now?"

"Yeah, there are a couple of leads on his location." Ryker's words were tight, the earlier ease and warmth gone. "He wants his team to lead when we find him."

By the tightness of Ryker's jaw, she knew that bothered him. Because Ryker wanted to be the one who killed Saad. He'd told her as much a number of times.

They'd just stepped into Mercy Ring's back parking lot when he stopped suddenly and tensed. Fear shot through her and she glanced around, expecting to find Saad and his men, a myriad of weapons aimed toward them.

What she actually saw had her blinking in surprise.

The two guys who'd been at the bar with Janice last week were standing across the parking lot. They didn't have guns or knives…but they did have baseball bats. And the expressions on their faces left no guessing as to what they planned on doing with those bats.

Ryker pushed her behind him before shoving keys into her hand. "The second you have a safe path," he said just loudly enough for her to hear, "go to the car and lock yourself inside."

～

Thick cords of muscle bunched in Ryker's chest and arms. He was already having a bad fucking week. These assholes were choosing the wrong day to be idiots.

He took a small step forward, making sure he still covered Blakely's body with his own. "I want you to think really fucking hard about what you're doing, boys." He kept his voice low, barely containing his raw anger. "Because I'm not joking when I say I'm not capable of mercy right now."

He was armed, but he didn't want to pull a gun, scare them away and have them return in a week or a month with more deadly weapons of their own. And yeah…a small part of him wanted them to know exactly who he was and what they were up against. To know he could ruin them without blinking. Without hesitation. And without a weapon.

Though, when it came down to it, to keep Blakely safe, he'd do anything. Kill or maim any man.

The guy with the tattoos stepped forward, a smug look on his face, handle of the baseball bat gripped between his fingers and the business end smacking against his palm. "Oh, we've thought about it. And we've decided we didn't appreciate what you did at the bar the other night. In fact, we're pretty damn pissed about it, asshole."

These morons didn't know the definition of pissed. "Then grab a tissue for your tears and fuck off."

The jerk's eyes narrowed.

The guy behind him took three steps forward. He also had a bat, and he wore the same stupid expression on his face as his friend. "You won't be cracking jokes in a few minutes."

"I don't joke."

Both men rushed forward.

So did Ryker, wanting to put distance between the violence about to erupt and Blakely.

The second they were within reach, Tattoo Guy swung.

Ryker dodged the bat easily and grabbed the end. He yanked

hard so the guy fell forward, and Ryker threw an elbow into his face.

The guy cried out when he landed on the ground, blood pouring from his nose.

The second guy swung at him from behind. He expected it. These idiots were nothing if not predictable.

Ryker crouched. The guy's entire body spun from the momentum when his bat didn't connect. Ryker straightened, wrapped an arm around his throat from behind, and squeezed. The asshole choked, dropping the bat and grabbing at Ryker's arm, but he didn't let up. He was deadly serious when he said he had no mercy. Not a single fucking scrap of it.

From his peripheral, he saw Blakely running toward the car. When the guy bleeding from the nose rose to his feet, he didn't run toward Ryker—he ran toward *her*.

Dark rage welled up inside Ryker. He threw the guy in his arms to the ground and took off running.

Tattoo Guy reached Blakely first, grabbing her. She cried out as he wrenched her arm hard. The asshole didn't even notice Ryker behind him.

Like he had with the other guy, Ryker wrapped an arm around his neck and squeezed. "Let her go before I break your fucking neck."

He didn't let go. And it fueled every ravenous urge inside Ryker.

He tightened his hold. There was an audible choking sound. A few long seconds passed, then the asshole finally released her arm. Blakely ran, and the second she was out of reach, Ryker dropped the guy. He fell on his ass. Without hesitation, Ryker punched him in the face so hard, the asshole blacked out.

The second man was already sprinting across the lot, running away.

A part of him wanted to give chase, but the bigger part of him wasn't willing to leave Blakely alone and unprotected for a second. The police would get him.

He turned to see Blakely in the car, phone to her ear. He took a moment to breathe deeply. He needed at least a shred of calm before approaching her. Touching her. When he finally had a hold of himself, he crossed the distance to the car. She threw the door open, was just lowering the phone to her lap when he crouched and touched her thigh.

"Police are coming," she gasped, her breathing too fast.

He lifted her wrist, seeing the red fingerprints on her skin. His blood boiled, and suddenly, he didn't want to feel calm. He wanted to turn around, grab the man who'd marked her, and murder the fucker.

Blakely touched his cheek, bringing him back to her.

"Are you okay?" she asked, words quiet.

"No."

"Hey," she said, her soft voice, her gentle touch grounding him. "I'm all right. We're both here and unharmed."

He watched her eyes for another beat, letting the deep green lighten his rage to something he could manage. Then he tugged her close and held her.

CHAPTER 20

*B*lakely layered turkey on the bread, making sure to include extra slices for Ryker. In the days since the guys had tried to jump them in the parking lot, Ryker had been more on edge than ever.

Memories of how easily and efficiently he'd disarmed and injured those idiots flickered through her mind. She shuddered. The man was dangerous. He'd always *looked* dangerous. Big and muscular and intimidating, with a look on his face that warned he could kill at a second's notice. But sometimes she forgot. Sometimes he was just Ryker to her. The man she'd met in the Middle East with the smiles, sweet words, and the kindness.

She opened a jar of sun-dried tomatoes and placed some on top of the turkey.

Even though there'd been this underlying tension in Ryker these last few days, there'd also been tenderness. She remembered it so well, like the old Ryker was seeping through the cracks of the new one.

They'd slipped into a new normal. Of sleeping while wrapped in each other's arms. Of *both* now offering touches anytime they were near each other. Looks so intense, her tummy twisted and turned all goddamn day, and her feet forever itched to go to him. Kiss him. Give him all of herself.

She spread cranberry sauce on the other slice of bread, then set it atop the sandwich. She was slicing it in half when the knife slipped from her grasp and nicked her finger.

"Dang it!"

She turned to grab a towel—and gasped when a hard chest was suddenly in front of her. Where the heck had Ryker come from? "I didn't hear you come in."

Instead of responding, he wrapped his fingers around the back of her hand and lifted it to study the cut. Without a word, he opened a drawer and grabbed a napkin, which he pressed to the wound.

"You okay?"

His deep, raspy voice slid over her skin, prompting the familiar tingling in her belly. "I'm fine. It's just a small cut."

His gaze rose to hers, and she felt it all. Connection. Longing. And something else. Something more complex. Hotter.

The sexual tension had been building all week. And right now, it was a thin string about to snap.

He took a small step forward, his mouth lowering to her ear. "It's getting harder and harder not to kiss you, princess."

Her breath shuddered from her parted lips. She opened her mouth to respond, but then his lips pressed to her cheek, causing the words to dissolve on her tongue. It wasn't so much a kiss as it was a lingering touch of his mouth to her flesh.

He shifted his head, lips drifting closer to her mouth, and did it again.

The heat of his breath on her cheek was a tease of what could be. The softness of his lips so different from the hardness of the rest of him.

She pressed one palm against his chest, while the other remained in his hand. She wasn't sure if her intent was to push him away or pull him closer. She did neither. Instead, she slid her palm up and down, slowly, feeling every hard ridge through his shirt. Memorizing him.

His lips dropped, and he sucked at her neck.

Her eyes closed. "Ryker—"

"Please don't ask me to stop," he whispered, his breath grazing her flesh with each word.

"It would be smarter to wait…" The words tumbled from her lips with absolutely no conviction.

He nipped her ear. "I don't want to be smart. I want to be reckless and fearless and hopelessly drowning in you."

She closed her eyes, letting his words and the vibration of his voice pebble her skin.

She shifted her head, giving him better access to her neck, and he took it. When his hands shifted to her hips, skirting under the material of her top, her skin blazed at the contact.

One of his hands slid up, until his fingers covered her ribs. It wasn't enough. She covered his hand with her own and shifted it up that final inch so it cupped her breast.

She moaned as he kneaded her. A deep, melting-where-she-stood moan.

When that still wasn't enough, she pressed her palm to his cheek and pulled him to her. Their lips collided, finally finding each other, like two magnets that had been separated for too long.

His tongue slipped into her mouth, dancing with hers. They kissed like this was their first and last. Like they needed to make up for every lost moment.

His hands went to her hips, and he lifted her to the kitchen counter before stepping between her thighs. She clung to his shoulders, almost scared he'd turn away if she released him. But he didn't attempt to escape. Instead, his hand once again slid under her shirt, and when he cupped her through her bra, she moaned.

"Fuck, I love those sounds you make," he growled between desperate kisses.

They kissed for so many minutes, she almost forgot where she was. She forgot that she'd deemed these kisses off limits. That this moment was supposed to be saved for later.

It was only when he shifted her body forward, and she felt his hardness at her core, that sanity returned.

She pressed at his chest. "Ryker."

He lifted his mouth but didn't move away. He remained exactly where he was, his chest moving up and down, holding her like *she* might run this time.

She swallowed. "I'm sorry—"

"Don't say that. I was the one who pushed you away. Ignored you for over a year. I fucked up, and I need to work hard to regain your trust. I know that. I *understand* that. And I will."

The force behind his words, the intensity, almost knocked the breath from her chest. God, she loved this man. She wrapped her arms around him and touched her head to his chest. The pounding of his heart was so distinct beneath her ear it almost beat in time with her own. Strong beats. Powerful.

"Thank you," she whispered.

She was just raising her head when something moved outside. She looked toward the window, frowning at the teenage boy headed toward the door. Ryker followed her gaze—and immediately any ease slipped from his face as his eyes narrowed.

He lifted her from the counter and set her on her feet. Then he opened the bottom drawer beside them, rummaged beneath the tea towels, and pulled out a gun. Her eyes widened but she remained silent.

"Stay here," he said quietly.

Her fingers itched to pull him back. To keep him right where he was, in the safety of the four walls of his home. But she knew he wouldn't do that. So instead, she tried to stop the trembling in her limbs as she watched him cross the room. He pulled the door open, and she listened to the exchange between him and the kid.

"Who's this from?" Ryker growled.

"Some guy paid me to drop it off."

"What did he look like? Did he speak with a foreign accent?"

She heard the guy splutter. "Uh, short. Dark haired. And yeah, he had some foreign accent."

An accent? *Oh, Jesus.*

Ryker cursed. "Where is he?"

Ignoring his warning, Blakely slid off the counter and walked to the door.

"I don't know, he drove off."

"Do you remember the car he was in?"

The kid frowned. "Uh, a dark one…"

Ryker's fingers whitened where he gripped the doorframe. He looked up and down the street, then cursed before slamming the door closed. Blakely looked down at the envelope in his hand. Ryker opened it and pulled out a note. It was in Arabic. She quickly pulled out her phone to translate the message.

This was just a tease of what's to come. Are you ready?

Ryker's eyes seemed to hold the same question she had.

What was just a tease?

The whispered question had barely flittered through her mind when Ryker pulled something else from the envelope.

Blakely's heart stopped and all the blood drained from her head.

It was a Polaroid of River. On the ground. Bleeding.

Ryker's curse was vicious. Before he could even open the contacts on his phone, Jackson's name flashed on the screen.

Ryker answered to Jackson's angry voice. "The asshole attacked her in the front yard while she was bringing the trash cans in. We're at the hospital. He fucking *beat* her, Ryker."

Nausea crawled up Blakely's throat, and for a moment, she

thought she might be sick. She forced it down, needing to be strong for Ryker.

"Where is she?" he asked, his voice choked with barely concealed rage.

❧

THERE WASN'T a single fucking shred of Ryker that was okay. The asshole had hurt his *sister*. Made her bleed outside her own fucking home.

He strode down the hospital's corridor, Blakely's hand secure in his grasp. In River's room, Jackson was sitting beside her. Her left eye was black and her jaw bruised.

For a moment, he froze. Unable to move forward or back. Barely able to exist in his current reality.

His baby sister had been hurt by his enemy.

It was only when River's gaze rose, eyes so similar to his, and when Blakely touched a hand to his back—not pushing, just comforting—that he finally propelled himself forward, pulling Blakely behind him.

Ryker went to the side of the bed opposite Jackson, sat on the edge, and tugged River into him. When she groaned, he instantly pulled back to see pain etched on her face. He wasn't used to seeing it. His sister was the strongest person he knew. Hell, she'd been shot, and they'd barely been able to force her to rest.

She touched her abdomen. "Cracked ribs."

The asshole's men had cracked his little sister's ribs. He was going to find the guy and break every fucking bone in his body. "Tell me what happened."

She swallowed. "The garbage truck came by, so I went out to take the cans back to the house. I shouldn't have. Jackson told me not to go outside without him. But I thought it would only take a moment. That I'd be safe in my own yard."

She *should* be safe in her own yard, dammit. She should be safe everywhere.

"I was just wheeling them back when I heard something behind me. I turned in time to see a fist flying toward my face. I didn't have time to recover before he hit me again. Then I was on the ground, and I managed to scream before getting a boot to the ribs."

Ryker clenched his fists, trying to stop the shaking in his limbs.

"They were just driving off when I made it out there," Jackson said, lips thinned, words not coming close to concealing his anger. "The assholes must have been watching the house, and when they saw her go out, seized the opportunity."

"I'm going to kill them," Ryker said. Kill was probably too tame a word.

A warm hand touched his back. He wanted to lose himself in Blakely. In the refuge only she provided.

River set her hand over his. "He said something. It was in broken English so I could barely understand, but he asked me to tell you…"

She stopped, looking unsure about whether she wanted to share whatever it was. Ryker braced to hear something he would rebel against. That might make his body, already shaking, threaten to tumble apart.

"Tell me," he bit out.

"He said he was letting me live, but only because he needed me alive for the finale."

Finale? What fucking finale?

He met Jackson's gaze. His friend had the same question in his eyes.

The door opened, and Cole and Declan entered the room, Michele and Aria with them.

Ryker stood and stepped back, letting the women take his place and check on River.

Cole, Declan, and even Jackson moved over to him.

"We need to find them," Jackson said through gritted teeth. "They got to her while I was right inside the fucking house."

"That's exactly why they did it," Cole said quietly. "To prove nowhere's safe."

Ryker's breath hissed from his teeth. "I got a note delivered to my door." He pulled it from his pocket and showed his team. "It says that this was just a tease of what's to come."

The guys cursed.

"I called Davis on the way here for an update," Declan said, gaze moving to the women, then back to the men. "He just said the same thing he's been saying for days. That they have leads they're chasing."

It wasn't enough, and they all knew it.

CHAPTER 21

The sound of fists hitting a bag was loud in the otherwise quiet house. It was the middle of the day. Ryker had been angry and distant since yesterday. Since he'd walked into that hospital room and seen his injured sister.

He was shouldering the blame yet again. He didn't need to say it outright for Blakely to know.

She'd tried talking to him. Tried breaching the wall he'd rebuilt. Nothing had worked so far. By now, she fully understood that wall was his defense mechanism whenever something went wrong, when he needed to protect himself. Understood it...but hated it.

With a long sigh, she grabbed a glass from the dishwasher and placed it in the cupboard. It was happening again. He was getting scared and shutting her out.

When talking to him hadn't worked, she'd tried to keep busy, but there was only so much she could do within the walls of this house.

This was exactly what she'd feared. The very reason she'd tried to keep their physical need for each other at bay. When things got hard, he shut her out, rather than letting her in. He *chose* to suffer alone.

She tried to push the unease and hurt from her mind as she unloaded the dishwasher, but too soon her gaze caught on the man in the car on the street. The FBI, an extra layer of protection. This town was crawling with men, all armed and ready for war.

She put away the last clean glass, then exhaled loudly, looking for the next thing to keep her mind busy. River had been discharged from the hospital this morning and was home now, with Michele and Declan staying with them. She'd expected Ryker to want to go over and visit her. He hadn't. They hadn't left the house since yesterday. Hell, he'd barely left that damn workout room. The guilt was keeping him away.

More loud punches filtered into the kitchen.

She lifted her phone and sent a quick text to Michele.

How's River doing today?

She'd just set the phone back down when the response came through. But it wasn't Michele, it was River herself.

Hey! I'm okay. Forced bed rest, which is kind of relaxing, but also kind of driving me nuts. How's my brother?

Did River want the truth? That he was pounding the shit out of a bag in his gym like that would somehow wipe away his problems?

No. The woman had just been assaulted. She didn't need to worry about her brother on top of everything else.

He's doing okay.

That was the best she could do. The three dots appeared on her screen but quickly cleared. It took a few beats for River to respond.

Look after him for me, Blakely.

Her gaze lifted to the hall that led to the gym. How did she look after a man who didn't want to be looked after? Who preferred to suffer in silence?

Screw that.

River was right. He needed someone to look after him whether he could admit it or not. Straightening her shoulders, she followed the thuds of gloves hitting the bag and stopped in the doorway.

Ryker was shirtless and barefoot, sweat dripping from his body. She wasn't sure if he didn't see her or just didn't care that she was watching, but he didn't stop. Didn't even pause. And every time his fist connected with the bag, his muscles rippled. The look on his face was dark, but there was also agony. Torment. And it filled her with sadness.

For a few long seconds, she just stood there, not sure how best to reach him.

"River's okay, Ryker." The words were all she could think to say.

He paused, chest rising and falling so quickly, she knew he wasn't getting a single deep breath. He responded without looking at her. "This time. What about next time?"

More hits to the bag.

Damn him. "Why do you do that? Why do you shoulder the blame for crimes you don't commit?"

Another pause. This time he took a bit longer to answer. "Because it's my job to protect the people I care about. And when I fail, I feel guilty."

She stepped forward. "You can't protect everyone, and you can't escape failure. Both are unfortunate facts of life."

He pulled the gloves from his hands. She wished he would look at her.

"Trust me, Blakely. I know. Life has made that abundantly clear."

They were back to Blakely. Great.

"I just need some space right now."

Her heart skidded. "Really? You're pushing me away *again*?"

"I can't…" He stopped, frustration clear on his face, and God, she ached for him. It was like he didn't know what to say. What to feel or do.

She couldn't stop herself. She crossed the room and stood behind him, then pressed herself firmly against his back. "You feel my heartbeat? It beats for *you*, Ryker. Only you. Don't push me away every time things get tough. Let me feel your pain and let me help you heal."

The room was quiet. She waited for his response. Waited for him to turn. Give her something.

When he didn't utter so much as a word, she swallowed the lump in her throat and stepped back. She couldn't keep doing this. Couldn't keep begging the man over and over and over to let her in, to trust her, only to have him snatch away any progress they'd made the moment something went wrong.

She waited one more beat, and when he still offered nothing, no splinters of hope, she let the heaviness propel her away.

She made it two steps before fingers wrapped around her upper arms and halted her. Then she felt him at *her* back.

"I'm sorry."

She swallowed. "For what?"

"For not being the man you deserve." He stepped closer and pressed his lips to her neck, sounding completely wrecked. "I have to do better. I *want* to do better. Because I want you…all of you…all the time."

She closed her eyes, letting those words settle heavily in her chest. Slowly, she turned in his arms and looked up into his tormented face. "Then why do you push me away when things get hard?"

"Because it's the only way I can think to protect you from this shit storm that's become my life. I love you too goddamn much to hurt you."

Her heart stuttered, and it took longer than it should have to get words out. "You love me?"

"Princess…there is not another soul on this planet who I love more. I love you so much that I hurt when I'm not with you. It's a physical ache inside me. I've ached since the moment I last saw you in Beirut. Even before that awful fucking mission." He lowered his head, his breath brushing her ear. "A part of me wishes you'd find someone safer. But the selfish part of me hopes you don't. Hopes you're as hopelessly tethered to me as I am to you."

Two breaths. Two heartbeats. The world continued to turn, the minutes ticking by, while everything in her stopped. Tears she had no control over burned her eyes. She'd waited so long to hear those words. And so many times she'd feared the day would never come.

She cupped the side of his face and held his gaze like he was all that existed in the room. "You *are* the man I deserve. You're deserving of love and happiness and a future we can create together. My heart will always belong to you."

His eyes darkened, his chest rising and falling on a deep breath. Then in one swift move, she was in his arms and his mouth was on hers.

THE SECOND RYKER had Blakely in his arms, her lips under his, he felt it. Just like every other damn time he touched her, she was his breath of peace. The first heartbeat of calm in days.

Her sweet scent surrounded him and made his blood roar between his ears. His hand went to the back of her head and the second her lips parted, he plunged his tongue into her mouth. She tasted of citrus and cinnamon. So damn sweet.

He needed that sweetness. He needed everything this woman would give him. She was the calm to his storm. The cool water on his burning soul.

He'd tried to free her. Save her from the mess that was his life. But she refused to give up on him.

He spun her toward a wall and pressed her against it. She groaned, and that sound caused fucking havoc on his insides.

With desperate fingers, he grabbed the hem of her shirt and wrenched it over her head. The heat of her skin soaked into his chest. The scars beneath his fingertips, marks of her strength and survival. Her courage.

You feel my heartbeat? It beats for you...

Her words destroyed him. They were everything his starved heart needed to hear.

He moved his lips from hers, sliding them down her neck. As he did, he shifted the strap of her bra down her arm, then lowered the cup. The second her perfect breast was on display, he swooped, wrapping his lips around her hard nipple and sucking.

Her cry shot through the air like an arrow. It hit him in the chest and he welcomed the jolt. He continued to suck as his hand moved to her other breast, thumbing her nipple through the material of her bra.

Every sound she made pierced him deeper. Made parts of him he'd thought dormant scream to life.

He wanted to feel all of this woman, and he wanted to be for her what she was for him. The love. The hope. The light in the dark that showed him the way to salvation.

He reached behind her and removed her bra, letting it fall to the floor. Then he lowered her to her feet, but only long enough to tug down her jeans and panties. A second later, she was back in his arms and completely bare.

He kissed her again, but this time soft, gentle kisses. His lips swiping against hers in a cherishing caress as he shifted his hand between their bodies. He stroked a finger against her bundle of nerves.

She trembled and gasped in his arms, so damn responsive, he wanted to touch her for endless hours.

So beautiful. And his. So fucking his.

He continued to stroke. Nibble on her lips. Her fingernails

scraped down his chest, digging into his flesh. She kissed across his cheek to his ear before whispering, "Mine."

His heart pounded at the word. At the vulnerability in it. "Yours."

He pushed his shorts down, positioned himself at her entrance, then watched her eyes darken to emerald as he slid inside her tight walls.

She clenched, causing white-hot fire to ripple through him.

He pressed his head to hers. "God, I love you."

~

BLAKELY CLOSED HER EYES, letting those words and the weight they carried change her world.

Then he shifted his hips back before thrusting. She cried out at the feel of him. So thick and perfect. Made for her.

He thrust again, his mouth returning to hers. The man made her feel safe. A safety that had no business being there, not with the danger that hustled around them and his habit of running when things got hard. But right now, in the arms of the man she loved, finally feeling loved in return, she couldn't possibly feel anything else.

She threaded her fingers through his hair, trying to anchor herself to him as he took what was his. What would *always* be his.

"Ryker..." She breathed his name as his hand returned to her breast. Kneading. Running the pad of his thumb over her peak.

His mouth moved to her neck, where he bit and sucked, as his hand moved from her breast down to her core. When his thumb ran over her clit in a firm, almost circular motion, her back arched and she broke. Shattered into so many pieces, she wondered how she'd ever be whole again.

Ryker kept thrusting, faster and harder, his thumb never pausing. He growled, his muscles bunching. She felt him thicken and his hot seed shoot deep inside her.

He thrust a few more times, until finally there was stillness. A quiet that not only saturated the moment but eased the anxiety in her chest that had been so loud all day.

She held his head to her neck and closed her eyes, letting the moment muffle the world around them so it was just her and him. The way it should be. The way it felt right.

She loved him. And he loved her. It was everything she'd wanted for so long. And now she had it.

CHAPTER 22

Blakely knew before she opened her eyes that she was alone. The sheets were cold and the room too quiet. Slowly, she opened her eyes, and yep—empty bedroom.

She let her lids flutter closed again as the events of earlier that afternoon played over in her head. Ryker's declaration of love. The sex against the gym wall before Ryker carried her to the bathroom and they showered together. Then he'd slipped into bed with her. And even though it had been the middle of the day, she'd drifted into a sleep so restful, she doubted anything could have woken her.

But now, she was waking up alone. Why?

She opened her eyes and rolled to her side to find a note on the bedside table. She lifted it, smiling at the sight of Ryker's handwriting.

I'm just visiting River. Erik's here. Alarms are on. You're safe. Text or call if you need anything. Love you. R x

Those two words had tendrils of happiness multiplying inside her. He loved her. She wanted to hear those words again and again. To go to sleep with them in her mind. Wake with them in her heart.

She'd waited so long for them. In Beirut, there were little things that made her suspect he already loved her. She'd seen fewer of those things here, but every so often, sparks of affection snuck through the cracks in his wall.

With a long exhale, she climbed out of bed. After splashing some water on her face, she slipped into some yoga pants and a T-shirt before going in search of Erik.

He sat at the dining table, brows slashed together as he worked on his laptop. He looked so serious, she hesitated to enter the room.

Yet again, she wondered what exactly he did for a living. Beyond that night at the twilight market, she'd rarely seen a smile lift his lips. Sometimes it seemed as if he carried the weight of the world on his shoulders. It wasn't hard to see he kept parts of himself locked up tight.

What had he said? That he was a government contractor? She knew he was both former Special Forces and a former professional boxer. But what did his job as a "contractor" entail? And did he have family close by? Friends outside of Ryker's group?

"Are you planning on standing there all day, or do you want to come in?"

A smile kicked up the corners of her lips. Whoops. She *had* been watching him longer than intended. And yeah, it had probably been naive of her to think he wouldn't notice her skulking in the shadows. She was pretty sure the military had trained all of these guys to see the most insignificant movements. Anyone or anything that didn't belong.

She moved into the room and perched on a seat beside him, pulling a knee up to her chest. "Sorry, I... Sorry." She cleared her throat, having no excuse for spying that wouldn't come off as intrusive or stalkerish. "What are you working on?"

He closed the laptop. "Just looking over the specifics of a job."

She raised a brow. It was a silent question. *A job for...?*

When he didn't give her any more information, she nodded.

He didn't want to share. Fair enough. Ryker and his team trusted the man, so she would too.

"How are you feeling?" he asked.

Good question. She should be feeling bad, right? There were so many reasons to *not* be okay. But after what she'd just shared with Ryker? "I'm good, considering."

Erik didn't respond, but he gave her a look a licensed therapist would envy. It made her want to spill every secret she'd ever locked inside her.

She tugged at a small thread that had come loose on the bottom of her shirt. "I finally broke through to Ryker, and that's... God. It's everything. He's been shouldering so much blame, for so long, and he just doesn't need to do that. It's like he's determined to stay in this self-created hell."

The gray specks in Erik's hazel eyes brightened, and the eyebrow ring that he only wore occasionally glinted in the light. "It can be easy for hell to take root in the mind. And that's the worst kind, because you can't escape it."

Sympathy swelled in her, but Blakely kept her expression neutral. Clearly, he'd lived through his own hell. Maybe he still was. "You sound like you know from experience."

He gave her a smile that didn't reach his eyes. "There's a little bit of hell in everyone, isn't there?"

That didn't really answer her question.

She looked away, then inhaled sharply when she noticed his hands. They rested loosely on his keyboard, but the knuckles were raw, like he'd hit something—or someone—recently. Without boxing gloves on.

"Your hand... Did you get into a fight?"

His gaze lowered but he didn't try to cover the abrasions. "They're just flesh wounds."

Again, didn't really answer her question, but before she could ask any more, he lifted his phone. "I ordered some food. Figured we can pick it up and take it to River and Jackson's house."

She perked up. "I could eat."

Right on cue, her stomach growled. It wasn't a quiet or subtle growl. It was a let's-tell-the-entire-world-how-hungry-you-are growl. *Oh, Lord.*

Heat bloomed in her cheeks, but Erik laughed, and the sound was genuine and light. That alone made her embarrassment almost worth it. When the man laughed, he wasn't quite so intimidating, and the hard edges of his face looked a lot softer.

"I hope you're a fan of pizza, because I ordered six."

Ha. Ryker could easily eat an entire pizza by himself. All the guys could. "Please tell me you ordered Margherita."

Erik didn't look like a cheese pizza kind of guy. Nope, he seemed more the how-many-toppings-can-you-fit-on-the-pie type. So when he nodded, her spine straightened in happy surprise.

"I did. And a couple of supreme, a couple of meat lovers, and a pepperoni."

"And when will this pizza be ready?" If the man said it would be a while, she might just—

"We can go now."

Thank the Lord above. She was starving. Erik jingled his keys, and she followed him to the garage door. Usually, it was just Ryker's car in there, but they'd obviously decided walking through the enclosed garage was safer than walking on the street.

When she stepped inside, she came to a dead stop at the sight of his car. Holy crap. It was beautiful. And it looked as expensive as she was sure it was. "A Corvette?"

He opened the passenger door for her. "I'm a car guy."

Uh, yeah. She could see that. You didn't invest in a beautiful vehicle like this if you weren't. She slid onto the cool leather of the passenger seat, wanting to moan at the softness. The upholstery was as smooth as butter under her fingertips. The brushed steel accents. The display screens. The black and red steering wheel.

Yep, the inside was as beautiful as the out.

Erik slid behind the wheel. The engine was loud and made her think of power.

She tapped her fingers on the seat. "I, uh, didn't know government contracts paid so well."

He pressed a little button on a remote to open the garage door. "My department does."

Cryptic.

He pulled out of the garage and headed down the street. She caught sight of the agent in the side mirror, pulling out behind them. The idea of a tail made her hands clammy. She hated that there was enough danger to warrant extra eyes on them twenty-four hours a day.

"So," she said quietly, trying not to think about that. "Any great loves in your life?"

His jaw tensed. It was subtle, but she saw it. Ah, crap. She was not doing well at asking this guy the right questions. But then, was any question the right one?

"No," he finally said. There was a short pause, then he added, "I was married."

Was...as in, not anymore. His fingers clenched the wheel, whitening his knuckles for a moment before he loosened his grip. Whatever had happened to that relationship was painful for him. She didn't need him to spell it out.

Okay, personal question time was over. "It's really nice of you to come and watch me. I can't imagine stepping into a dangerous situation like this is any fun."

"I don't mind helping. The guys are friends. And danger doesn't scare me."

Yeah, probably because he looked like he could end a man with a single punch. But he was dangerous in a good-guy way. It wasn't so much about what he said that made her know that, but how he made her feel. Safe. Like Ryker.

"How's your head feeling since the incident?" he asked.

She touched the old graze, which had almost healed. "I barely feel it. But when I do, it's mostly a reminder as to how lucky I am. Basically, all the good luck fairies had to be on my side that day, and they were. Thank God those guys didn't manage to get away with me a second time."

Erik's eyes steeled. "Yeah, there are a lot of messed-up assholes in the world." He turned right. "It seems like these guys are enjoying messing with Ryker for the moment. We need to work out what their eventual plan is."

They really did.

"I'm glad Ryker has you back," he added. His words had Blakely's eyes widening and shooting toward him. "I've only known him a short time, but obviously he's been holding onto a lot of heavy shit. It's still there, rippling under the surface, but there's less of an edge to it with you around. I don't worry so much anymore that he's going to go and do something stupid."

Oh, she definitely still worried about that. "Like fight in an underground boxing ring?"

She still couldn't believe everything that had happened since his return to the States. That he'd been declared dead and she hadn't even known. But it hurt a little less now than it had when she'd first learned about it.

Erik's chuckle was a rumbly baritone. "The fights themselves weren't all that bad. If the club was still open, I'd still be participating."

"Yeah, but you used to be a professional boxer. Did you enjoy it?"

"In a way. I spent a bit of time doing that after the military for similar reasons as Ryker."

She tilted her head. Because he was angry too? "How old are you?" The question popped out before she could stop it. She quickly tried to backtrack. "I just ask because you seem to have done a lot, but you don't look that old." Early to mid-thirties, perhaps?

"Thirty-six."

So, older than he looked, but still, not very old at all.

She was just opening her mouth to tell him exactly that when his gaze went to the rearview mirror. His brows pulled together sharply. A trickle of unease slid down her spine.

Then he sped up.

She turned her head to see the FBI agent still there, and behind him was a pickup truck. The windows were tinted, so she couldn't see the driver, but the truck was huge.

"Is everything okay?" she asked, turning back around.

"I'm not sure."

He took a sudden hard right. In the side mirror, she saw the FBI agent hadn't seen the move coming, and he kept driving forward—but the truck followed. When Erik accelerated, so did the other vehicle.

Her belly cramped.

Erik sped up again, going so fast, the trees and buildings outside the windows lost their shape. He pressed a button on the wheel.

"Everything okay, Erik?" Ryker's voice was clear through the car's speakers.

"I have a Ford F-350 Super Duty Chassis tailing us."

Ryker swore as Erik continued.

"Windows are tinted so we can't see inside. They're not trying to stay hidden."

She swallowed. Was the fact they weren't trying to remain hidden good or bad? She was thinking bad.

The sound of jingling keys came across the line, then a car door opening and closing. "I'm leaving now. Where are you?"

"I've changed course. I'm heading toward the police station, currently on Oakley."

Ryker's engine started. "I'm driving. Is Blakely okay?"

"I'm okay—"

Her words were cut off when the truck hit them from behind. Erik cursed, spinning the wheel and working hard to keep control of the car. He did—*just*. Then he sped up again. They were driving so fast, her heart stopped every time they veered close to a car or pedestrian or pole. He passed other vehicles with ease, like he'd been in a hundred car chases before.

"What was that?" Ryker demanded.

"They hit us," Erik growled. "What's their fucking game?"

Blakely's heart pounded so hard in her chest, it stole her breath. The only thing keeping her calm was that Erik looked completely in control. Angry, but in control.

"Hold on, Blakely."

She didn't understand Erik's request until he took another hard right. Her body swung to the side, the seat belt digging into her, locking her in place. Pain twinged in her chest, but she held in the groan. And the second they were straight again, she shot a glance behind them. God, the truck was so close.

Erik took a left this time, only he didn't warn her about the turn, instead grabbing her arm to pull her back to the center of the car just before she cracked her head on the window.

He cursed loudly, and she looked around. A second truck, this one somehow even bigger, was coming from a side street on their left—fast.

Her heart jumped to her throat when he slammed his foot on the brake and swerved.

It was too late. The Corvette hit the truck.

She slammed against the seat belt, then bounced off the headrest.

Immediately, Erik released both their belts, reached over, opened her door, and pushed her out while shouting their location to Ryker.

She scrambled out of his way as he followed her to the pavement. Darkness shadowed his entire face, making him look as deadly as she knew he was.

"Stay down and don't move," he growled, as bullets started pelting the car.

Then he rose, pointed a pistol, and started firing.

CHAPTER 23

$\mathcal{A}$drenaline, anger, and fear pumped through Ryker's body, creating a deadly cocktail. A perfect fucking storm.

They'd *hit* Erik's car while Blakely was inside, and now they were firing. Each gunshot blasted through the line, causing his lungs to seize and icy panic to flood his system, until he'd been forced to hang up and call the police and his team. Jackson was contacting Davis while remaining with River. But no one else was as close as him.

How many people were in those trucks? Would Erik be able to hold them off and protect Blakely?

He took a hard right, thinking of all the ways he planned to murder the fuckers who dared hurt the people in his life. He was going to make damn sure they regretted the decision to cross him.

Police sirens sounded in the distance. They were too far as well.

He squealed through another turn. The only reason he was able to function right now was due to years of specialized training.

Why hadn't he waited to visit River? Or even woken Blakely and taken her with him?

Because she'd fallen asleep the instant her head hit the pillow, and he'd known she needed the rest.

Right now, he just had to trust Erik, a man he'd known for less than a year, to protect the woman who meant the world to him.

He took the last turn and came upon the scene—the Ford F-350, a second huge white truck, and perpendicular to both, Erik's car. Erik was hiding behind his Corvette on the passenger side, the engine block between him and the oncoming bullets.

One of the FBI agents was on the side of the road, crouched behind his vehicle and engaging one of the shooters from the white truck.

Bullets came at Erik from both directions. He was taking cover behind the car but shooting back every chance he got.

Ryker drove as close as possible before slamming to a stop, swerving his car so he could use it as protection. He lifted his Glock and climbed out, immediately aiming at the Ford. One man inched his head out from behind it, and Ryker fired.

One round to the head. The asshole dropped.

A second man behind the same truck swung his gun toward Ryker. Before he could get a shot off, Ryker fired, hitting him in the neck.

"Two down," he shouted to Erik. Just the assholes in the white truck to go.

He ducked behind his car again, waiting for a break in gunfire from the large truck. When it came, Erik yelled, "Go!" and provided cover fire while Ryker rushed across the street.

He dove behind the Ford as bullets peppered the air. He heard the thud of a body hit the ground, but it didn't come from the truck or Erik's Corvette—it was the agent.

Fuck.

A second thud sounded, but this time from the other side of the truck. Their enemies were another man down.

Staying behind a wide tire, he quickly glanced beneath the truck. Two sets of legs on the other side. He pulled the trigger but the angle was awkward, and both men quickly dodged behind the passenger-side tires.

Erik fired again, hitting one of the men in the side. He cried out and fell back. Then everything went quiet for a moment, each man waiting to see who would break cover to shoot first.

Ryker caught quick movement from the sidewalk.

Shit. The second man was running—fast.

Erik popped up and put a round in the injured asshole's head as Ryker took off running.

"Don't leave Blakely's side!" he shouted back, not slowing or pausing. He couldn't let the shooter get away, not when he might have information on Saad.

He turned into an alley, but the man was already on the other side of a fence, turning a corner. Ryker lunged at the chain link and climbed over, feet pounding the pavement as he rounded the corner. But he was too late—the guy wrenched open a door at the back of a building and disappeared inside.

Ryker pushed his legs to move faster, then shoved through the same door. It was a small restaurant. Waitstaff cried out while customers sat shocked as the man raced through. Ryker stopped and took aim, ignoring the screams, but the guy made it out the front door.

Fuck. He ran to the street, but the asshole was gone.

There was another narrow alley two stores down. That was where he'd gone. Had to be.

Ryker moved toward it quickly but cautiously, keeping his gun raised and his steps silent. He paused against the wall just to the right of the alley. He only had to wait a second before hearing the crunch of feet against pavement.

Ryker swung around the corner, identified his target, and fired.

The guy hit the ground hard and rolled, ending up on his back, blood blooming from his stomach. Ryker rushed forward and stepped on the wrist holding the gun, aiming his Glock at the man's hand.

"Drop it or I put a fucking hole in your palm."

The guy sucked in a breath, anger and pain marring his features.

"Now!" Ryker yelled.

One more beat, then his fingers released the weapon. Ryker kicked the gun away, lowered to his knee, and pressed the muzzle of his Glock to the man's forehead. "Are you a contractor or do you have ties to Saad?"

"The others were hired. I am not," he spat.

So he'd captured the right asshole. "Where's Saad and what's his plan?"

The man laughed, a cackling sound that caused blood to splutter from his mouth. "You think I will tell you? There is far greater honor in death than in betrayal."

"Death will only be the beginning for you. I can make you *beg* to die. Shoot your fucking fingers off one by one and watch you bleed and scream. Break your bones until every single one is snapped in half."

"Do it! I do not fear you."

Ryker removed his gun from the asshole's head and pointed it toward his thumb.

Before he could pull the trigger, another shot fired—this one from the street.

Ryker rolled to the side, taking cover behind a large trash container as bullets peppered the guy's body. He eased his gun out even as the car drove away.

Then there was silence.

Dead. The guy on the ground was fucking dead, his body

riddled with bullets. Ryker wouldn't be finding out anything. Not today.

He ran his hand through his hair and cursed. His phone rang in his pocket, and he ripped it out, seeing Erik's name on the screen.

"Is she safe?" Ryker growled, his breaths sawing from his chest.

"She's safe. We've had no more visitors, and the police and FBI are here."

Ryker closed his eyes in relief. One fucking reprieve from this nightmare. Blakely was secure.

"Are you okay? Did you catch the guy?"

"I'm fine." A new vein throbbed in his temple. He looked down. "The guy's dead. A car passed the alley we were in and shot him."

"Shit. They must've had a tracker on him or something. They didn't aim at *you*?"

Ryker could have laughed, even though there was nothing even distinctly funny about this mess. "No. I wasn't the target."

The shooter from the car could easily have killed him before he took cover. He didn't. But Ryker already knew the reason for that. Saad didn't want him to die. He wanted something else. Something that would hurt more than death.

Blakely's death? Was that why Erik's car was targeted?

Whatever his goal, one thing Saad had proven was that he wanted Ryker to be acutely aware that no one he loved was safe. And that was a hell far worse than death.

CHAPTER 24

*S*mall *stones crunched below Blakely's shoes as she made her way across town. She had three family visits today, all general health checks.*

Man, she loved her job. Connecting with people. Helping in big and small ways. It never grew old.

She turned the corner and her feet slowed at the sight of two people beneath a cedar tree. Cyrus, one of the local children, and Ryker. Ryker was on one knee, putting him at eye level with the boy, who was handing something to him.

She swallowed. Ryker wore cargo pants and a black shirt that hugged his thick, muscular arms. His skin was bronzed with a slight sheen, like he'd been in the hot sun for a while.

God, he was gorgeous. Especially wearing a smile that wrinkled his eyes and softened the masculine planes of his face. But it wasn't just his looks that shortened her breath and made her steps falter. It was literally everything, inside and out. He was so kind to the locals, not because he had to be or because he got anything in return, but because that was him. He did the right thing because that was who he was.

She remained still, not moving forward to avoid disrupting the moment.

She and Ryker had grown closer during his missions here. He had even taken to texting her...and texting often. She lived for those texts.

She was still standing there, just watching, when little Cyrus turned his head. His eyes lit up when they found her.

"Blakely, come!"

Cyrus spoke English well. It was impressive for a kid so young. But then, his parents spoke fluent English, so it wasn't a surprise.

When Ryker's gaze lifted and hit her, her mouth went dry and her heart gave one giant thud. She swallowed, then moved forward. The second she reached them, Ryker stood and leaned forward, touching her elbow while kissing her cheek.

Her belly flopped and she was sure her cheeks were the shade of a tomato. At least he didn't know how fast her heart was racing.

"Hey," he said quietly, his gravelly voice tickling her insides.

"Hey." Geez, her voice was so quiet, she wasn't even sure he could hear it. That was what he did to her. He stole her words. He stole her damn sanity.

At a tugging on her pant leg, Blakely lowered her gaze from Ryker's beautiful eyes to see equally dark ones gazing up at her. She knelt beside Cyrus, a genuine smile stretching her lips.

"Hey, champ."

"I just gave Ryker the present we have been working on."

She grinned wider. "Is that right?" She snuck a peek up at Ryker, who had a hint of a smile on his handsome face, before looking back at Cyrus. "And did he like it?"

She was pretty sure she already knew the answer, but...

"He loved it! He said he was going to take it home and put it in his house."

Her voice lowered conspiratorially. "I knew he would."

"I do love it," Ryker said softly. "Thank you."

She rose to her feet. "All I did was help choose the rock."

Although, that in itself had taken a full day. The kids had been very picky.

"And you helped us come up with the idea," Cyrus added.

That was true. The kids had asked her to help think of a gift they could give Ryker. She'd mentioned he might like something handmade, then pointed out that he often skipped rocks across the water with the kids. That led to the idea of painting a rock for him to take back to the US. She already knew Cyrus and Ara were talented young artists.

Ryker opened his palm, and her gaze brushed over the painted cedar tree on the rock's wide surface. Beneath the tree stood Cyrus, Ara, Ryker, and her, all holding hands.

She rose to her feet and stepped closer. Then, without thinking, she placed her hand beneath his and traced the paint with a finger. She didn't think about the burn of Ryker's skin against hers, or the way he made her chest feel unbelievably tight, as she normally would. Instead, she focused on the art.

Beautiful. The artwork was beautiful.

"You and Ara did such a great job, Cyrus! It's amazing."

And so lifelike. They'd captured the steely brown of Ryker's eyes. The kindness in his features. Even the intricate lines and shadows of his face.

"We'll make one for you next!"

She finally dragged her eyes away from the rock to look at Cyrus. He beamed at her.

"I would love that," she said softly.

When she looked up at Ryker, it was to see he wasn't looking at Cyrus or the rock. His entire focus was on her. And it made her want to squirm. To escape the heat, even as she wanted to pull it around her like a cloak.

She sucked in a breath and dropped her hand, losing the contact. "I should get going." She ruffled Cyrus's hair. "Your mom invited me over for dinner tomorrow night. See you then?"

He grinned and nodded. She gave Ryker a final smile. He winked at her, and damn her traitorous heart for thumping so hard she almost doubled over.

With a quick nod, she turned and walked fast, certainly faster than normal, to get away before she did something stupid—like kiss the beautiful man who made her heart race.

She was several yards away when an explosion boomed through the air. It was so loud it deafened her and caused the ground to tremble beneath her feet.

Her heart stopped. She turned back, opening her mouth to tell Cyrus and Ryker to run. But she didn't see them.

Instead, she saw flames. Hungry, violent flames surrounding the tree. Her chest heaved, panic like a fist around her lungs. Clenching. Tightening.

"Cyrus? Ryker?"

Desperate, she searched the street for help, but suddenly the flames were everywhere. Burning through the town like wildfire. Every house. Every building. There was nothing left.

Everything in her began to shatter.

She ran toward the tree, the heat of the fire intensifying with each step. She yelled their names again, knowing it was futile. Hopelessness and desolation carved into her chest, hollowing her.

She screamed so loud her lungs ached. She was looking around frantically, searching for someone, anyone to help, when a heavy branch from the tree crashed down, pinning her to the ground. It burned through her clothes to her skin, turning her screams of heartache to ones of searing pain.

Suddenly, the limbs of the branch turned into a hand with fingers, grabbing her upper arms, shaking her.

"Blakely! Open your eyes."

RYKER'S EYES shot open at the sound of frantic whimpers. Blakely's whimpers.

He swiftly sat up and switched on the light. Within the blink of an eye, he'd opened his bedside drawer and pulled out his Glock. When he turned back, he expected to see people in his room, the firefight from earlier that evening still fresh in his mind.

Instead, he just saw Blakely, lying beside him, her eyes scrunched shut, pain on her face.

It was another nightmare. And this one sounded worse than usual. Her cries were filled with deep, dark anguish.

She screamed his name, the desperation in her voice like a tangible sword cutting into his flesh. Then she said another name...

Cyrus.

For a long moment, he froze. His skin went cold, the chill reaching into his bones, almost making him grab his chest.

He tried not to think about that boy or his sister. Every day, he made the conscious effort to keep them as far from his mind as possible. He wasn't strong enough to relive his memories of them. He might *never* be strong enough. It was why he'd spent so long funneling every ounce of energy he had into finding Saad.

Blakely twisted, flailing, the sheet falling from her body. Now, instead of screaming names, she just screamed. Long, terror-filled cries.

He cursed under his breath, depositing the weapon back into the drawer and taking hold of her shoulders. "Blakely."

Her twisting became more aggressive. She arched her body, writhing.

He didn't release his hold, but it was damn hard to grip her firmly enough without risking bruising her. He'd never seen a nightmare so intense. So all-consuming. He lowered his head and touched his lips to her ear.

"Blakely. Open your eyes."

After a tense minute, her twisting stopped, body muscles unclenching...and her eyes opened slowly. She looked at him without moving. Heavy seconds ticked by, and with each one, her body grew more calm until her breathing was almost normal.

Her eyes were dark, like a forest with no light, and so damn tortured, he swore he could feel her agony.

"Ryker…" She swallowed, her voice thick. "You're here."

His heart tore in two. "I'm here, princess."

She sat up and leaned into him. He wrapped his arms around her and held her as close as he could. His heart still beat too fast, and his chest still felt tight, but he refused to let go. He let their closeness bring him a small semblance of peace.

"Your nightmare," he finally said, not wanting her to think about it but needing to know. "It was about Beirut, wasn't it? About the bombing."

The shudder that cascaded down her spine vibrated against his arms. He tightened his hold.

"Yes and no," she whispered. "The nightmares came every night for the first few months. They've lessened…but I'm not sure if they'll ever leave me completely."

A muscle ticked in his jaw. He *hated* that.

"This one was different," she continued. "Usually, my nightmares are an exact replica of that day. This time, it started somewhere else. We were under the cedar tree and it was the day Cyrus gave you the painted rock. It was an exact memory…until I walked away." She swallowed. "Then a bomb went off. And when I turned, there were flames. First surrounding the tree. Then everywhere."

"I'm sorry, princess. So damn sorry." He wished he could take it all away. The memories. The scars.

She clung to his shirt. "The worst part is always the silence. I remember seeing the flames and waiting for screams. The cries of people calling for help, so I could go to them. Because sounds mean life. But there was nothing but that roar. I was a nurse…but I couldn't save anyone."

He understood that helplessness. The need to do something but completely unable. It was crippling. "I was a soldier, trained to protect, yet I couldn't protect a single person from what happened to them."

"You can't save people you don't know are suffering," she said quietly, fingertip trailing over the ink on his chest. The tattoo of flames. He wasn't there to see them that day, but he'd carry them with him forever…just like Blakely.

"Do you know what really happened after you walked away from us that day?" Ryker asked quietly.

"What?"

He hadn't allowed himself to think about this in so damn long, and he didn't know if it would help her now, but he told her anyway. "I told Cyrus that I loved you. That you were mine, and we were going to build a life together in the States."

That had been his plan. Even before their amazing night together. Then everything had changed.

She looked up at him, eyes glazed with tears. "And what did he say?"

The corners of his lips twitched. "He looked at me with a face that was so serious, he seemed a hell of a lot older than his age. And he told me I'd better not hurt you."

A tear trickled down her cheek. "They were such good kids."

He swiped it away with the pad of his thumb. "They were."

Ryker pressed a kiss to her head before settling her on the mattress and rising from the bed. He walked to his dresser, lowered to his haunches, opened the bottom drawer, and reached to the very back. His fingers wrapped around cool, hard stone.

The second he brought it back to her, her eyes widened.

"The rock." Tentatively, she took it from his palm, running the tip of her finger over the paint. Over Cyrus. Then Ara. "I'm so glad you kept it."

"Out of all my possessions, this is my most valuable." He could lose every other fucking thing in this house. He didn't care. But this rock meant the world to him. It was irreplaceable.

Her eyes rose to his. There was so much emotion in their

depths, he could have drowned in them. When he sat on the bed, she climbed into his lap, wrapped both legs around his waist, her arms around his shoulders, and whispered, "I'm sorry you lost them."

For a moment, he was completely still. Not even breathing. People had said that to him before, but they didn't know *what* he had lost, making the words feel empty. Blakely knew exactly what had been stolen from him. From both of them. And her words allowed the emotion, the pure, unadulterated devastation, to cripple him. To slip through every crevasse of his chest, find the vulnerable parts, and clench tight.

He wrapped his arms around her and, for the first time in a year and a half, finally let himself feel more than a need for revenge. He let himself feel the loss. The pain. The heartache. And it was so fucking heavy, it crushed him. The only thing that kept him anchored to the world in that moment was her.

CHAPTER 25

*B*lakely used mitts to take the muffins out of the oven. Steam billowed and the room thickened with that fresh-baked-goods smell. She wasn't an amazing baker, but hey, as long as she added enough sugar, they tended to taste okay.

River leaned forward. "They smell a-*mazing*. Please tell me we get to eat them before the boys return and steal them all."

She grinned at the woman. They were in River and Jackson's kitchen. Jackson and Ryker had disappeared from the room a few minutes ago when Ryker received a call. She was trying not to think about that, though. The look on Ryker's face had told her it was serious. Probably about Saad.

"What's the fun in baking muffins if they're not burn-your-tongue-off hot when you eat them?"

River laughed. "Trust me, there's no fun in making muffins for me—ever. Unless you call setting the smoke alarm off and taking blackened mounds out of the oven fun."

"Oh, I know that feeling. Believe me when I say this is the one muffin recipe I can actually pull off. I do have a semi-successful banana bread as well, but every so often even that betrays me and comes out with the inside raw and the outside burned."

She used the same recipe every time. The same oven. The same temperature and cooking time. The blueprint for creating perfect food repetitively had never revealed itself to her.

"I'm a strong believer that baking is best left to the wizards who have the magic wand," River said, already eyeing the muffins. "Michele's one of those wizards, and not just with baking. Anything in the kitchen. Lucky, because she's been keeping me and Jackson alive this last week."

Blakely used a tea towel to take out one of the hot muffins. "How are the ribs?"

The bruising on River's face was still visible, but fractured ribs would take a lot longer to heal.

"Honestly—and don't tell Jackson this—it's worse than when I was shot. If I move the wrong way even slightly, it hurts like a mother trucker."

"Wait, you were *shot?*"

River tilted her head. "Ryker didn't tell you? Yeah, a rookie cop was aiming for the bad guy and got me instead. Jackson had me on bed rest for *weeks*. But the day I was shot was also the day I learned Ryker was alive, so I almost have fond memories of it."

Her heart skidded. "I'm glad you're okay. And I can't imagine the pain of thinking he was dead."

Just thinking about what River and everyone else went through made her knees weak and her tummy sick. She set the muffin on a plate and pushed it to the other woman.

River started to peel off the liner. "I didn't believe it for a long time. I remember standing at the funeral with everyone around me, crying. I couldn't even muster a tear for show, because I was *so certain* he was alive and so fixated on finding him." She swallowed, and dark demons played in her eyes. "It wasn't until Homeland Security came to my house and insisted he was dead that I started to wonder if I'd been wrong the whole time. And when I tell you it was the worst moment of my life, I'm not lying."

The pain in her voice made hurt ripple behind Blakely's own ribs. A deep, tear-the-soul-apart kind of hurt. "I'm sorry."

River inhaled a deep breath and met Blakely's gaze. "No, *I'm* sorry that I didn't know about you so I could call and tell you. If that had been real, and you hadn't even been told he was gone…"

"It wasn't real. And you don't know what you don't know."

It had definitely hurt for a while, but the pain had really stemmed from feeling unimportant to Ryker. Things were different now, and that had turned the hurt into gratitude that she hadn't had to mourn his death and go through the heartache of losing him.

"Thank you."

Blakely paused with a second muffin half out of the pan. "For what?"

"Coming here. Recognizing that he wasn't okay and fighting for him."

"I love him. That's what we do for the people we love."

River's eyes glistened with moisture. Then she rose from her stool, moved around the counter, and slid her arms around Blakely's waist. Blakely hugged her back, gently, knowing Ryker's sister needed this. The woman had been through so much. Thinking she'd lost her brother, then getting him back, only to really have just a part of him. A broken part. A shell of the man he once was.

River had kept fighting for him, though. And Blakely knew the woman would never stop.

"TELL me the FBI has some leads to this asshole's whereabouts, Davis."

Ryker ground the words out. Yes, the FBI had agents on the streets. But as long as Saad was breathing, no one he loved was safe. And that was fucking terrifying.

Davis sighed over the phone line. "We had some leads—"

"Had?" Jackson interrupted. He was just as on edge as Ryker.

"We find the locations too late. After he leaves. It's usually with friends or connections in the area. But each time we get a lead, he's already moved on, and the people who gave him sanctuary claim to have no idea where he's gone."

"Do you think that's true?" Ryker asked.

"They were all questioned extensively. They seemed shocked to hear he was a wanted man."

"Bullshit! One look at him and you see he's pure evil," Jackson growled.

"His community is loyal," Davis said quietly. "When they look at him, they see a hero."

Ryker leaned back, scrubbing his hands over his face. "He keeps sending these messages that he's planning something. I need to know what. I know it involves the people I care about. It's why he hasn't just blown up our fucking house or car. There's something he wants more. And at this rate, we won't find out until it actually happens."

Then it would be too damn late.

"You're right," Davis agreed. "And before you learn his plans, he wants you scared. He's still got about seven men, best we can determine, who arrived in the country with him. Probably more allies stateside. He obviously has easy access to weapons."

There was a heavy pause.

"But you've got my guys and the FBI on your side," Davis continued. "We're watching locations we think he'll try next. Intercepting communications. His time is limited."

Yeah, but you didn't need much time to destroy fucking lives.

Davis went through more details about the agents on the street. His men crawling through the town. Ryker listened, but his mind also raced. Because for everything Davis said he had covered, Ryker could think of a million ways Saad could sneak through the cracks.

When they finally ended the call, Ryker leaned back in his seat, the heaviness of his enemy sitting like a weight on his chest. Pressing. Suffocating.

"I know, brother," Jackson said quietly, obviously seeing that Ryker was not okay. "I feel it too."

"I can't lose either of them. And fuck, I can't lose you guys or your women either."

Jackson gripped his shoulder. "You're not losing anyone."

Words that should hold some weight. Yet, right now, they were so damn light they bounced right off him.

They remained in River's home office a bit longer to call the guys. By the time the calls were done, he was itching to get back to Blakely and his sister. He didn't like them being out of his and Jackson's sights, but at the same time, he didn't want to be talking about this shit in front of them.

The second Ryker opened the office door, he caught the sweet scent of baked goods. When he stepped into the kitchen, the women were laughing and eating. The smile on Blakely's face was everything.

He crossed the room to slip his arms around her waist and kiss her cheek.

She murmured a soft groan and leaned back into him. Some of the weight on his chest lifted, and for a moment, he could actually breathe.

"I missed you," he whispered.

She laughed, a soft, lyrical sound. "You were out of the room for less than twenty minutes."

"Too long." He kissed her again, and she tilted her cheek.

A deep sigh came from the other side of the kitchen island. River watched them, elbow on the counter and cheek in her palm. Jackson stood beside her, arm around her waist.

Ryker scowled. "Aren't you supposed to make a choking sound or something at the sight of your brother kissing a woman?"

Another sigh from River. "Don't know. Don't care. I could watch my brother be happy and smitten all day, every day."

There was humor in her voice, but there was also something else. Something that ran far deeper. River worried about him. Hell, everyone did. He'd done a shit job pretending he was okay, and he was only just realizing it.

He gave River a soft smile. "I like seeing you happy too, little sis."

She scoffed. "Little? I'm only one year younger than you."

"Yeah. Little." His gaze went to the muffin on Blakely's plate. "These look and smell incredible. I'm guessing River didn't make them."

His sister threw a chunk of muffin at him. "Hey. If I wanted to learn to bake, I could. It's just not a priority."

Nope. He didn't believe that for a second. He'd seen his sister's attempts at baking. In fact, he'd almost gotten food poisoning from them more than once growing up.

"Of course you could." Jackson's lie was smooth as silk, especially when he followed the words with a kiss on her cheek.

Blakely started to move away, but Ryker tightened his arms. "Where are you going?"

"To get you a muffin."

"You're not going to share yours with me?"

Both she and River scoffed.

"Um. No," Blakely said firmly. "I've seen you eat, Ryker. I'd be lucky to get a bite in."

True.

As she moved toward the tray of muffins, his phone vibrated. He lifted the cell, frowning when he saw it was a text message from Janice.

Wait, not a message. A video.

He opened it and clicked play. The second he realized what he was watching, his breath seized in his lungs.

The village in Beirut.

For a moment there was stillness, bar the swaying of the trees with the wind. It happened so fast, he didn't have time to click out.

The explosions. The fire.

Fuck! The sick asshole had filmed it?

And why the hell had it come to him through Janice's number?

A gasp sounded behind him, then the shattering of a plate. He swore again, dropping his phone to the island and spinning. Blakely's face was pasty white, her gaze still on the phone on the island.

Jesus. He hadn't realized she'd been so close behind him. "Blakely..."

The stool on the other side of the island scraped against the floor. River said something, but his entire focus remained on Blakely. He grabbed her arms, scared she'd fall, she trembled so badly.

Her mouth opened and closed, her gaze still on his cell. "That was—"

She stopped, the remaining color leaching from her face. Then she wrenched herself from his hold and ran to the sink, where she threw up.

eclan: We found her.

Ryker took a second to inhale deeply before responding. Before asking the question he was almost certain he knew the answer to.

Ryker: Alive or dead?

Declan: Dead. Slit throat.

His fingers tightened around his phone to the point he almost crushed it. The fucker had killed Janice. For what? Just so he could send a text from her phone? As another damn warning that he could do what he wanted with the people in Ryker's life?

They'd called Davis and the team, and while Ryker had brought Blakely back to his house, Declan had gone with the FBI to Janice's apartment. They'd known what they'd find. But thinking you knew something and having it confirmed were two different things. And knowing another person had lost their life because of a connection to Ryker made the very breath that kept him alive fight to flow through his lungs.

He dropped his phone to the kitchen table and glanced down the hall. Blakely was in his bedroom, but she wasn't okay. She hadn't been sick again, but the color hadn't returned to her face by the time they got home and her shaking hadn't subsided. The second they'd stepped inside, she said she needed to lie down. She'd needed silence and some time alone to process.

Alone. He hated that word. She shouldn't have been exposed to that video. Shouldn't have been forced to relive that moment all over again.

His feet twitched to go to her. Check on her. Make sure she was okay. But he had no idea what he'd fucking say. Were there even words to comfort a person when they'd witnessed the depravity of evil? When death had been shoved on their fucking doorstep?

No. There were no words.

He moved over to the closed blinds and looked outside. The FBI agent sat in his car on the street. Ryker then systematically checked every window and door in the house, as well as the alarm. He'd already checked the bedroom windows before allowing Blakely in there.

Once he was certain they were secure, he called his parents, something he'd made a habit of doing every day since they'd left.

His mother answered on the first ring. "Ryker, darling, are you safe?"

He'd intentionally ensured they were aware of the danger and why they had to stay away for the time being. But he wouldn't be telling them about Janice. Not right now. Not only because he didn't have the energy, but because that would spike their fear and maybe even make them want to come home to personally see that he and River were safe. They'd already wanted to come back after River was attacked.

"River and I are safe, Mom."

"And your team and their partners? And what about Blakely? Tell me everyone's okay."

He ran his fingers through his hair. "Everyone's okay. Blakely's here with me, and the guys are all protecting their women."

His mother exhaled loudly. "Thank God."

"How are you and Dad?"

"Oh, the boys at Blue Halo Security have been taking such good care of us."

He'd known they would. Exactly why he'd called in the favor.

"I spoke to River this afternoon," his mother continued, her voice a notch quieter. "She said you received a video of what happened in Beirut."

He closed his eyes, a tension headache forming behind his lids. Why had his sister gone and told his mother? "Yeah, that happened. We're dealing with it. I don't want you or Dad to stress about anything."

"Darling, when you and River and the people you love are involved, we'll always be stressed." Her voice softened. "She also shared some good news. That you and Blakely have made it official?"

He was going to *officially* kill his sister. She always seemed to share his news before him. Probably because she knew it would take him too damn long himself. "We're...dating."

The word wasn't entirely accurate, and he could say a hell of a lot more about that, but now wasn't the time.

When Saad was dead, and he could enjoy his new relationship without fear, he was going to propose to Blakely and let every fucking person know she was his. He just needed to keep reminding himself that the time would come.

"Oh, Ryker, I'm so happy for you. Sometimes, it's in the midst of the hardest times of our lives when we find the person we're supposed to be with. How's she doing with everything?"

"She's a fighter." It was the best answer he could give right now. And it was true. So damn true.

"The poor dear. It must be a lot. I'm glad she has you."

"If it wasn't for me, she wouldn't be in this mess." He hadn't meant to say that out loud, but dammit, he was past the point of having the energy to censor.

His mother's voice firmed. "You are a protector, Ryker. You have *always* been a protector. But do *not* make the mistake of thinking that just because harm slips through your armor, you wielded the sword. You didn't."

Jody Harp always had been, and always would be, the wisest woman in the goddamn world.

"And if you two are meant for each other," she continued, "then you are a gift to Blakely, just like she's a gift to you. Never forget that."

"I love you, Mom."

"I love you too, darling. Please stay safe for me."

"Always."

BLAKELY LOOKED from the bathroom mirror to her bare feet. She was still partially wet from her shower, small drops of water glistening on her skin.

She could almost feel the world rocking beneath her. *Had* been feeling it since she saw that video clip.

She closed her eyes, but the darkness didn't help, it just gave the memory a better backdrop.

For months, she'd known the feeling of the explosion intimately. The shaking of the Earth. The plumes of dirt in the air like thick fog. The heat of the flames. But she hadn't actually seen the homes break apart. She'd never witnessed buildings standing one moment and collapsing the next.

In a fraction of a second. One single moment. The world could shift from stillness to utter devastation. And the most painful part? The detail from that video that *really* haunted her body and soul?

She'd seen movement in the windows of those houses.

And it brought into sharp focus the reminder that it wasn't

just bricks and mortar that had been destroyed. It was people. Humans who'd loved and laughed and deserved to *live*.

She bent over like she'd been sucker punched, her lungs refusing to let air in. Those poor souls had taken a breath they hadn't known would be their last.

She grabbed onto the counter, trying to hold herself up, keep the pain inside instead of letting it leak from the darkest corners of her chest and crumble her to the floor. The ache was so intense, it felt physical. Like someone had dug their claws into her flesh and kept twisting, wanting her to bleed out until she was nothing but bones and organs.

It wasn't just pain. It was agony. And there, right beside the agony, was a fury so red and so raw that for the first time in her life, she felt violence tremble through her limbs. The desire to kill. Destroy. Bring the lost souls the justice they so desperately deserved.

She forced herself to straighten and looked at her reflection.

She finally felt what Ryker felt. And it was crippling. Crushing. Made her heart feel like it was disintegrating into ash.

Suddenly, she couldn't breathe.

Footsteps sounded from the other side of the door, then a knock.

"Blakely."

She opened her mouth to ask him to leave. To tell him that he couldn't see her like this...internally breaking, externally destroyed.

But her stolen breaths turned into stolen words. Stolen like the future that had been yanked right out from under her.

The door slid open, and she watched through hazy vision as Ryker stepped in, wrapping his arms around her from behind. Noted the way he towered over her. The incredible breadth of his shoulders. And that face. So much concern...

"I can't breathe," she finally gasped out, an admission that came out weak.

His mouth heated her ear, his breath brushing her skin. "Breathe with *me*, princess."

As his chest pushed against her back with an exaggerated inhale, she did as he said. When he exhaled, she blew out a similar breath.

It took ten long breaths. Then he applied some pressure to her hips and turned her. She focused on the pulse in his throat, watched it pump life through him. Then his thumb and forefinger went to her chin and lifted it until she met his gaze.

"I'm so sorry you saw that, princess."

His other hand rose, and he used the pad of his thumb to swipe a tear from her cheek she didn't know had fallen.

She swallowed, letting the near-black of his eyes anchor her. "I'm not."

His frown deepened.

"This whole time, I've felt such deep sadness. Such devastation for all the lives lost. But I've never allowed myself to feel *anger*. I've never really allowed myself to focus on the man who caused all of this."

She pressed her hands to his chest, allowing his warmth to flow through her limbs like a hot waterfall.

"I feel it now," she breathed. "This…blinding rage. The need to destroy the person responsible. I finally feel what *you've* been feeling."

He shook his head. "I don't want you to feel what I've been feeling. It can ruin you."

"I *want* it to ruin me!" The muscles beneath her palm were hard, developed to protect and provide. "I want to sink into the depths of the hell you've been living, then I want us to rise together. I want us to put that asshole so deep in the fucking ground, he can never find his way out and hurt another soul."

Ryker looked almost pained. "Blakely—"

"People were stolen from us, Ryker! But you and me…we're

still here. We're still breathing. We *will* get justice for them. And we will *live* for them."

His eyes shimmered like black pools. Then in one swift move, he lifted her to the counter and stepped between her thighs, touching his forehead to hers. "You destroy me."

"Then I'll make you whole again."

His mouth crashed to hers and he kissed her with so much emotion and passion, she felt him in every empty part of her. Residing. Healing.

The towel fell from her body, and he cupped her breast. She groaned as his thumb brushed over her hard peak, his tongue continuing to work hers.

When his hand lowered to the apex of her thighs, she arched, trying to push herself against him. It wasn't enough. She wanted to feel all of him and let her love and lust for this man overwhelm every other emotion.

She grabbed at his jeans, undid the button and zipper. Then she reached into his briefs and tugged him out. He was large and hard in her hand, and he growled when her fingers circled and pumped him.

She shifted her lips to his ear and grazed his lobe. "Now, Ryker! Ruin me."

Another deep, sexy growl, then he thrust inside her.

She threw her head back and screamed.

"Fuck, you're so beautiful," he rasped.

He thrust again and again, deep thrusts that took her somewhere else. A place where no one existed but her and Ryker. Somewhere devoid of pain and panic and devastation.

They were damaged, but they were still here. Blood still flowed through their veins. And she was going to live and love this man like she was born to do.

His mouth tore from her lips, and he latched onto her neck while his hand returned to her breast. He rolled her nipple between his thumb and finger.

She wanted this moment to stretch out. For them to be entwined for so long, she didn't have to return to the world around them. But her body betrayed her, and too soon, she threw her head back and cried out as her walls convulsed around him.

He kept thrusting. Kept sucking and rolling her nipple. Then, finally, he shattered along with her.

CHAPTER 27

*R*yker kept his fists raised as he danced around his opponent. Danger thickened the air while dread crawled inside him. The dread wasn't from the man in front of him, though. It was a dread he'd been feeling for days. A thick, ugly trepidation that sat in his gut like a weight.

Lindeman had been too quiet since Janice's death. He hated the quiet. He wanted noise. Motion. To hear the footsteps of his enemy.

The one possible spark of hope? That today, things might end. Davis had yet another location for Saad. This time, he was so certain the guy was there, he was sending a massive team of men in to raid the place.

Jackson swung, and instead of dodging the hit, Ryker raised his fists and used the high guard to block. The force dispersed through his back and lats. It felt good. Jackson swung again, and again, Ryker blocked.

Boxing was an intricate balancing act between offense and defense. Teeter too far to one side or the other and lose. He'd learned that as a kid, and as he'd gotten older, he'd realized the same rules applied to every battle he'd ever fought.

Jackson swung a third time. Ryker blocked with one arm and swung with the other.

Defense—offense.

The punch landed, but Jackson didn't pause, and he didn't fold. Instead, he struck back. Ryker ducked just in time to feel the glove graze the side of his head.

Then they were back to dancing, waiting to see who threw the next punch.

From the corner of his eye, Ryker kept Blakely in his sights. She sat with the women. All four of them were eating pizza on the floor of the gym. But even though Blakely was smiling, he saw the unease behind the expression. The effort it took for the corners of her lips to lift.

He hated that. She didn't deserve any of what had been thrown her way, and when this was over, he was going to make damn sure she lived the happy life she'd more than earned.

Jackson jabbed. Ryker slipped to the side, narrowly avoiding contact.

His entire team was here tonight. The men. The women. Anthony and Zac. They'd lain low for a few days, but today, because he wasn't taking down his enemy like every part of him screamed to do, Ryker needed to spar. He needed to be up and on his feet. He needed to expel some of his pent-up energy. And by the looks of it, his team felt exactly the same, especially Jackson.

Jackson threw a combination Ryker's way, and he bobbed and weaved, avoiding each one. Then he lunged with two crosses and a jab. Only the jab hit Jackson. He didn't so much as bend over.

Still, they both stopped, each knowing the other man was done. Their chests heaved with their panting breaths.

"You okay?" Ryker asked.

Jackson nodded, pulling his gloves from his hands. His gaze flicked to River, then through the glass window on the door to the gym. Day was turning to evening, and they were losing light fast. They couldn't see them, but two FBI agents sat outside Mercy Ring in their car, and some more were in the back lot.

His phone vibrated from the floor. He pulled off his gloves and lifted his cell to see a message from Erik.

Be there in ten. I've got beer.

He slid the phone into his shorts pocket. Good. He was glad Erik was coming. Not just because he liked having his friend around, but because the man had protected Blakely the other night, and almost died doing it. He owed him a debt he could never repay, and now, Erik not only had his trust, but Ryker wanted him around if shit hit the fan.

"How are *you* doing?" Jackson asked, pulling Ryker from his thoughts.

"Want the truth or a lie?"

"Truth. Always."

He ran his fingers through his hair. "Not great. I'm battling between wanting to be here with Blakely, and out there with Davis's team, raiding the location."

The target was a house a few miles outside of Lindeman. The FBI had been keeping tabs on the phone line, and when they'd heard a voice in the background of a call that had sounded like Saad, they'd moved to phase two—stealing some trash sitting outside the house and fingerprinting it. Sure enough, they'd found the man's prints. That confirmation came through just this morning.

"You want to be here," Jackson said quietly, so the words only reached Ryker's ears. "If something went wrong, and you weren't with Blakely, you wouldn't be able to forgive yourself. When River was out of my reach, and I couldn't protect her..." He shook his head. "It was hell. Pure fucking hell."

Ryker remembered that day well. It was the day he'd returned to his loved ones. And River ended up with a bullet wound. It could have been worse, and he was grateful every day that it hadn't been.

He looked at the women. As if she felt his gaze, Blakely met his eyes. She gave him a small smile. He didn't want a small one. He wanted a full, uncensored, effortless rise of her lips. He wanted her smile to squint her eyes and reach every little corner of her face.

His phone rang and he dug it out of his pocket, chest tightening when he saw who it was. "Davis, did you—"

"It was a fucking setup!"

Ryker's body locked, tension so thick he could taste it. "What?"

Wind blew in the background. "Where are you?"

"Mercy Ring." His gaze moved to his team to see all three guys were now looking at him, giving him their full attention.

"I can't get in touch with any of my guys who were tasked to watch you."

Ryker's gut twisted, his throat closing.

"Ryker—he's coming for you."

BLAKELY TRIED to concentrate on the conversation around her. Aria was talking about how the boys were doing at school. Blakely made an effort to smile at all the right times and throw in a nod every so often. But the second the echoes of fighting silenced from the ring, she looked over to see Ryker and Jackson talking. She didn't need to hear their words to know they were talking about Saad. Ryker had been off all day. Agitated. Like he was uncomfortable in his own skin.

She nibbled her bottom lip, trying to work through the heaviness of the last week. Not just the video, but also Janice's death. She hadn't liked the woman, but she certainly hadn't deserved to die.

River nudged her shoulder, dragging her out of her thoughts. "Hey. You okay?"

She swallowed and opened her mouth to say yes, but the lie twisted into a truth before it hit air. "I'm worried."

"About Ryker?"

"Yes. And everyone else." She was worried about every person she'd come to love in this town. Every person who could be hurt by Saad.

Emotions flickered in River's eyes. Dread. Anxiety. Fear. Blakely's stomach turned. That's when she realized she'd been wanting the other woman to tell her everything would be fine. That they were safe, and the FBI would make sure of it. Not to mention they had four former Delta operators in the room. But just as Blakely couldn't lie, River couldn't either.

Then she felt the heat of eyes on her. She turned her head to see Ryker watching. The look on his face made her throat close and the fine hairs on her arms stand on end. He looked at her like he was moments from grabbing her. Shielding her from the world.

They both knew the reality of that would be futile. Nowhere was safe. Not until the enemy had been caught.

And maybe that would be tonight, a voice whispered in her head. Ryker had told her his former commander was hopeful.

Then why did her gut feel so uneasy? And why did *Ryker* look so tense?

She knew he wanted to be there. He didn't need to say the words for her to know. He'd done nothing but plot Saad's death for the last year. But he was choosing *her*. And honestly, she was grateful. Not just because she felt safer when he was around, but because she wanted him as far from Saad and his evil as humanly possible.

When Ryker looked away to answer a call, she blew out a long breath, realizing air hadn't moved through her lungs the entire time their gazes had been caught. But she didn't take her eyes off him. Something inside her told her to keep watching. That whoever this call was from, they would either provide the salvation they needed…or tip them the other way.

Ryker's muscles visibly tensed. A sick feeling churned in her gut.

It wasn't salvation.

Slowly, she pushed to her feet, unable to stay down. River said something to her, but she didn't comprehend the words. All she could focus on was Ryker. The way his body went deathly still, his knuckles white around the phone.

His gaze moved to the door. Then, whatever the person said on the other end of the call caused a fear like she'd never seen to sweep over his face. It swirled through the dark depths of his eyes like a storm.

The room went quiet, and she realized she wasn't the only one standing and watching him. Everyone was. Because everyone felt the shift in energy? The danger?

He hung up and opened his mouth—but whatever he was about to say was lost as glass shattered from both the front of the building and the kitchen at the back.

Cries rang out through the room. Cole and Declan pulled guns from their holsters while Ryker and Jackson made a run for their duffel bags, but they only made it a few steps before men rushed in from the front and back of the gym. Eight men, four from each end, all armed, with guns pointed at both the men and the women.

"Stop, or we shoot them!"

Blakely sucked in a sharp breath. Saad. One look at the man, and suddenly she knew—he was the face she'd seen at the market. A calm, dangerous authority rippled from his features.

The terrorist stepped between two of his men. He was shorter than any other man in the room, but it didn't take away from the pure menace that all but poured off him. The danger and the calculating coldness.

"Put the guns on the floor, or we shoot your pretty ladies one by one," Saad said in his heavily accented voice. "Or maybe one of the kids."

Beside her, Aria grabbed both boys' arms and inched in front of them.

She looked back to Cole and Declan, their jaws granite.

Saad raised a brow. "You think I won't?" He lifted a shoulder and looked at one of his men like he was about to give them the go-ahead, but Cole growled.

"Fine." He lowered his gun to the floor first. Declan quickly followed.

Her heart skidded. Oh God. Now they were completely at Saad's mercy.

The man's lips curved. "Good."

Rage shot through her, heating her veins to boiling point. *Arrogant prick.*

"What the fuck do you want?" Ryker growled.

Saad studied him. "You know what I want."

Ryker's eyes narrowed. Saad moved farther into the room. He was closest now to Blakely and the women. And every step drew him closer still.

"The death of my brother cost me and my family dearly. That offense cannot go unpunished."

"Killing dozens of innocents in your own country wasn't enough?" Blakely asked, voice almost quiet.

She felt Ryker's gaze cut to her like a knife. A silent command for her to be quiet. To not pull attention her way.

Saad's gaze shifted to her, and there was another curl of his lips. "I was feeling…emotional that day. I had just lost my brother, and when I could not kill Ryker and his team, I eliminated people he cared about."

Emotional? The guy killed people because he felt *emotional*? Jesus, this wasn't a man, it was a monster.

"But it was not enough," Saad continued. "You see, I lost a man who was not only family but an ally. My most valuable ally. Our losses were not equal."

"Why Ryker?" Blakely asked before she could stop herself. It was clear Ryker had been Saad's target from the beginning.

"Blakely, *stop*," he growled.

"No. I am glad you have asked." Saad took another step toward her. "I target Ryker Harp because he fired the bullet that took my brother's life. He took something precious and valuable from me. And I will not stop until he feels the same crippling loss."

CHAPTER 28

Ryker thought he knew anger. He thought he'd felt the hot embers of it in all its worst forms. He was wrong. Seeing this asshole's men point guns at the women, the two teens, and his teammates…this was the height of fury.

"Shoot *me* then," he growled, needing this sick bastard to switch his focus.

Blakely and his sister both gasped, and he felt their desperate looks like laser beams on his skin. He ignored them. He'd do whatever it took, say whatever he had to, to get the guns aimed somewhere else.

Saad shifted his gaze back to Ryker. "Although that offer is tempting, I have something better planned. A revenge so beautiful and poetic, justice will *finally* be served."

Blood roared between his ears as he fought for calm. To not tear across the room and rip the guy's head off.

"What?" The word hissed between his teeth.

Loud thumps sounded above them. Then footsteps. His gaze rose to the ceiling, a new dread poisoning every inch of his body. The roof was angled, with a row of windows providing plenty of light during the day. It was dark outside, so he barely saw the men.

He *did* see the red laser sights beaming through the glass.

His gaze flew back to Blakely and River to see both had a laser pointed at their heads.

Kill shots.

His mind slowed, a blinding darkness catapulting his world into something else. Something he didn't recognize.

His attention returned to Saad. Two of his men had shifted their guns to Anthony and Zac.

"What the fuck are you doing?" he forced out.

Saad ignored him, moving his gaze to Cole. "Kick that gun to Harp."

The asshole was trusting him with a fucking gun? It should make him happy that he'd have a weapon in his hand. It didn't. Because he could already feel what was coming next.

Cole met Ryker's gaze. For a moment they were each as still as the other, then Ryker gave a sharp nod, and his friend kicked the pistol across the floor. It landed at Ryker's feet.

"Pick it up," Saad said, voice so quiet, Ryker almost didn't hear the words.

"Tell me why first."

A gun fired.

Zac fell to his knees with a deep groan while blood bloomed from his shoulder.

Aria screamed and dropped to her son's side. Cole took a single step before Saad spoke.

"Move, and I shoot the woman."

Cole stopped, his chest rising and falling heavily as rage consumed his features.

Saad raised a brow at Ryker. "Shall we try again? Pick it up."

With a clenched jaw, Ryker bent down and lifted the gun.

"Good. I have considered many scenarios in my head of how

to end this. I could kill everyone you love right before your eyes and watch you mourn their losses."

Ryker's fingers twitched on the trigger. Every part of him wanted to just shoot the asshole between the eyes. But he knew that would only get everyone else killed.

"But then I thought of something better," Saad continued, taking another step toward the women, his gaze never leaving Ryker. "I want you so fucking tormented for the rest of your life that you cannot even function."

Suddenly, he knew what the man was going to say. And it made every part of him rebel. Every breath, every beat of his heart, a fresh slice to his chest.

"Choose," Saad said quietly, his eyes burning into Ryker's. "Shoot the woman you've been living with…or your sister."

Hot waves of fury practically radiated off Jackson beside him.

"I'm not shooting anyone," Ryker hissed.

"Then they both die. Either way, death will be on your hands."

"You fucking animal," Jackson growled, inching forward.

"Jackson, no!" River cried out. "Don't give them reason to shoot you too."

There was fear in his sister's voice, but Ryker knew the fear wasn't for herself. It was for Jackson. For him. Blakely. Everyone else.

Ryker forced himself to take a calming breath and respond cooly. "You know I'm not doing that, Saad."

The man chuckled, the sound grating against Ryker's raw nerves. "You are. Because what other choice do you have? Even if somehow you got the upper hand with my men in this room, there are shooters on the roof who will kill your women without blinking."

"I'm going to kill you," Ryker growled. "Tear you apart with my bare fucking hands."

"You won't. People you love, whether of your choosing or not, will die today, and you will understand that your greatest mistake was underestimating me and my people. The lengths to which we will go to destroy you." He smiled cruelly. "I have many allies in your country. The blood of my people runs thick. And we will get the vengeance we seek."

Blakely laughed, but it was a dry, humorless sound. "Your people? The same ones you murdered in cold blood and filmed while you did it?"

"They were casualties of war."

"No. They were *your* casualties. Innocent Lebanese families *you* murdered. You think Ryker killing your brother, one man, a known threat to millions of innocent people, was bad? You killed *children* in your own country. You're a monster."

"Blakely. Stop!" The woman had a damn laser sight trained on her. She needed to be quiet before Ryker lost his mind.

Saad's eyes narrowed, but instead of responding to her, he turned to Ryker. "I'm giving you ten seconds to choose before I give my men orders to kill them both, as well as your three teammates. You will live—but you will wish you hadn't."

Ryker's chest rose and fell as an utterly reckless idea began to form in his head. The only option he could think of…

Shoot the skylight glass.

As it shattered, and people scattered to miss the shards, shoot the enemies in the room.

He was a breath from doing just that, heart racing, praying his loved ones would remain safe.

Then two thuds, nearly simultaneous, sounded above.

The red laser dots were gone.

Saad's men looked up at the ceiling, and Ryker fired.

Erik ran his fingers over the wheel of his new Corvette. The leather was crisp and cool beneath his touch, the engine rumbling with a loud purr.

He slowed slightly as he took a right, heading toward Mercy Ring.

Insurance would end up paying for the replacement, but if it hadn't, he still would have gotten another. Money had never been an issue. Not just because his family came from money, but because he'd earned a lot over the years, first during his stint as a professional boxer, and now as a government contractor.

He took another right. She cornered beautifully.

He hadn't shared with the guys at Mercy Ring the finer details of his job, and they never asked. It was one of the things he liked about them. They didn't push for information he didn't want to give. The friendships were easy, and they didn't need to know every little detail about each other to build trust.

Which was good, considering his job was classified. Even if it wasn't, not sharing came easy to Erik. He didn't let people get close enough to know his business. Not anymore.

Memories tried to weave their way into his consciousness, slipping through the cracks that had become his armor. They did that often. Usually in the quiet moments. The moments when his guard was down and his mind relaxed.

He shut them out like he always did. It was something else he'd become good at. Not letting the ruin of his past seep into his present and annihilate him.

The message he'd received from his mother this morning played in his mind. A message about his father's health. A few months ago, the man had a heart attack, and even though he'd survived it, he wasn't doing well. His mother wanted Erik home. Hell, his whole family wanted him home. His brother. His sister. And maybe it was finally time he returned.

Every part of him rebelled against the idea. He wasn't the same man he used to be. He'd stayed away because the idea of going back hurt too damn much. It was a physical ache that filled his chest, reminding him of his old life. But he'd been away for so long. And if the world had taught him anything, it was that life was fragile and people had a limited number of days on this Earth.

His fingers tightened on the wheel as he turned onto the street where Mercy Ring was located. His gaze cut to the gym—and something immediately caught his attention.

Even from down the street and surrounded by darkness, he could see two figures climbing onto the roof.

The muscles in his arms tensed. The men bent forward slightly, attention on the windows looking down into the gym. What they were doing at the moment didn't matter. They weren't supposed to be there at all.

Instead of continuing to Mercy Ring, he pulled over. There were three buildings between him and the gym. He ignored the beers on his passenger seat and grabbed his Glock from the middle compartment instead and attached the silencer.

He knew the enemies Ryker and his team were up against. They were deadly. But so was he. And more than that, he didn't fear death or danger.

He climbed out of the car and moved quietly down the street, sticking close to the shops. He was grateful for the darkness. It was a constant in his life. Having insomnia meant he and darkness had become intimately familiar.

He stopped at the side of the building. His eyes narrowed on the car across the street. Two men sat inside. No doubt the FBI agents who'd been tasked to watch the place.

Even from where he stood, Erik could see the small holes in the windshield, the spiderwebbed glass. And the blood trailing from their foreheads. Someone had shot them from a distance.

He forced his tense muscles to ease and let the familiar training take over. Then he slipped along the side of the building, searching for whatever means the men had used to get onto the roof. He spotted the access ladder halfway down.

Silently, he moved toward it. If the assholes were on the roof, they no doubt had weapons trained inside. He had to be quiet.

He climbed the ladder with ease. Near the top, he peeked at the roof to see the two men hunched over the window. He could just make out the Walther PPK .380s with laser sights aimed through the glass.

Erik silently aimed his Glock, and with pinpoint accuracy earned from years of experience, before either man could even look up, he shot the two men in the head, one after the other.

Then he climbed to the roof and ran over to the window to see utter fucking chaos.

 yker fired three times—three kill shots—in the space of two seconds before a single man had time to realize what was happening. Then Saad's men dropped and scattered, some taking cover behind the desk, others rolling and shooting as they went.

Bullets rang through the cavernous space. He didn't need to look to know Declan had picked up his gun and was also shooting. From his peripheral vision, he caught sight of Jackson and Cole lunging toward the duffel bags for more guns. The women had dropped to the floor, making themselves small targets. But Saad's men weren't focused on them, all their attention remained on him and Declan.

He moved closer to the boxing ring for cover and aimed for a shooter, but the guy got a shot off first, hitting Ryker's exposed shoulder. He growled as he dropped low, raising his pistol as he went and returning fire. He got him in the gut. The guy went down.

He scanned frantically, his insides icing when he finally found Blakely—in Saad's hold. The asshole was using her to shield his body as he dragged her back toward the kitchen.

A stormy rage fogged his vision. He shifted his pistol, but the man with the gut shot suddenly reached for his weapon and fired at Ryker. The lucky shot hit the Glock and sent it flying.

He lunged forward even as the guy took aim again. Ryker grabbed his wrist before he could shoot and slammed his hand to the floor until he released his grip on the weapon.

The man grunted and rolled Ryker to his back. A fist flew at his face, but he dodged, feeling the knuckles barely skim the side of his head. The man howled when he punched into the concrete floor. Rolling again, Ryker gained the upper hand once more. He landed a jab in the terrorist's face, his nose crunching with the force of the blow. Blood splattered, and the guy cried out louder. Ryker threw another punch.

He was about to go for a third when pain seared his side. The asshole had stabbed him.

With a growl, Ryker grappled the guy's wrist away, tugged the knife out of his side, then used his body weight to force the man's hand until the knife plunged into his heart.

The second the life left the asshole's eyes, Ryker glanced around wildly.

Gone. She was fucking *gone*!

Acid burned through his veins. He rose to his feet just as a man to his right dropped from a bullet wound…on the top of his head? Ryker's gaze flew up.

The shot had come from Erik, who was on the roof.

He barely let that thought sink in before he was running toward the back exit, where Saad had pulled Blakely.

BLAKELY KICKED her feet and dug her nails into the thick arms that were wrapped around her from behind. Cool air whipped across her face as Saad dragged her outside.

He wasn't tall, but his arms were like steel. His body granite. It was like he'd trained to disable and take people as quickly and efficiently as possible. He kept her close, plastered against him as he pulled her across the back lot.

When she saw him heading for a car, shock froze her limbs for a moment. It was the car from her hotel. The one that had followed her to the bar.

He'd been *stalking* her. She'd been prey almost from the moment she arrived in town, and she'd had no idea it was Saad.

A fresh wave of terror tinged with anger hit. This was it. Her last-ditch effort to escape. If he got her into that vehicle, her chance of survival drastically decreased. He would make her disappear for good.

Saad wrenched open the car door and tried to shove her forward. The second she had a tiny bit of space between them, she lifted her foot and slammed it down on his with everything she had, feeling the effect ricochet up her leg.

He growled. She quickly followed it with a grab and twist of his balls. With a shout of pain, he instantly released her.

She ran for her life. Let the weight of her fear propel her forward. The need to survive power her legs.

But it wasn't enough. She'd almost made it back to the door when iron fingers grasped her shoulder and swung her body into the building. Her head slammed into brick, rattling her teeth and shooting pain through her skull.

She tried to blink it away. But the second her vision cleared, she saw a fist flying toward her.

It was too late to move. Hard knuckles collided with her forehead with so much force that her ears rang and her knees buckled. She would have hit the ground, but Saad grabbed her once again and dragged her back to the car.

She wanted to fight, her mind screaming at her to claw and kick until she had nothing left. But her brain was foggy from his strike, not a single cohesive thought translating to action.

Too soon, she felt the cool leather of a car seat beneath her. Heard the door slam. Then the engine.

She breathed shallowly, fingers shaking as she touched her forehead, feeling the stickiness of blood. Her vision was still blurry.

"He's going to come for you, you know," she gasped out, ignoring the pain that accompanied each word. The sacrifice was worth it. If she couldn't fight with her fists, she'd fight with her words. "They all are."

"Shut up!"

She blinked, forcing her vision to clear. When she saw Saad looking in his rearview mirror, she turned—and gasped at the sight of Ryker running out of the building. He lifted his gun. But before he could shoot, Saad had raced around a corner.

She turned back to him, fighting for calm. "The FBI know where you are. They're coming," she bluffed. She had no idea. But Ryker had received a call from *someone* before all hell broke loose. And she was praying it was Davis sending help. "It's just you against a small army. Just let me go and run."

"No." The single word came out as an aggressive sneer. "Harp will fucking *pay* for what he did!"

He glanced at the rearview mirror again, and let out a string of Arabic. She looked back also, ignoring the ache that came with the movement.

A car was gaining on them—fast.

She didn't recognize the vehicle and couldn't make out the driver, but she knew it was Ryker.

"So what?" she gasped. "You kill me. Then what?"

"My goal has not changed," he said, eerily quiet now, speeding up and watching the rearview mirror. "Once you are dead, I watch the man crumble. He will blame himself for your death."

Her chest tightened, a small band wrapping around her lungs and heart, choking her. "You're going to crash the car while he's chasing us, aren't you?"

"Yes."

She shook her head, the dread inside her like a wide chasm. "How can you ensure that I die and you live?"

He took a hard left, and she only just saved herself from hitting the door by grabbing onto the dashboard. When he didn't respond, just tightened his fingers around the wheel, she suddenly understood.

"You don't care if you die." The words were a whisper.

Again, he didn't respond. But his silence was loud.

Jesus. The man wasn't just a psychopath, he was a psychopath willing to die for his cause. He would rather his enemy suffer, even if that meant dying himself. And that made him so much more dangerous.

Saad sped up again, pushing the car to race so quickly down the streets, she feared each time they grew too close to another vehicle. She shot another look over her shoulder, and sure enough, Ryker sped up with them.

"He won't blame himself," she tried desperately, dragging her attention back to Saad. "He's not getting close enough to cause us to crash, just to keep us in his sights. He's smarter than that. You crash, and he'll know where the blame lies."

The man just smiled like he knew a secret Blakely didn't.

"Just stop the car," she said, voice shaking, the pressure inside her suffocating. "Accept that you've lost."

That got a bit of emotion from him. "*La.* I do not lose!"

Shit.

Her mind scrambled to come up with a desperate plan to somehow get out of this alive. Her head throbbed and she was dizzy as hell, but she wasn't bound in any way, not even with a seat belt. She was mobile, had the use of all her limbs, and she could and would use that to her advantage.

Her gaze flicked to the door handle. Before she could even touch it, the click of the lock sounded.

A small smile spread the asshole's lips, and it made her want to throw herself at him. Hurt him. Attack.

She looked through the windshield and saw the road ended at a cross-street up ahead. He was going to have to turn. Left or right, she wasn't sure. But to turn, he'd have to slow down, at least a little.

Her belly soured at the idea forming in her head. But what choice did she have? Leave it up to him to choose when they crashed? Probably while driving at high speed, and in a way that left her no chance of surviving?

If she did this, she'd get hurt, but she'd maybe survive…hopefully. And Saad might be hurt too, giving Ryker the advantage he needed.

Her heart sped up, its rhythm so fast and uneven, she thought she might pass out. She counted in her head to calm herself and kept very still, not willing to give herself away.

Then, just as they turned right, she reached over and wrenched the wheel so the car kept turning.

Saad lost control and the vehicle spun—before jumping the curb and crashing into a building.

CHAPTER 30

Ryker cursed loudly as he stomped on the gas harder. Not *his* car. He'd had to pull Davis's dead agent from behind the wheel of a vehicle in the back lot before taking off after Saad. A bullet hole cracked the glass, a reminder of another death on the terrorist's hands, but he didn't let that stop or slow him.

He clenched the wheel so tightly that the leather creaked beneath his fingers. Blakely was in that fucking car in front of him, and the asshole was veering back and forth, getting too damn close to parked vehicles.

He barely touched the brake as he turned the corner, his tires squealing against the asphalt. He was working hard to keep the car in his sights but also not edge too close. He was all too aware that Blakely likely wasn't wearing a seat belt.

Memories of that laser trained on her head made his temple throb and acid drip in his gut.

His cell rang from his pocket. A cell he'd forgotten he even had.

He tugged it out and put it on speaker. "Are they all dead?"

"Yes," Declan answered quickly. "And Davis and his guys have arrived. Where are you?"

Saad turned again, this time wider. Faster. Ryker's gut tightened at how dangerously close the man came to a building. He let out a slew of curses.

"Driving down Jader Street. Saad's got Blakely and he's driving like he has a fucking death wish."

This time, Declan cursed. "We're coming."

Ryker opened his mouth to respond, but the end of the road appeared ahead.

Ryker slowed, giving Saad more space to take the turn.

He watched, his breath catching in his throat when the vehicle veered sharply to the right—too sharp. It did a complete three-sixty before the passenger side slammed into a brick building.

The fear inside Ryker became so vivid and vile that his heart stopped.

"Saad crashed at the end of Jader," Ryker managed, each word pulled from somewhere deep and dark inside him. "Blakely's side hit a building."

He didn't hear what his friend said. The vehicle ahead of him took all his focus. He needed eyes on Blakely. He needed confirmation that air still flowed through her lungs and her heart still beat in her chest.

He slammed his foot hard on the brake, watching as Saad stumbled unsteadily out of the car. But he wasn't alone. One hand was fisted in Blakely's hair. The sight of her had the blood in his veins turning to ice. She had a black eye and blood dripping from her forehead. Even from where he sat inside his car, he could see the black eye wasn't from the crash. The asshole had struck her.

She was blinking like she was trying to remain conscious and pain riddled her features. When Saad pressed the muzzle of a gun to Blakely's temple, Ryker grabbed his Glock and slowly climbed from the car.

He aimed at the asshole. "Let her go."

"Why would I do that when I have nothing to lose and you have everything?"

The accuracy in that statement threatened to cripple Ryker. Made his knees want to buckle where he stood. But he didn't let the asshole see it.

"Come on, shoot me," Saad said. "Shoot me, or I shoot *her*."

Saad was playing a dangerous mind game. Ryker knew exactly what he wanted. He wanted him to shoot. And for Blakely to become collateral damage. Wasn't going to happen.

"You think he cares if I die?" Blakely said softly, each word more pained than the next.

His gaze whipped to her. "Blakely—"

"I got injured in Beirut, and he never came for me," she continued, her words firm despite her visible pain. "He never called. Never visited. This is the first time he's seen me in over a year. The man *tolerates* me. That's it. Your plan is flawed, Saad."

The man's brows slashed together. Ryker could see the anger in his expression, but also…doubt.

Blakely scrunched her eyes, then opened them. "He killed someone *you* loved. Your brother is *dead* because of him. And now he's going to kill you. Are you really okay with letting him live?"

"Blakely. *Stop*," Ryker demanded.

She ignored him. "You lost everything because of Ryker. And now you want to waste your one shot on me—and not him?"

Visible indecision brewed in Saad's eyes.

"If he lives, you lose." Each of her words seemed to stir turmoil in their enemy, becoming more and more pronounced. "I mean *nothing* to him, so you will die having achieved *less* than nothing."

Ryker knew the exact moment Saad's plan shifted. His eyes tightened, his knuckles whitened. Then the muzzle left Blakely's head.

Before Saad could even take aim at Ryker, Blakely's arm was already flying back, her fist digging into his gut.

When Saad grunted in pain, Ryker realized she hadn't used her fist. She had a weapon.

Saad doubled over behind her, and Ryker fired.

THE SECOND GUNFIRE sliced the air, the fingers in her hair released, and she almost fell with them. Would have, if Ryker hadn't caught her seconds before she hit the ground.

Her vision hazed as he swept her off her feet and pressed her to his chest. Air moved around her as Ryker walked them away from Saad. Then her feet were on the ground, a cold wall pressed to her back, but warm hands on her cheeks.

"Hey, talk to me, princess! Stay with me!"

She swallowed and squeezed her eyes shut, forcing herself to remain conscious. Everything hurt. Her chest. Her lungs. And her head…*God*, her head hurt. Not only from Saad's punch but from smashing into the Mercy Ring building, then hitting the passenger window in the crash.

She touched her hairline near her right temple, feeling wetness. Her fingers came back coated in crimson.

She swallowed, blinking three times to make the outline of Ryker switch from a blur to a solid image. Then, there he was. The man she loved. Alive and whole in front of her.

"You're alive."

He blew out a breath, almost looking like he was going to fall to the ground in relief. "I'm alive. And so are you."

Her gaze shifted to the man in the street. The blood from the bullet wound in his head painted the asphalt red.

Dead. He was *dead*.

And she couldn't look away from him.

The warm hand on her cheek applied pressure, until she faced Ryker.

"He's dead," she whispered.

"He is."

He wrapped his fingers around hers, gently unfolding them. It was only then that she realized she was still holding the shard of glass she'd used to stab him. She'd grabbed it as Saad pulled her from the car, desperate for any weapon she could get her hands on.

God, was she glad she did.

Carefully, he slid the glass from her hand. A deep growl reverberated from his chest when her open palm revealed blood where it had sliced into her skin.

"I'm okay." When he didn't meet her gaze, she used her good hand, tugging his chin back to her. "Ryker, I'm okay."

He blew out a long breath, and now that she was focused on him, she saw what she'd missed earlier. Blood—staining his shirt at his shoulder and on his side.

She gasped. "You're hurt!"

"I'm fine."

She didn't believe him. Neither of them were okay right now.

But they would be.

He tugged her into his chest, and she leaned against him heavily. His hands lowered to her backside, then he lifted her into his arms once again. Without hesitation, she wrapped her legs around his waist and finally allowed herself to breathe.

Saad was dead. The danger was gone.

Sirens wailed in the distance and cars raced toward the scene. Ryker's team arrived first. Then the FBI. Everything was a blur. Even the words spoken by paramedics.

Her one constant was Ryker. She made sure to hold onto him the entire time, almost scared that if she let go, she'd blink and he'd be gone, and her new reality would shift to what could have been.

Blakely watched as the flames danced before her eyes. They were bright against the dark evening sky, and their heat coated her skin like a warm blanket.

A month ago, those flames would have brought her pain and heartache and nightmares. Made her thoughts turn to darker things. And there were still shadows of that in the hollows of her chest. But there was also something else. Something lighter. Because the man who had caused the pain was gone. Dead, along with the men who'd supported and served him. None of them would ever breathe another breath, harm another innocent soul, or taint another life.

Conversation was a hum around her in the quiet evening. Declan's voice across the fire as he recounted a story to Cole and Jackson. River, sitting beside her, saying something to Aria and Michele.

Zac and Anthony argued over whose bullet wound had been worse. Zac was still recovering, of course. It had only been a couple of weeks since that awful night, but he was doing well, considering.

They sat in Ryker's backyard around the small fire. Well…her and Ryker's yard. Because only a week ago, he had asked her to move in with him. She'd probably broken records with how quickly she'd said yes. With how fiercely she'd jumped into his arms and planted her lips on his.

They both had war wounds and grazes. But they were alive, and they had each other. After everything they'd gone through, they knew how lucky they were to have so much.

She scanned the group for him. He sat between Jackson and Erik, the flames dancing in the reflection of his eyes.

He'd been lighter this week. Remarkably so. The guilt that had been weighing him down since she'd arrived in town almost appeared to be gone. He still wasn't the man she'd met in Beirut. He'd probably never be. Neither of them would be those people again. Life had changed them. Carved new versions of them. It was impossible to experience everything they had and come out unscathed, but they were stronger. More resilient.

His gaze cut through the fire to hers, causing the beat of her heart to spiral into a new rhythm. Then he winked, and the heat of the flames suddenly felt cool compared to the burn he ignited inside her body.

A small smile touched her lips. The man had been her everything over the last couple of weeks. Caring for her while she recovered from her wounds. Holding her through the worst of her nightmares.

Life felt surreal some days. After spending so long having the man she loved push her away, she almost expected to wake up and find she'd lost him again. That he'd slipped through her fingers like sand.

Ryker had seen that fear. Of course he had—he saw everything. And each time that worry tried to claim her, Ryker used soft words and gentle touches to reassure her that she had his heart, and he wasn't going anywhere, emotionally or physically.

He'd actually used the word *forever*. She was his forever.

A shoulder nudged hers. "You look happy."

She turned to smile at River. While she'd been on forced bed rest, River had visited almost every day. The love the woman had for her brother and everyone in her life was so tangible, you could almost touch it.

"I am." Blakely wet her lips. "I keep thinking I'm going to blink and realize this isn't my reality. I'll be back in my apartment in Minnesota, loving a man who won't return my calls. Ryker will be here, still angry and hurting. And Saad will be alive somewhere in the world, plotting who he'll hurt next."

She almost shuddered at the sound of the man's name. He might be dead, but it would take her a while to speak of him without physically rebelling. Without every part of her stomach souring.

River's mouth curved into a soft smile. "I felt like that for a while after Jackson came back into my life. I'd loved him since I was a teenager, and having him love me in return felt surreal." She chuckled, her gaze moving across to the man. "Some days, it still does. But I don't think that fear's a bad thing. It helps me appreciate what I have. When I remember what we had to endure to get where we are, I let my touch linger a bit longer. I remind him I love him a bit more often."

It was like she'd plucked the words from Blakely's heart. She'd been feeling and doing the exact same.

God, she loved Ryker's family and friends. His parents had returned to Lindeman only a week ago, and they'd not only said the most beautiful things to make her feel welcomed into their family, they were also very free with their hugs. Those warm, you're-already-family kind of hugs.

Blakely reached over and squeezed River's hand. "Thank you. Not just for always saying the right things, but for welcoming me with such ease."

River shook her head. "No. I should be thanking *you*. All I've ever wanted was for my brother to be happy. For a while, I wondered if that was even a possibility anymore. It felt like I was asking for a miracle." She looked across the fire at her brother, and Blakely thought she saw moisture in the woman's eyes. "Now he *is* happy. And you have everything to do with that. Thank you."

Blakely let those words filter into her chest and just sit. They felt good. Warm. Comforting.

For the next hour, she enjoyed the company of the group, her gaze forever wandering back to Ryker. Eventually, she stood and moved inside to heat some milk on the stove. A few people were drinking tonight, but she'd opted out. Her headaches from the concussion had only just ceased, and she didn't want to give them a reason to return. So hot cocoa it was. She'd make extra, see if anyone else wanted some.

She was just pouring the milk into a pot when she felt his heat from behind. His warm breath. His familiar comfort.

RYKER SIPPED HIS COLD BEER, letting the liquid wet his throat and warm his gut.

He was trying like hell to concentrate on the conversation around him, but it was impossible when Blakely sat across the fire, like a shining light in the darkness.

Two weeks had passed since Saad had died, but he still couldn't get the events of that day out of his head. The red laser on her forehead. The car chase. The muzzle of the gun pressed to her head by a man who'd had nothing to lose.

He'd watched her so closely over the last two weeks, it was becoming an obsession. To make sure she was okay. To make sure she was alive, safe, and in want of nothing.

He'd almost expected her to complain that she felt suffocated by his careful scrutiny. That she needed space to breathe. And, God, he'd dreaded hearing those words. But they'd never come.

The sound of her laugh reached him. It had become his

favorite sound. Like a cool breeze on his heated skin.

"You doing okay?"

At Erik's question, Ryker faced his friend. He owed the man a lot, more than he could ever repay. If it hadn't been for Erik, there was a very real chance none of them would have made it out of that gym alive.

"Most of the time." There were still the odd moments when he wasn't. "That day will forever haunt me."

"I know, brother." And Erik looked at him like he really *did* know. Like he too had been touched by evil and had similar scars etched inside him. "But she's here. She's okay."

"Thanks to you."

Erik shook his head. "You would have figured a way out of it."

Yeah, he would have shot the damn glass, then prayed like hell the people he loved survived. "Still, thank you. Twice now you've saved my woman. You ever need anything, I'm there."

"You repay it with your friendship."

He squeezed Erik's shoulder. "Always." He took another sip of his beer, dropping his hand. "You gonna tell me what you do one of these days?"

"Nope." His head dipped, and he looked at the beer in his grasp. "But I *should* let you know that I'm moving. Only about an hour north of here, but it'll make my visits to Lindeman and Mercy Ring a lot less frequent."

Ryker's brows rose. "You're leaving us?"

He swallowed. "My grandfather died a year ago. He had a few different properties but left me the home he lived in. It's just been sitting empty since then. I wasn't planning on going back, but my dad's health hasn't been great, and I think it's time I went home."

Home. The way Erik said the word made it sound like both a blessing and a curse. "I'm sure they'll be happy to have you back."

Erik's fingers visibly tightened on the bottle. "I haven't had a lot of communication with them for a while now. They deserve more from me."

It sounded like that sentence was unfinished. Like he had more words to share but couldn't speak them. And they left Ryker with a lot of questions. Why didn't he have much contact with his family? Why did he seem reluctant to move back home, when he could hear in Erik's voice that he loved them?

He wanted to ask those things, but he didn't. Erik's business was his, and if he wanted to share one day, he would.

"Let us know if we can help with the move. If the house has been unoccupied for a year, it may need some work, or at least a cleanup. We're all happy to pitch in."

Erik's white knuckles regained their color, and he turned to Ryker. He wasn't smiling, but that tense expression on his face eased. "Thank you."

This time, Ryker nodded.

The group continued to talk and drink and laugh around him. Ryker stayed where he was and participated in the conversation where he could, until he saw Blakely rise and move to the house. He watched her right until she stepped inside, then he rose and followed.

She was like a magnet he was drawn to. Where she was, he needed to be.

He found her standing by the stove. The second he was behind her, he slipped his arms around her waist. She softened in his hold and leaned into him.

Fucking perfect. Like they were made to fit together.

He dipped his head and whispered into her ear, "That distance out there was torment."

She laughed, a low, sexy sound. "We were sitting in the same circle."

"But you weren't within touching distance. Too far."

She turned, then her green gaze bore into him. "We've been stuck at the hip for two whole weeks. Hell, even before that, we were spending all our time together. Aren't you tired of me yet?"

"Tired of you? Princess, that's like asking if a man could grow tired of water in a desert." He lowered his head, placing a light kiss on her cheek, beside her ear. "Not possible. You have become essential to my existence."

She hummed. "I didn't like being out of arm's reach from you either."

Good. Another kiss on her cheek, then he lifted his head, his gaze wandering over her face. The bruises had faded, but he knew the headaches had taken longer to subside. "Are you doing okay?"

"I'm perfect, Ryker. Because of you…I'm perfect."

She really was. Still, he shook his head. "Not because of me. Because of your strength. Your smarts."

The woman had almost killed him with her words to Saad that day. She'd been trying to get the man to move the gun away from her head so she could stab him. He knew that, of course. And it had been a risk. A risk that had paid off. She'd saved herself, and in the process, saved him.

Her hands grazed up his chest before locking behind his neck. "I love you, Ryker Harp."

The woman had no idea. There was no end to his love for her.

He lifted her and sat her on the counter beside the stove. Then he stepped between her thighs and touched his forehead to hers. "I love you more than I thought possible."

Her eyes softened, then closed. It was while her eyes were closed that he dipped his head and kissed her.

Immediately, her lips parted, letting him slip in. And he felt everything. The peace that had evaded him for so long. The whispered reminder that this was it. This was as good as it gets…and Blakely was his…forever.

Order ERIK'S SALVATION today!

ALSO BY NYSSA KATHRYN

PROJECT ARMA SERIES

Uncovering Project Arma

Luca

Eden

Asher

Mason

Wyatt

Bodie

Oliver

Kye

BLUE HALO SERIES

(series ongoing)

Logan

Jason

Blake

Flynn

Aidan

Tyler

Callum

Liam

MERCY RING

Jackson

Declan

Cole

Ryker

BEAUTIFUL PIECES

(series ongoing)

Erik's Salvation

Erik's Redemption

Erik's Refuge

JOIN my newsletter and be the first to find out about sales and new releases! CLICK HERE

ABOUT THE AUTHOR

Nyssa Kathryn is a romantic suspense author. She lives in South Australia with her daughter and hubby and takes every chance she can to be plotting and writing. Always an avid reader of romance novels, she considers alpha males and happily-ever-afters to be her jam.

Don't forget to follow Nyssa and never miss another release.

Facebook | Instagram | Amazon | Goodreads